About the Author

Peter Ward was born on the Wirral but, as a young child, moved to the south Yorkshire town of Doncaster where he was introduced to three great future strands of his life... soccer, cricket and music.

The author qualified as a biologist (Botany and Zoology, Joint Hons.) at the former London College of S.Mark and S.John before taking up teaching in ILEA Secondary Comprehensive Schools. With this experience, he applied for a production post in BBC Education's School Radio Department. Peter also produced Current Affairs items for BBC Radio Four *Woman's Hour* and directed the live national phone-in, *Tuesday Call*, presenter Sue McGregor. He completed his broadcasting career as Chief Producer and Editor, BBC Education.

The author now lives on the Kent-Sussex border in the heart of the High Weald and continues his lifelong passion for natural history and conservation matters. He has also sung in a number of choirs, including Tonbridge Philharmonic, Royal Tunbridge Wells Choral Society and Kent Chorus. Currently, he sings Tenor with Wadhurst Polyphony and has piano and choral compositions publically performed.

Books by the Author

***The Adventures of Charles Darwin* 1982 CUP**
(Translated into seven languages.)

'an excellent introduction for young readers…' *Times Literary Supplement*

'this is children's writing at its best.' *Nature*

'If Darwin sounds a bit heavy for children, think again…' *The Sun (Australia)*

***Freedom of the Waves* Trafford USA 2012**

'Mixing elements of Norse mythology, adventure, cheeky humour, romance and magic, this page-turning read follows a young band of Viking tweens as they try to escape a destiny of violence.' *blueink REVUE*

'The next few days of the absconders' lives are filled with a steady stream of demons, serpents, killer fogs, a poisonous purple haze and one angry sea god. All of which keep the pace scooting up in the red zone.' *Foreword Reviews*

'…the story becomes a high seas adventure to rival Homer's Odyssey. The gang encounters sea witches, hostile Norsemen, duelling giants and treacherous mermaids as every chapter brings a new adventure and a certain brush with death….Lush settings and exciting adventures make for a read kids will love.' *Kirkus Reviews*

'The book serves as a golden-rule message for young readers to absorb.' *Foreword Reviews*

***Trouble with Toads* Trafford USA 2014**

A black adult comedy set in post-Brexit UK. An erstwhile sleepy, rural village in the English Weald seethes with corruption as power-mad Russian oligarchs seek to bribe local dignitaries in the pursuit of environmentally ruinous fracking operations. The villagers hit back, inadvertently aided by genetically-modified giant toads.

The Music of Freedom

WWII ESCAPE FROM NAZI TYRANNY

Peter L Ward

Copyright © 2019 Peter L Ward

The moral right of the author has been asserted.

Apart from any fair dealing for the purposes of research or private study, or criticism or review, as permitted under the Copyright, Designs and Patents Act 1988, this publication may only be reproduced, stored or transmitted, in any form or by any means, with the prior permission in writing of the publishers, or in the case of reprographic reproduction in accordance with the terms of licences issued by the Copyright Licensing Agency. Enquiries concerning reproduction outside those terms should be sent to the publishers.

This is a work of fiction. Names, characters, businesses, places, events and incidents are either the products of the author's imagination or used in a fictitious manner. Any resemblance to actual persons, living or dead, or actual events is purely coincidental.

Matador
9 Priory Business Park,
Wistow Road, Kibworth Beauchamp,
Leicestershire. LE8 0RX
Tel: 0116 279 2299
Email: books@troubador.co.uk
Web: www.troubador.co.uk/matador
Twitter: @matadorbooks

ISBN 978 1838591 809

British Library Cataloguing in Publication Data.
A catalogue record for this book is available from the British Library.

Printed and bound in Great Britain by 4edge Limited
Typeset in 11pt Adobe Garamond Pro by Troubador Publishing Ltd, Leicester, UK

Matador is an imprint of Troubador Publishing Ltd

To Dr Charles Armour, former Head of BBC School Broadcasting (Radio)

Introduction

Silesia, Poland. Last day of August…1939
A light breeze rustles the soft cushions of pine needles on the forest floor. Autumn's mellow sunlight bathes the sleepy pastures bordering the trees. In the distance, chickens peck in the dust and white geese crane their enquiring necks. A peasant boy herds his cows towards a field gate and calls to milkmaids carrying pails. Without a care in the world, they chat to each other as they head towards an old barn. It is time for the afternoon milking.

An untidy dog sprawls and dozes in the heat. It half raises its shaggy head and barks without conviction at the milkmaids; more recognition than threat. One of the maids puts down her wooden pail and ruffles the old dog's neck. The animal responds, lapping up the affection. Tenant farmers and their families work hard on the land. Even in the harshest of winters, there is always enough to see them through the bitter Polish winter.

i

Ubergrenadier Heinrich Müller manoeuvred into a concealed position at the open edge of the forest. Raising military field glasses to his eyes, he took in the scene. So commonplace… or so it appeared. He swept the primitive buildings and adjoining fields. Rippling wheat ripening in the sunshine. And in a fenced enclosure, spotted pigs churning up their terrain with muddied snouts.

It reminded Heinrich of childhood visits from his Viennese home to the surrounding countryside. Now, events had transported the twenty year-old to the border of a foreign country. The young *Wehrmacht* conscript worked hard to adapt to the novelty of military discipline. He had slept rough and endured heavy rain. Heinrich's boots had become clogged with clay, his *feldgrau* uniform soaked through. Thank God the rains had ceased over the last few days and the forecast for September was good. It made border scouting easier. Although not without risk.

In idle moments when there was no activity to report, Heinrich permitted his educated mind to wander back to an earlier, softer existence. Reared by well-connected parents in a privileged district of the Austrian capital, he had performed well at his academic *gymnasium*. Majoring in violin studies, Heinrich had temporarily left Vienna to study at Salzburg. In his brief time in the ancient city on the Salzach he had occasionally explored the verdant countryside. Grassy meadows and lakes; timber houses bedecked with summer flowers.

On one occasion, he and his new friends had taken the bus to the foot of the Untersberg mountain. Rising some few kilometres from the city, its towering lop-sidedness spoke of dominance and mystery. Heinrich smiled as he recalled the cable car ascent to the summit. Some hesitated to board the vehicle, watching in trepidation as it made its descent to the ground station. But anxieties were dispelled once the summit was achieved. Stepping out into crisp mountain air, the young city-dwellers gazed in wonder at spectacular mountain peaks. An ogre's domain of weathered crags stretched before the musical adventurers; the very highest tops still bound in snow. The youngsters thrilled at the seemingly endless mountain chain linking Austria to its near neighbour.

The girls had been content to sit and chat, picking bunches of wild flowers. This encouraged the boys to go off and explore. They planned to snatch a glimpse of the Obersalzberg, across the border, rising above Berchtesgaden. It was rumoured the *Führer* had arrived with an entourage of Nazi High Command, including Goebbels and Bormann. Hitler also invited his top military commanders to a meeting that would determine future action. Discussion of war was high on the agenda.

On that perfect day, Heinrich and his pals hoped to spot the summit of the Kehlstein mountain; Hitler's Eagle's Nest with its high tea room built by slaves. But the student friends had not thought to bring binoculars. It was maddening to imagine the great Leader so close – present at his Berghof retreat, but distanced from ordinary mortals by terrain and hierarchy. Disappointed, the friends turned back to find the girls idling on the high meadows. Yellow-beaked alpine choughs wheeled and circled in the hot sun. These slender, acrobatic crows landed close to the picnickers, seeking left-overs.

That was months ago. Heady days of music-making in Mozart's own city and far from the threat of war. Even on active army duty it was easy to daydream. *Ubergrenadier* Heinrich Müller came to his senses, concentrating his mind on the present scene. He lamented his lapse of concentration. Heinrich's colleagues in the Patrol were more focussed and experienced less difficulty in responding to military demands. Once more, he peered through his field glasses, observing the pedestrian routine of the agricultural workers. In truth, these people were little more than uneducated peasants. He was aware they offered no threat to the world and were content to indulge in their rural ways. Heinrich kept the matter to himself and did not share it with his fellow troopers. It disturbed his inner thinking.

'These Poles appear oblivious to the storm that's about to hit them. Why doesn't their obstinate government sign a pact with us? They'll never withstand invasion. The border between our two nations is ludicrously undefended. Our *Führer* seeks simple justice for the *Volksdeutsche,* the German speakers trapped inside Poland by history.'

To Heinrich's naïve mind, a straightforward resolution to the problem seemed perfectly possible.

'Return Danzig to its German minority. Rule from Berlin. Simple!'

The young lance corporal smiled to himself.

'War's a waste of time. I'd rather go home!'

Unlike his colleagues, Heinrich was highly conscious of his doubts and uncertainties. If his companions grew suspicious he would be mocked. He shifted his position and pressed up against a mature pine. The forest provided a dull monotony of perfect cover. Heinrich's scouting party had been ordered to observe and report activity. In particular, any sightings of active Polish border units. He turned to his nearest companion, crouching in trampled bracken.

'Nothing's happening,' he whispered. 'No activity. D'you think the Poles know we're watching?'

Uwe Walter made a face that was difficult to interpret beneath the mud markings streaked across his forehead and cheeks. Leaf camouflage woven into netting covered his coal scuttle helmet.

'Don't know, *Ubergrenadier*,' he mumbled. 'Calm before the storm. If one of them spots us they'll send for back-up. None of these lads have seen action.'

Walter was shocked at his own indiscretion and hurriedly corrected himself.

'But we'll fight if we have to! Germans are better than Poles. Our instructors tell us that. *Polskis* are inferior. Not fully human.'

Heinrich grimaced. Since his unexpected promotion to the lowest rank above *grenadier*, he and his companions had been forced to attend daily lectures. But despite indoctrination, he continued to struggle with recent responsibilities thrust upon his unmilitary shoulders. He stayed silent, his mind plagued by whirling thoughts.

'My friends at University would find this strange,' he pondered. 'I wonder what they're doing?'

Heinrich felt uneasy about the reliability of one of the border scouts in his team. He suspected Hassler was a Party member planted on them and encouraged, no doubt, to report back.

'Just a few months ago,' he reflected, 'I studied violin… Bruch, Mozart, Mendelssohn. Now, I'm reckoned to be a trained soldier in the *Wehrmacht*. Crazy! Why did they select *me* for promotion?'

It was unthinkable to share his anxieties with the lads. When Heinrich's thinking ran deep, he was able to recall certain events of his teenage years. Ironically, they now stood him in good stead.

'At my *gymnasium*, my father insisted I joined the *Hitler Jugend*. I should have refused. He said it would make a man of me. All that marching. Drill sergeants and flag-waving. Outdoor camps and jumping to command.'

He snorted, cynically.

'How did I survive that nonsense when all I wanted to do was concentrate on my violin?'

Heinrich lifted the field glasses, once more. By now, the milkmaids had disappeared into the patched wooden barn. Passive cows queued, almost courteously, to enter the old building.

'*Ubergrenadier!*'

An excited, high-pitched whisper.

'Over to the right. Lane behind the farm...horses!'

Day dreaming Heinrich snapped onto alert, ordering the others to retire to the trees. He edged back, seeking the cover of a stout trunk. Uwe was right. A puff of summer dust rose from a winding lane connecting the farm to a metalled road. Four horses and riders. Heinrich felt the tingling of hairs rising on his neck.

'Polish cavalry? Tough professionals.'

He focussed his glasses on the leading horseman. A young officer in khaki wearing a soft military cap. Raven-haired and fully moustached, the cavalryman handled his fine charger with skill. Heinrich noted a rifle slung over the officer's shoulder. The other riders were similarly armed. He continued observing as the Polish troopers eased themselves out of their saddles. They then led their mounts to tie up at a stone water trough.

The peasant farmer stepped out of the cowshed to hail the unexpected arrivals. Heinrich could just make out indecipherable banter. The soldiers were invited into the primitive, thatched farmhouse. They entered willingly, unaware of the young Germans' presence on their border. A bottle or two of the local spirits would be passed round.

'Routine visit?' Heinrich speculated.

He turned to his companions, lying flat on the forest floor.

'Four troopers. Looks like a regular patrol checking our sector. Make a note of numbers and how they're armed. We must be ready to move back. No confrontation. Wait for me to give the signal!'

His comrades remained in their places, recalling the day's set orders.

Go out on patrol. Observe and report back. In no circumstances get involved in fighting. Withdraw. Above all, remain unseen.

To Heinrich, the scene was taking on a children's fantasy, like the games he once played at *kindergarten*.

'Just the four of us,' he thought. 'And four Poles. We have no quarrel. Yet they're the enemy.'

Heinrich knew he was far from alone questioning the presence of German forces massing secretly on the Silesian border. After a few minutes, the camouflaged patrol witnessed the Polish cavalrymen trooping back into the yard. They strolled over to the trough to unhitch their horses.

'*Ubergrenadier!*'

It was the weaselly Hassler. Suddenly alert.

'Behind us!'

Two peasant boys crashed through the wood, pausing at the tree line. One draped a shot rabbit over his arm. The other sported a gun. Their faces dropped the moment they spotted the statuesque Germans. Neither party moved. Hassler reacted first and levelled his rifle.

'Don't shoot!'

Heinrich's plea came too late. Hassler ignored him and pulled the trigger. He missed and let out an expletive. The two young Poles sprang into life and dashed down the slope. Hassler re-loaded.

'I ordered…*don't shoot!*'

Heinrich hurled himself at the young *grenadier*. They grappled in the thick undergrowth. Uwe and Georg Ulbricht piled in. Hassler's elbow struck the ground. He lost his grip on his weapon and Heinrich vented his fury.

'Stupid oaf! You'll have those Poles on us!'

He scrambled up again.

'Pick up your rifle…we're retreating!'

Hassler swore under his breath, felt his bruised jaw and broken tooth, and heaved himself off the forest floor.

Uwe, too, scrambled to his feet, powerless to prevent the Polish youths from reaching the farm. They gesticulated wildly at the emerging cavalrymen pointing up at the trees. The moustachioed officer barked out a command. In an instant, the armed soldiers leapt into action, turning their horses towards the unexpected threat. The Poles' blood was up as they charged the hidden German look-out post. Heinrich reacted with speed.

'Run!'

His scouting party needed no telling. They turned tail, heading towards a ride leading to the heart of the forest. Heinrich's heart pounded, lungs fit to bursting. He fought desperately for every painful breath.

'Make for cover on the far side!'

Out of his eye he saw Hassler blubbing.

'Control yourself, soldier. Follow me!'

Heinrich plunged into a stand of dark pines. A sharp crack rang out. Momentarily, he glanced round to see the leading horse and rider galloping along the path. A second shot and Uwe cried out. He twisted and tumbled to the ground, left thigh shattered by a well-aimed bullet.

'Keep going!'

A third shot struck Georg Ulbricht, low in the back. The youngster staggered a couple of metres before sprawling head first. Dodging between the trees, Hassler and Heinrich ran for their lives. Hassler flew headlong over an unseen stump and collapsed in a heap, clutching his ankle. Ignoring his comrade's plea for aid, Heinrich ploughed on. Approaching hooves thundered in his ears. He zig-zagged between the trees, his only advantage over the riders.

Another shot rang out and a whining bullet flew past his helmet. Badly shaken, Heinrich plunged deeper into the forest. He was stunned by the loss of his unit, soldiers under his command, wounded or captured. Should he go back and support them? He opted for escape. In minutes, the Polish cries grew fainter, gradually fading out of earshot. The cavalrymen appeared to have given up, satisfied with their successes. Heinrich knew he must get back to his lines.

Silent escape was impossible. Snapped branches, underfoot, resounded like pistol shots. Sick with fear, he pulled up to give his heaving lungs the chance to recover. But Heinrich's blood ran cold as an awful realisation dawned. He had deserted his own comrades. When he got to base he would face searching questions. The young lance corporal broke down and wept.

Brandishing an automatic weapon, a sturdy figure stepped out from behind a trunk.

'*Heben sie Ihre hände!*'

A harsh voice.

'Stay where you are!'

The man spoke Heinrich's language, betraying a Hamburg accent. Heinrich obeyed, his hands held high. Blinded with tears he shuffled forward, all the stuffing knocked out of him. He was past the point of caring. The swarthy newcomer, iron jaw and bristle beard, pierced him with narrowed eyes. A sergeant's stripes denoted his rank.

'*Mein Gött!* He's one of ours. Step forward, soldier!'

A trembling Heinrich subsided to his knees.

'Identify yourself. Unit?'

The *Unteroffizier* in camouflaged battledress squared up, menacingly. Heinrich found himself staring down the barrel of the gun.

'17th Infantry,' he mumbled. 'I've lost my unit. Polish cavalry charged us.'

The burly sergeant took a further step forward. His expression changed swiftly from outright aggression to disbelief. He turned to two fellow soldiers, hard faces camouflaged with mud.

'We've caught one of our own!'

The sergeant made little attempt to conceal his wry amusement. One of his companions spat on the ground.

'*Ubergrenadier*, is it? Hmph! They make 'em young, these days!'

The irony was not lost on the unhappy soldier. He shrank back as the *Unteroffizier* approached him.

'This place is getting too lively for boys! Better come with us, son. Don't want the whole *Polski* army poking around.'

He pulled Heinrich up by his lapels.

'You can stop your snivelling. At least you kept your rifle. Report to HQ. You'll have to answer questions. We heard shooting. You weren't supposed to engage the enemy. Stirred up a hornet's nest, you have.'

Heinrich's regular *Wehrmacht* captors reluctantly lowered their weapons.

ii

As darkness fell over the small Silesian town, a thick cloud of acrid smoke spiralled over its burning buildings. Crackling flames leapt high into the sky. A fierce red glow settled over the wreckage created by the morning's artillery assault. A vision from Hell. Transfixed by the awful scene before him, Heinrich Müller prepared to bivouac down for a disturbing night. Earlier that day, his unit had set out from its starting position. Mopping up, they had encountered sparse resistance.

Since the moment of Heinrich's demotion to the ranks there had been little time to ponder his personal humiliation. Broken by interrogation, he readily admitted the loss of his scouting patrol. The *Major* in charge of questioning accused Heinrich of dereliction of duty. He added the warning that a guilty verdict meant facing a firing squad. Against his instincts, the examining officer allowed himself to be persuaded to spare Heinrich's life. The lance corporal's punishment was to lose his humble stripe. A defending officer desperately thought up reasons to defend his client.

'Our future operations, *Herr Major*, require every man. Even Müller. It was his first live action leading men.'

With studied reluctance, the examiner gave way.

'Why waste a bullet on him?' he asked, grimly. 'We'll stick him in the firing line. Cannon fodder. He can take a bullet meant for one of his comrades. Let the Poles snuff him out!'

The Major cast a contemptuous glance towards the humiliated Heinrich.

'Get out of my sight, *grenadier*! You'll be on patrol at first light. We go in after the *Panzers*. Dismiss!'

The sergeant who had rescued Heinrich, the previous day, marched him out on the double. There was no sleep, that night. When dawn broke, its innocent rays pierced the eastern horizon to reveal a new theatre of war. After a rushed camp breakfast, Heinrich's new unit received the order to go into action. He slung a heavy pack over his shoulders. Cold-shouldered by hostile, new companions, he sensed he could rely on no-one. If shot and wounded in a skirmish, Heinrich suspected he would be left for dead.

Cautiously approaching the blackened ruins of a provincial town, the patrol fanned out whilst keeping a wary eye out for snipers. The bloated corpses of cows caught in cross-fire lay strewn across a meadow. On reaching a narrow lane they stopped to re-group. From a distance, muffled sounds of artillery fire cannon reached their ears. A sharp shot rang out. Crisp and near.

'Down!'

The men dropped to the ground. *Obergfreiter* Hessler, corporal in charge of the advance party, remained in a kneeling position and lifted his field glasses.

'To the right. Two o'clock. Take cover!'

The soldiers squirmed on their bellies, gaining the scant protection offered by twiggy roadside bushes. Merging into the leafy background, the grenadiers grew tense. Hessler pointed beyond.

'Corner of the field. Farm out-buildings. Split up and advance. Heinz…you take the right. I'll lead the left. Go!'

Crouched low on the right flank, Heinrich followed third in line, gripping his *Carabiner 98K*. Beads of sweat broke out on his brow. The firing ceased. Yet with every passing second he felt vulnerable. Suddenly, a crackle of gunfire burst from a line of bushes opposite the buildings. Bullets zinged over the attackers' camouflaged helmets.

'Hold your fire!'

Hessler's terse order was passed along the lines. They crept forward, stealthily. In an instant, the brief lull was lifted by a prolonged burst of fire. The grenadiers threw themselves to the ground. Heinrich's heart racing.

'My God!' he thought. 'Machine gun nest. All we have is rifles!'

The *Obergfreiter* signalled for the patrol to head for the protection of a crumbling stone wall.

'One at a time. You…Weber…run!'

Bent double and gripping his weapon, the young German raced for cover.

'Now you…Luther. Go!'

A short burst of fire spurted from the dug-in Polish position. A burst of bullets bit into the dusty lane and Luther flung himself behind the wall.

'Hold it!'

Hessler realised the Poles were anticipating the next runner.

'Cover fire. You, Müller…Krauss. Small shed by the gate. That's where they're holed up. Target it when I give the order. You…Kramer… you're next. Go!'

The two riflemen obeyed, firing at the enemy machine gun position to give the next man across a fighting chance to reach the wall.

Eugen Kramer, an eighteen year-old from Halle, tore across the unprotected gap. The machine gun started up again and Heinrich watched in horror as the callow youngster pirouetted, before collapsing to the earth. The firing ceased but its threat remained.

'We're sitting targets!'

Heinrich desperately tried to force back panic as Kramer lay twitching on the spot where he had fallen. Blood seeped from the young grenadier's trousers, a dark pool forming in the dust. The *Obergfreiter*, little more than a couple of years older than the rest, froze. At this moment of hesitation, Heinrich reacted. Flattening himself on his tummy, he crawled across the open gap towards the wounded soldier. No enemy shots were fired. The moment he reached Kramer, he felt for the first aid kit carried at his waist. His hands shook as he fumbled for a bandage, winding it tightly round the victim's groin. The only way to stem the immediate loss of blood. Heinrich secured the binding and struggled to drag the semi-conscious Kramer after him. The near lifeless body resisted his best efforts.

The other grenadier recruits watched helplessly as Heinrich pulled Kramer to safety, inch by inch. He felt, at any moment, the machine gun would open up again. After what seemed an eternity, Heinrich succeeded in getting his fallen comrade back under cover. An experienced first-aider crawled over to offer assistance. *Obergfreiter* Hassler regained control and pointed to the sky.

'Keep your heads down, boys!'

Two planes circled low, before turning and targeting the enemy position.

'*Ju87s*. They're ours!'

The fighter-bombers dipped their noses, engines roaring at full throttle. Heinrich ducked as the '*Stukas*' switched on their terrifying sirens. He did not dare raise his head as each plane dived down to release their deadly loads. Heinrich clasped his hands over his ears. The aircraft skimmed over his head. 150 metres beyond, two mighty explosions took out the enemy machine gun nest. A plume of smoke and debris rose in the air. Did he hear muffled screams? The *Stukas* wheeled away and headed back to base.

Within a minute or two, all was silent. Smoke drifted in the light breeze and there was no sign of activity. Accurate, low-level bombing had eliminated the Poles to a man.

'*Mein Gött!*'

Hessler shook as he spoke.

'We're saved!'

He signalled the two men cringing behind the wall to rejoin the patrol. His attention switched to the plight of the hapless Kramer. By now, the upper parts of the grenadier's battle trousers had been cut away and a proper tourniquet applied. Hassler spoke quietly.

'Kramer will live. We'll get him back to our lines.'

He turned briefly to Heinrich.

'Müller...how stupid can you get? We nearly lost two killed!'

He looked the new recruit in the eye and offered his hand.

'You saved his life.'

There was no more time for niceties. Hessler knew they had to get going.

'We need to move. Four men to carry Kramer. Not you, Müller. You've done your bit!'

There was new respect in the *Obergfreiter*'s tone.

'Lift him, boys. Easy! He's lost a lot of blood.'

The bedraggled patrol finally gained the shelter of the under canvas Field Headquarters, camouflaged in a neighbouring wood. They handed over the wounded man to an *Oberartz*, the medical officer with the skills to save a life. That evening, pork soup, black bread and coffee were issued to the infantrymen who had penetrated deep into Polish territory. Within the camp, Heinrich's reputation had risen from zero to grudging admiration. The demoted lance corporal found himself accepted into his new company.

Next day, the unit skirted round the still smoking town. Their objective was to take a hill summit overlooking a railway tunnel and to set up an observation post for artillery. To reach it, they were ordered to climb a winding road blocked by fleeing Poles. Small carts, pulled by exhausted mules, blocked their progress. Whole families pushed at the rear to help the unfortunate beasts drag their over-packed burdens. The elderly fell behind, some using sticks to support their feeble frames. Women wept and herded children to one side as the intimidating Germans passed by. Many evacuated villagers shouldered large bundles. They were all they could rescue from their shattered homes.

The patrol pressed on. The hill had been the site of a fierce battle during which the Polish army had put up fierce resistance. But craters along the roadside displayed the accuracy of targeted bombing. The *Stukas* had done their work, causing the defenders to abandon hastily excavated positions. Baggage wagons were crammed together in a muddle. Wounded horses lay collapsed in harness, writhing in their death agonies.

Heinrich was astonished at the abandonment of Polish weaponry. It appeared that the adversary had piled up heaps of munitions; rifles, gas masks and bayonets. An abandoned armoured car smouldered, turned over on its side.

'They must have cut and run,' he thought to himself. 'Germans would never do that.'

The chaotic scene spoke of panic and desertion. A cluster of nervous cavalry horses ran riderless across over the hilly terrain.

'If it goes on like this things'll be over in days. Where's the opposition?'

Heinrich was about to be answered. He and his comrades were walking blindly into a trap. Suddenly, all Hell let loose as a cannonade of shells fell just short of the intruders. The townsfolk fled for cover, abandoning possessions and terrified animals to whatever fate might befall them. Children screamed as mothers grabbed their hands to pull them away from the bombardment. A second fusillade fell amongst the Germans. Red hot pieces of shrapnel tore through the patrol. Hessler and Krauss fell to the ground. In seconds, life ebbed away. Heinrich felt a terrible blow in his shoulder. Clutching his open wound, he stumbled over to an exposed rock to find Ludwig Beck cowered and whimpering. It seemed to Heinrich that his head was splitting open with the pain. Splinters of bone bespattered his battledress jacket. He was in a bad way and there was no escape route.

'We can't fight shells,' he told the unhappy Beck. 'Heads down and hope for it to stop.'

A third volley of shells passed over them, exploding further down the hill.

'Don't know what's happened to the others. Stay still 'til dark.'

He feared being taken prisoner but kept it to himself. Heinrich took a quick swig from his water bottle, wincing at the torture of such a simple task. His right shoulder was bloodied and exposed. Beck began to regain his senses. They appreciated only too well their isolated position.

'No-one's going to take me,' Heinrich muttered. 'I'd rather die than be captured.'

He had not yet figured out that his left shoulder had been rendered useless, unable to fire a rifle. Beck offered to apply anti-septic and a field dressing. Heinrich screwed up his courage and permitted his colleague to administer crude first aid. The inexperienced grenadiers kept cover for some hours, not knowing the Poles had retreated.

Towards evening, it appeared they were isolated. Grimacing with pain, Heinrich permitted Beck to help him to his feet. It was a risk to move in the final hours of daylight but leaving things until dark increased the chances of getting lost. Ludwig Beck risked exposing himself by crawling out of the shadow of the protective rock.

'I think we can do it,' he said urgently. 'There's nothing out there.'

The two soldiers backed their decision and moved out. Beck, who had avoided being wounded, steadied Heinrich as they made their way slowly down the hill. The dumps of accumulated goods and weapons, left earlier in the day, sat jumbled at the roadside. And there was no sign of civilians. Without a map, they attempted to retrace the steps of the morning's patrol.

'*Halt! Hande hoch!*'

The brusque German command sounded almost sweet to their ears. Beck immediately raised his hands in surrender. Heinrich stood by, unable to obey.

'*Hande hoch!*'

The command was more urgent and directive.

'He can't!' Beck pleaded. 'He's wounded.'

Two burly *Wehrmacht* sentries stepped out into the road, rifles pointing straight at the fugitives. They relaxed and lowered their weapons.

'You look in a bad way. We'll get you to the dressing station. D'you want a hand?'

Heinrich accepted and the four German infantrymen followed a track through a dense wood.

'Oh no!' Heinrich gulped. 'They're going to question me again. What can I say?'

iii

'You did very well!'

Heinrich Müller shuffled his feet, attempted to stand to attention. His badly damaged shoulder had been given only temporary treatment. Sheathed in a full sling strapped across his breast, the injury continued to give him acute discomfort. The prognosis was depressing. *Hauptmann* Kempff, his company commander, eyed the young soldier with a degree of sympathy.

'Day Four of this war, Müller, and you're already on your way out!' he suggested, cynically.

'You're likely to be sent home. Or maybe the Division will come up with something else for you. Desk job? Which hand do you write with?'

Heinrich turned over his right hand. It belonged to the undamaged side of his body.

'This one, sir. I'd prefer to stay and fight.'

Kempff eyed him, ruefully. He did not wish to sound cruel.

'Highly commendable, young man. But there's nothing for you in this active unit. Things are moving too fast. The

Poles have shown spirit but our next offensive will rout them.'

He clenched his fist over the rickety table.

'We'll be in Warsaw before the winter sets in. Danzig's already on the brink of surrendering.'

He paused and scrutinised an army document on the folding table in front of him.

'So, what do you do in peacetime?'

Heinrich had spent a sleepless night, mostly in pain but agonising over his future.

'Student, sir. Salzburg.'

The *Hauptmann* showed interest.

'Austria, eh? I skied on the borders only two years ago. Zugspitze mountain. Top glacier. Good sport!'

Heinrich suddenly felt shy.

'I play the violin, sir.'

There was an awkward silence between the senior officer and demoted grenadier. The *Hauptmann* picked his words with care.

'I see. Well, I'm no musician, Müller, but I hope you'll get back to your violin. Have you discussed this with the medical people?'

Heinrich shook his head and sounded glum.

'I'm too confused.'

Kempff motioned Heinrich to be seated on a canvas chair. He picked up a pair of rimless spectacles and pushed his desktop papers to one side.

'The Panzers are sweeping all before them. We'll overrun this sector during the next few hours. The enemy's getting knocked about by the artillery. We follow up with the hand to hand stuff. But it means we're creating a vacuum in our rear. That's the danger. There's already been resistance and they're going undercover.'

The *Hauptmann* warmed to his theme.

'Our *Führer* demands all Poles must submit to German direction. From now on, they'll be working for the benefit of the *Reich*. A dynasty to last a thousand years. So we need to set up top class organisation.'

He sounded contemptuous.

'Not my thing! But there's also the problem of Polish prisoners. Surrendering in droves. More than we can cope with. We need to set up temporary camps.'

Heinrich wondered where the conversation was leading.

'Besides,' the *Hauptmann* went on, 'we must gain a quick victory. It's rumoured the French are already manoeuvring in Alsace. Responding to the Polish cause. If you ask me, it's all sabre rattling. We certainly don't want war on two fronts.'

The young wounded soldier was hardly in the mood for a lecture on military politics. Kempff, however, had the bit between his teeth.

'As Infantrymen on the front line, we can't stand still.'

There was a gleam in his cold eyes.

'Press on and deliver victory for the *Führer*. The *SS* can mop up the civilian chaos in our wake. They're already occupying ground gained.'

Kempff coughed. With impeccable manners he raised his hand to his mouth.

'The paramilitaries could use a bright lad like you. Wound or no wound. You could help out with the paperwork, maybe? No need to get involved with the dirty stuff. Leave that to the fit troops.'

Heinrich did not respond but waited for his superior to continue.

'You know what they're like, these people. They're not like us. Have a different set of values to the *Wehrmacht*. We'd never lower ourselves to their…'

He hesitated.

'…persuasive methods!'

He cleared his throat for a second time.

'The Poles will soon learn to come round to our demands. Yes…I'm sure the military police could make use of you in a "paperwork" capacity. What d'you think?'

Heinrich felt uneasy. He had heard vague accounts of Himmler's *SS*; the army of black shirts working directly to the *Führer*. At school, a particularly fearsome bully had volunteered for the *Schutzstaffel*. Hitler's special protection guards were already expanding into fully-fledged military units. He had stumbled across the term '*Waffen SS*' but was unsure of its role. The young grenadier's expression barely concealed his innermost doubts.

'With respect, sir, it doesn't sound like me. I'm not political and I never joined The Party.'

His superior sat up in his seat and appeared uneasy.

'Don't get me wrong, young man. I'm dyed in the wool *Wehrmacht*. And my father and grandfather before me. This new breed of troops is a bit new for all of us. Each to his own way!'

He dismissed Heinrich's anxieties with a cursory wave of the hand.

The Music of Freedom

'In times of war, we're forced to do things we don't anticipate. What matters is winning. Victory at all costs… and quickly. This Polish nonsense will be over before Christmas. Then, with your shoulder problem, you can be in the first draft for early discharge!'

The *Hauptmann* smiled and replaced his spectacles on the bony bridge of his thin nose. He searched for a file and opened it at the first page.

'There's something else I must tell you, Müller. Your colleague, Grenadier Beck, was instructed to write a full report on your unit's abortive mission. *Obergfreiter* Hessler was killed, we understand. Very unfortunate. Beck claims you went to the rescue of an injured comrade?'

Heinrich looked up, sharply as the *Hauptmann* flicked through the pages.

'You saved his life in the face of enemy fire? Word's got round, Müller. Your action has been noted at Army Group High Command.'

He looked Heinrich straight in the eye.

'We understand the *Führer* is proposing a new military award. The *Kriegsverdienstkreuze*. War Merit Cross. First and Second Class. A high honour at either level, especially for lower ranks. I'm authorised to tell you that your name is to be put forward to the General. He'll make the final recommendation to Berlin.'

Heinrich was visibly taken aback.

'I was only doing my duty, sir. Others would've done the same.'

Hauptmann Kempff laughed.

'I don't think so, *Grenadier!* From what I'm told, your

brave comrades stood by and watched. Is that not correct? To be fair to Beck, you both got back to our lines to report the military situation. Such an award will do the reputation of this company no harm. The *Führer*'s newest honour. Imagine! I've no doubt 14th Army and the Division will be proud to be amongst the first to receive it!'

Heinrich perceived where his superior was coming from. Such an award would reflect well on commanders and not just the lowly ranks.

'Beck was brave, too, sir. I don't see why I should be singled out for recognition.'

Hauptman Kempff terminated the interview and Heinrich winced as he stood for the salute with his good arm. His superior offered one final parting shot.

'Müller, I'm sending you back behind the lines to get proper treatment. After that, the military will assess your future. Dismiss!'

Walking over to the casualty tent, Heinrich reflected on the events leading up to such a turn of events. It was surreal. Merely days ago, he had been demoted for dereliction of duty. Now, out of the blue, resulting from the heat of battle, a recommendation for gallantry.

A confused Heinrich entered the casualty post for an overdue pain-killing injection.

iv

SS Standartenführer Willi Schneider surveyed the ruins of the captured town from his window, overlooking the market square. Three years prior to hostilities, he had been flattered by an oblique approach to join the *Schutzstaffel*. Already an enthusiastic *Nazi* supporter, the Munich lawyer had readily agreed to take the special training appropriate for Hitler's expanding paramilitary forces. With its leader, Heinrich Himmler, attending the Berlin initiation ceremony Schneider dedicated his life to the matchless *Führer*. Lucrative business contracts loomed. His chambers would rise to the top of Munich's legal establishment. Being in with the *Nazis* had its rewards.

Outside, an appalling scene of destruction greeted his reptilian eyes. Stone buildings blown apart; shattered windows and roofs burned out. Blackened timbers of undermined walls threatened to give way at any moment. Schneider had no time or patience for the local citizens. They came across as a sullen bunch. Barely polite when spoken to and less than willing to obey directives from their conquerors. A supervised work party of Polish youths humped rubble from the debris, whilst women in thin coats queued outside the surviving bakery. Many baskets would remain empty with children going to bed hungry.

These matters were of little concern to Schneider. The Poles were miserable failures, incapable of defending their nationhood and had dug their own graves. Had they not boasted their superiority at the start of the September offensive? He had seen Polish newspaper headlines of those uncertain days.

'We shall chase the Hun all the way to the gates of Berlin!'

Bravado nonsense! Their capital had now fallen under siege and a number of provincial cities had put up the white flag. In the east, the Poles were now threatened by the Russians. On the previous day, Schneider had got wind of a rumoured offensive. The Non-Aggression Pact signed by von Ribbentrop and Molotov permitted the Red Army to grab masses of Polish territory. True to their word, the Kremlin's mighty forces were knocking the stuffing out of the Polish defenders. The Nazi-Soviet binding agreement was now to be honoured. Two major nations collaborating in the total subjection of an inferior race.

Germany was left free to march into the Low Countries and threaten other parts of Europe. But would that provoke the French who had already pledged support for Poland? Schneider also agonised over the chances of the British responding to the Polish debacle. Yet, the *Führer* had stated Britain would never be his foe. On the contrary, the insular race was to be admired rather than provoked. It made sense to negotiate a peace deal between the two powers as soon as possible. The British were to be left free to run their world Empire, whilst the Soviets and Germans sought to gain territory, in continental Europe.

'*Lebensraum!*' Schneider concluded. 'Room to expand. The *Führer's* great promise to his oppressed people.'

He was roused from his mental ramblings by a sharp knock on the door.

'Come!'

An *Unteroffizier* entered the room.

'*Heil Hitler!*'

The two *SS* men stiffened and exchanged salutes. The *Unteroffizier* carried a thin file.

'*Standartenführer*, I have temporary lists of Polish troublemakers. Just a start. The local Police weren't especially co-operative.'

Schneider ordered his inferior to stand at ease.

'I hadn't expected less,' he said. 'Gaining collaboration of these people will never be straightforward. Tell me what you have, so far. Why not sit down?'

Unteroffizier Dietrich pulled up a chair and opened the file on the desk.

'It's been possible to gather details of most teachers in this town,' he said. 'We forced our way into the Education Office and caught their officials destroying files. Incinerating them behind the building.'

SS Standartenführer Schneider bit his lip.

'I suppose that was to be expected,' he said, icily. 'What about the professors at the University? They're the main danger. Too much to say for themselves. Respected by Slavic fools who think they're smart. I want them rounded up with immediate effect!'

The diligent Dietrich was ahead of him.

'I've already ordered arrests, sir. Many fled their posts to be with their families. We picked them up in their homes.'

Schneider nodded with satisfaction.

'Good work! And the godly priests who hold sway over the masses? You know these peasants are just about one hundred per cent Catholic? We can't accept dissident voices influencing brainless sheep. Signs of organised resistance are already springing up. I've received a report of a shooting of one of our men, on a house raid. We nabbed the criminal who's being interrogated as we speak. A woman, would you believe? She's in the hands of the *Gestapo* so we can expect quick results. They've set up in the local prison. The cells will be full, in no time.'

Schneider walked over to the window and studied the near-deserted market square.

'Our problem is lack of staff to do the back-up tasks. I don't know how we're expected to cope with such numbers.'

The *Unteroffizier* agreed.

'What about the *Juden* rabble, sir?' he said. 'The under race. Far more than we estimated. Breed like rabbits. I've sent two men down to the Synagogue by the river. They're sure to have records. The local Rabbi can always be "encouraged" to provide information!'

He joined his superior at the window as a gang of military prisoners marched miserably across the emptying square. German guards prodded stragglers forward with the butts of their rifles. Schneider sighed.

'So many problems, Dietrich! Not enough time. The *Berliner* bureaucrats have no idea of the scale of things.

Sitting on their arses, in luxury offices, with weightier matters occupying their great minds.'

He glanced round at the gloomy requisitioned office.

'We must make do with what we've got!'

Dietrich interrupted, courteously.

'We've been sent a young army fellow from 28th Infantry. They've no further use for him. Wounded in battle, so I hear, and declared unfit for active service. But educated. Comes with a high recommendation from his commanding officer so he might provide useful liaison with the *Wehrmacht*. They think they're above us. But this is the good chance for the *Waffen SS* to prove itself.'

The *Standartenführer* agreed.

'Let them think what they want,' he scoffed. 'Death and Glory boys. But they're not as good as they make out. The *Wehrmacht*'s sustained greater losses than they admit. I've seen trainloads of wounded ferried back to the Motherland. What they haven't caught onto is that there's quiet resistance mounting amongst these Poles. Thousands didn't turn in their weapons. That's where we come in. Sniff out resistance, arrest the perpetrators and…'

He paused.

'Well, you know the rest, *Unteroffizier*.'

He respected Dietrich as a true *SS* loyalist, never likely to challenge the *Führer*'s values.

'*Schnaps?*'

Schneider eased open a drawer and pulled out a small bottle.

'Local Polish!' he chuckled. 'Appropriated during a raid on the inn on the other side of the square. We rescued a good number of bottles before setting fire to the place!'

Dietrich grinned as Schneider produced small glasses.

'To the Poles!' his superior exclaimed. 'May their God protect them!'

'Jewish or Christian, sir?'

Dietrich snorted at his own witticism. Schneider did not permit himself to smile.

'I'm told,' he responded, grimly, 'they share out Jehovah at the week-end. Jews on Saturdays. Christians on Sundays!'

He raised his glass a second time.

'To the *Führer*!'

The *SS* colleagues downed a complementary dose of the cheering spirits. *Standartenführer* Schneider gazed into his empty glass.

'I wonder,' he said, slowly, 'if their common God provides protection during the week?'

There was menace in his eyes.

'It might be worth finding out!'

V

Heinrich Müller's shoulder continued to cause him discomfort. A Polish specialist had been summoned by the Infantry commander but was able to offer only minimal reassurance. The scapula had been damaged in several places. Heinrich listened in dismay to the doctor's explanation in broken German.

'I'm sorry, young man. Your shoulder will never mend. I hear you play the violin?'

The young soldier nodded, miserably. He tensed, anticipating the revelation he did not wish to hear. The bone specialist spoke quietly.

'To play the violin, I think will be impossible. I regret to be the bearer of bad news.'

Heinrich looked down at his feet. It felt like the end of existence. The Pole excused himself and wished his patient well. A German military vehicle returned the doctor to his over-worked and under-staffed hospital.

'Well, Müller!'

His senior officer, *Hauptmann* Kempff, started up a

cigarette. He inhaled deeply before exhaling a controlled cloud of blue smoke. His unit had expanded to requisition a villa on the outskirts of town. He examined a document on his leather-bound desktop. It was written in Heinrich's hand.

'So! You request to stay with us? Left to me, I'd send you home, immediately. However, we're learning there's more to invasion than we imagined. One thing is victory. The other is the aftermath. Poland is almost at the point of total surrender. But subjugating these people isn't easy. The German-speaking Poles welcome us with gifts but the majority regards us with barely concealed hatred. We shall never be loved!'

Heinrich kept his silence. The *Hauptmann* drew heavily on the cigarette.

'Unfortunately Müller, try as we might, we can find no further role for you in the *Wehrmacht*. As you know I've spoken to our friends in the *SS*. By co-incidence, I know the local commander…*Standartenführer* Schneider. We were at school, together. Played football in the same team. He was an average left back.'

He paused.

'Very average.'

Kempff drew another slow fill of nicotine into his lungs. Heinrich noted the officer's yellowed thumbs and fingers.

'Schneider is prepared to take you on. On trial, that is. If the work proves beyond you, because of the injury, we'll have to think again. How d'you feel about that?'

Heinrich hesitated. It would be only too easy to say the wrong thing.

'I'm not sure, sir. I've never had dealings with the *SS*. Don't really know what they do.'

The *Hauptmann* tried to put his mind at rest.

'From what I hear, they're simply involved in the final stages clearing opposition and getting certain local Poles on side. There are opportunists in every nation. People who know which side their bread's buttered on. Once we find locals prepared to collaborate, this wretched country will settle down again.'

He looked up sharply.

'Well, enough of this! You've done yourself credit. Don't forget that. If things don't work out, you can always come back to me. I make that promise. We can take it from there. So, for now, I wish you luck!'

Heinrich was no longer sure to which organisation he belonged.

'Do I remain in the *Wehrmacht,* or shall I be expected to join the *Schutzstaffel?*'

Kempff attempted to put the young grenadier's mind at rest.

'From what I hear, Müller, the *Waffen SS* is interested in building a positive relationship with the regular army. This is where you come in. Call it "liaison work." You'll be on our pay-roll. You will be the link.'

To Heinrich, the proposal sounded vague but he knew no purpose would be served if he pressed the point.

'Very well, sir. Whatever you suggest. I'm grateful for your support.'

He attempted to draw himself to attention and salute the officer.

'*Heil Hitler!*'

He turned slowly and made his way out of the room.

Then he proceeded carefully down the grand staircase of what, only days before, had been home to a wealthy Polish family. Shown into the street by a fellow private, he hesitated as a black limousine drew alongside. A Mercedes. The rear door opened and a thin, bony-faced officer called from the back.

'*Grenadier* Müller? Step inside. Take your time. We know about your injury.'

Somewhat startled, Heinrich felt his way gingerly into the waiting vehicle and was motioned to take a seat in the back. He felt uneasy to sit so close to a uniformed *SS offizier*. It surprised him that the man was not wearing the ceremonial black he had seen on newsreels. The uniform was closer to that of the combative *Wehrmacht feldgrau* – field grey.

'Drive on!'

The Officer settled back into the plush leather.

'I hope you're comfortable?'

Heinrich mumbled an affirmative and tried to smile. But it did not come easily.

'Thank you, sir. Forgive me. I don't know your name.'

The Officer looked at him through the thin slits of his grey eyes.

'Of course! How could you? Schneider. I'm sure you're intelligent enough to work out my rank by my insignia.'

The new recruit quickly took in the stark trademarks with which the German populace had come familiar. High-peaked cap sporting the party eagle at its centre and, immediately beneath, the chilling '*Danziger' Totenkopf* or death's head skull. The *SS* officer wore a scarlet band on his left arm, featuring the black Nazi *swastika* on a white background. Heinrich felt intimidated, cold shivers running up his spine.

'And how is my old friend, Kempff? We played football together. As boys. He kept goal. We called him *Fliegend Schwein,* the Flying Pig! Too keen on his *wurst!* I came to his rescue when he fumbled the ball in the penalty area…which he often did!'

Heinrich felt increasingly uncomfortable. He had never been a sporty boy and found those that were, generally threatening. He glanced out of the window as the car picked up speed in the hot sunshine. All of a sudden it screeched to a halt, pitching its occupants forward. The driver cursed. Scores of citizens, adults and children, swarmed towards the stationary vehicle. Many pushed home-made makeshift contraptions with wheels. Others shoved handcarts or bulging prams stuffed with bedding almost obscuring their tiny human occupants.

It was astonishing to see professionals of his own background. Well-dressed men had chosen to wear suits, ties and polished shoes for the journey whose end they could not envisage. Some women clutched handbags and tottered on fashionable high heels. Heinrich looked at the faces, all of which betrayed anguish. To where were these people fleeing? If they had abandoned their homes, where would they find new places to settle? Schneider cursed. He fingered the lumpy leather holster at his belt.

'Get a move on, driver! If we get stuck, I'll jump out and shoot a couple of these renegades. That'll clear a passage!'

The driver obeyed and headed the Mercedes into the face of the mob. At the last moment, the evacuees parted down the middle like frightened cattle. The accelerating vehicle plunged through, hands pressing against the side windows. Gaunt expressions betrayed the people's misery. The *Standartenführer* vented his spleen on the passing vagrants.

'Rabble! Blocking the roads. How will our army get through to the next objective? We must instil order into these people!'

The Mercedes reached the town centre and approached its near-deserted marketplace. It slowed as it turned into a parking slot at the central building taken over by the *SS*. A massive *Nazi* banner hung from an upper floor window. The driver jumped out to run round and open the rear door. As Heinrich stepped onto the cobbled square he heard shouting from behind the abandoned stalls. Two young, slightly bearded Jews walked together. A young German soldier sprang out from behind a barrier and cursed them. They had given him no cause. Heinrich watched on, helplessly, as the soldier spat at the young men and poked their ribs with his rifle barrel. He was joined by two comrades who yelled insults. One Jew was struck on the head. The other tried to restrain the bloodthirsty soldiers but was punched to the ground. The assailants swaggered on, but not before giving the cowering bodies a kicking. It was clear they had been drinking. *Standartenführer* Schneider watched on, laconically.

'You see the problem, Müller?' he said with controlled calm. 'Provocative Jews and under-trained soldiers! This is what we, in the *SS,* must sort out. Enforce discipline in our own fashion. In that way, we'll all get on. Of course…'

His gaze fell upon the retreating Jewish men, supporting one another as they limped away from the square.

'...if we can make life simpler for the Jews we'll all benefit. What they need is a place where they can be herded. I've heard Madagascar has been put forward.'

He guffawed.

'I'm quite serious! A crazy scheme dreamt up in Berlin. But how would we transport them there? In the meantime, we must restrict their activities. Keep the vermin out of sight.'

His voice grew in intensity.

'We call the shots! As long as these sub-humans remain in Europe, we'll grind them down man, woman and child. Why, only this morning, a new directive arrived from *Reichsführer-SS* Himmler. He sent instructions to remove all Jews from the streets.'

Heinrich felt shaken. He feared he was getting himself into something he had not anticipated. The former *Wehrmacht* soldier fought to conceal his pulsating heartbeats.

*

Three weeks passed. Early October. The *Wehrmacht* and Heinrich's unit had moved on, relieved of the responsibility to guard their rear. The *SS* was keen to accomplish the handover.

'You're doing very well, young man.'

Standartenführer Schneider stood overlooking his new recruit's assignment. Scattered over Müller's desk were neatly clipped together lists of local groups. Some invited further investigation.

'I admire the way you set about your tasks. Very commendable. Setting up a cross-referencing system of Polish individuals and organisations. It's the addresses we're most interested in. We'll soon be able to talk to anyone we regard as dissident.'

He stepped over to the town square window. Normality was beginning to return to the subjugated town. The Germans sought to encourage active co-operation. Certain prominent townsfolk were willing to negotiate personal freedom in return for helpful information about their erstwhile neighbours.

'I'm especially pleased with…what's his name…?'

Schneider shuffled papers to find the appropriate document.

'This…Wozniak. Marek Wozniak? A Mathematics teacher. Highly co-operative. What a sensible fellow. Without his information we'd have taken weeks to ferret out his colleagues who put about anti-German propaganda. Who'd have thought of such a thing? Professional schoolmasters prepared to subvert youngsters in the classroom. Now, this one…'

Schneider selected a single piece of paper.

'Jaroslaw Kowalski…aged thirty one. Married. No children. Graduated at Krakow; top honours in Economics. Nine years teaching at the Technical High School.'

He fingered his rimless glasses.

'Highly commendable. A fine record but spoilt, I understand, by recent utterances to his older students. I noticed Herr Wozniak reports Kowalski's comments.'

He examined the page more closely.

'*The Germans have no right to be in our homeland.*'

The *Standartenführer* grew angry.

'Very foolish. And what's this?

"*We must resist German culture by all means possible. The Nazis are to be challenged at every opportunity.*"

'Did he really say that? A Bolshevik without doubt! This fellow must be removed from his post of responsibility. He isn't fit to be in charge of young people. Doesn't he realise everything's changed? We Germans are naturally forgiving but we can't permit innocent minds to be polluted by seditious nonsense.'

Schneider cocked his head towards his new recruit.

'What's your opinion, *Grenadier* Müller?'

Heinrich gulped, pretending to examine the mass of paperwork scattered before him.

'I…really don't know, sir,' he stuttered. 'Perhaps Herr Kowalski's thoughts pass over the heads of his students? There's nothing they can do to alter the situation. I understand school attendance is rising now that terms of surrender have been agreed.'

Schneider glanced at him, sharply.

'We *welcome* opinion in the *SS*,' he replied. 'I insist you speak your mind, Müller! I know you haven't joined us by the normal recruitment route. Your privileged position is exceptional and the result of your injuries in battle. But we value your work – as long as you're one hundred per cent with us.'

Heinrich suspected he was being manoeuvred into a trap.

'I assure you, sir, I'm behind every action we take. My record proves this.'

His superior pulled out a silver cigarette case and selected a cigarette. He took his time over its lighting but made no offer to Heinrich.

'A non-smoker, I believe, Müller? Very wise. I regret I'm unable to resist the temptation.'

He peered at the setting sun settling over the remaining intact roofs of the town.

'Did you ever play music with Jews, Müller?'

It was a question out of the blue. Heinrich found himself almost tongue-tied.

'I think maybe…one or two…*Standartenführer.*'

He knew it was a lame response. Schneider drove in more deeply.

'One or two Jews, hey? You seem unsure. Did you not find them repellent?'

He turned from the window in the gathering gloom and pierced Heinrich with his cold eyes. The unwilling 'liaison officer' felt increasingly out of his depth. Any word he uttered was likely to dig deeper holes. To Heinrich's relief, the *Standartenführer* abandoned his line of questioning.

'Let's not waste time with trivialities,' he said. 'I have a present task for you. With your civilised approach you have a persuasive way with people. It hasn't gone unrecognised. I want you to put aside your current investigations and work more closely to me.'

Heinrich shuddered inwardly as Schneider warmed to his theme.

'You represent little threat to the indigenous Polish community,' he continued. 'Especially with your unfortunate injury. In any case, the Poles are growing accustomed to *Wehrmacht* uniforms. It's the *SS* they appear to distrust.'

He sneered.

'Why, I can't imagine! I want you to visit the local synagogue and speak to the Yiddish authorities. Of course, you'll go with proper credentials. I'll give you a letter of commendation. In this way, the good Rabbi will surely see sense!'

His thin lips curled into a cruel smile.

VI

'Welcome!'

The Rabbi in a long frock coat waited at the top of the steps of his synagogue, standing in front of its imposing carved door. He held his hand out in greeting, lively eyes smiling through round, rimmed spectacles. Heinrich noted the Rabbi's head was covered with a small *kippah*.

'I'm honoured to meet you, sir.'

He hesitated. Should he have called the Rabbi 'sir'? No matter. There was no-one else present. The spiritual leader regarded him with interest.

'I recognise your courtesy, young man. You'll forgive my German but it's some years since I studied in Mainz. For nine months. A happy time.'

Rabbi Wallenstein showed Heinrich into the temple of worship.

'Have you seen the inside of a synagogue before?'

Heinrich admitted this was his first opportunity. He was amazed at the beauty of the interior. The internal walls were adorned with ornate Hebrew designs in vivid hues.

He noted the formally arranged polished pews facing away from the entrance. Above him, on three sides, ran a balcony supported on pillars.

'We face East,' the Rabbi explained. 'Jerusalem, you know? Come...I'll show you round, if only briefly. I mustn't waste your time.'

They walked down the sanctuary, in silence, stopping at a table near to the front.

'This is the *bimah* where the scrolls of the sacred *Torah* are unrolled and read to the congregation.'

Behind the table, Heinrich's eye was taken by a wonderfully crafted wooden closet reached by a small flight of steps. Rabbi Wallenstein looked at him quizzically.

'Would you like to see the scrolls? They're contained inside the holy *ark*.'

He mounted the steps and unlocked the doors. Heinrich was surprised at the contents. The Rabbi revealed five large scrolls, standing upright, each clothed in hand-embroidered covers.

'These are the first five books of Moses. Our covenant with God is embodied in these...also the civil laws and religious obligations. Even the moral code by which we lead our lives.'

The Rabbi paused.

'I'm sorry. I can see I'm boring you. My apologies.'

The young German shook his head.

'No...no, Rabbi. Not at all. I had no idea. It's beautiful. My own church, back in Germany, is far plainer.'

Rabbi Wallenstein smiled.

'Ah...Lutheran, perhaps? Your founder was a great religious reformer.'

His dancing eyes shaded a little.

'Mind you, Martin Luther was no great lover of the Jewish race. Far from it. But that was centuries ago. Permit me to show you one or two other things you won't have seen.'

He pointed above the *Ark* where a small brass lamp burned quietly.

'That light represents God's eternal presence. It never goes out. And over on the left,' he went on, 'you see the *menorah.*'

Heinrich found himself looking at a prominent branched, brass candlestick.

'Seven branches,' the Rabbi continued. 'The oldest symbol of our faith.'

He stepped back from the *ark*. 'Well, young man, we must get down to business. Let me show you to my office.'

The two men, considerably apart in age and background, sat opposite at an open desktop.

'May I offer you something to drink?'

Heinrich politely declined. Rabbi Wallenstein rested his elbows on the desk and folded his hands.

'I think I may have some intimation of your visit. But you must explain more fully. I'll do what I can to help.'

It was the moment the young *grenadier* had wished to avoid. He was conscious of the dull ache in his shoulder.

'As you see, sir, I'm a *Wehrmacht* soldier. But, because of my injury, I've been assigned to clerical duties. And that duty is to liaise with the local *Schutzstaffel*. I think this may have been explained to you?'

The Rabbi nodded in the affirmative. Heinrich felt compelled to continue.

'We're attempting to put together lists of citizens in the community,' he said. 'For administrative purposes, I'm told. It'll help improve the smooth running of the town. Above all, we wish to work with local authorities so each group receives equal treatment.'

He sensed Rabbi Wallenstein's growing unease. The Jewish leader took out a handkerchief from his pocket and twisted it in his hands. Heinrich summoned up the courage to continue.

'What I've been ordered to do, sir, is request a full list of your members…worshippers. We understand the synagogue keeps such records?'

The Rabbi's response perplexed him.

'A list? Ah!'

He shook his head in the negative.

'I fear we don't keep records of our community as we operate on an informal basis. We all know each other, especially the regular attenders. And we ask those in need of help to inform us so care can be arranged. Of course, there are a number of frail members to keep an eye on.'

Rabbi Wallenstein pursed his lips.

'But as to a formal record, that isn't really in our remit. I'm afraid I'm unable to help you.'

Heinrich Müller felt confused. Was the Rabbi being fully honest with him? Or was he defending his flock? He had, after all, used the word 'members'. Heinrich feared returning to *Standartenführer* Schneider without the information he was sent to obtain. The Rabbi got up from his seat.

'I'm so sorry,' he smiled. 'Some matters are beyond my powers. I do hope you understand?'

Heinrich realised the interview was over. In a state of considerable mental confusion, he let the Jewish leader escort him back through the sanctuary to the great outer door. Rabbi Wallenstein held out his hand and smiled sympathetically. The young German bade him goodbye and descended the synagogue steps to the street. He suspected they would meet again.

*

'I'm furious with you, Müller!'

The *Standartenführer* paced up and down his cramped office.

'If you weren't injured,' he snarled, 'I'd be tempted to strike you. We sent you on a simple mission. How can you be so naïve to believe the Rabbi's telling the truth? Of course he wasn't! He's playing for time. I could've sent in my storm troopers and stripped the place bare. Turned it upside down. Now, you've given him the opportunity to conceal the records. Destroy them, even!'

He turned directly on Heinrich who stood to attention, too embarrassed to open his mouth.

'They're cunning, these people. He saw you coming! Why didn't you see through his game? This could set us back weeks and we have you to answer for it. What have you to say for yourself?'

He was boiling with rage.

'Well?'

Badly shaken, Heinrich pieced together an inadequate reply.

'I'm sorry, sir. Rabbi Wallenstein seemed so straight…'

'Straight?'

Fuming with anger, the *Standartenführer* stamped on the wooden floor. He fought to keep down his rising temper.

'Since when was a Jew "straight"? They're all crooked. Every one of them. And they'll pay for this insult. If they think they can play games with the *Schutzstaffel*, they've another think coming.'

Schneider kicked at a wooden chair. It rocketed across the office and crashed into a side cupboard.

'We'll show them a thing or two! Tonight, after dark, we'll break into the synagogue office and you'll be accompanying the raiding party. D'you understand?'

It was a rhetorical question requiring no response.

'Report to the armoury and get yourself a *pistole*. I take it you can still use your good arm?'

Heinrich stood confused.

'I've no idea, sir!'

He did not dare to ask why he needed to be fitted up with a weapon. Schneider fought to control his ire.

'You'll carry out orders that are given to you, on the spot, by your superior officer…whoever that may be. I've yet to arrange the details. Dismiss!'

Praying the floorboards beneath would open up, Heinrich marched stiffly out of Schneider's lair. An *SS* corporal passed him on the stairs and knocked lightly on the open door. He drew himself to attention and requested entrance. The *Standartenführer* ordered him inside, grumpily accepting a paper message. He glanced at it swiftly, froze, and read it a second time. His short temper finally got the better of him.

'Get out of my office!' he exploded, 'and let no-one up here. I wish to be alone!'

Schneider slammed the door shut. A third time, he glanced angrily at the paper to confirm its content.

'*Mein Gott!*' he raged. 'It gets worse! Those idiots in the *Wehrmacht* tell me they've received a message direct from Berlin.'

He read the words out slowly and deliberately

'*The name of Grenadier H. Müller has been put forward to the Führer for special recognition.*'

Schneider gasped, fighting to control his breathing.

'They're saying Müller is likely to receive the new medal issued by Hitler, himself. For outstanding bravery under fire!'

There it was in black and white…news of the award of the *Ritterkreuze*. The unhappy *Standartenführer* screwed up the flimsy note and flung it across the room. A second chair followed swiftly, smashing in pieces on the far wall.

vii

Darkness settled over the closed courtyard of the *Schutzstaffel* HQ. Grim-faced personnel dashed up and down the stairs of the building to check on last-minute instructions. Outside, the engines of two armoured cars ticked over and a nearby troop carrier stood by to move out.

The hard expressions of the *SS* raiding party gave little away. This was their first full-scale action since the occupation. A smaller covered truck pulled up and the driver jumped out to seek help to shift fuel containers into the rear. *Standartenführer* Schneider watched on, nervously fingering a pair of expensive kid gloves. He knew tonight's operation would be scrutinised by his superiors and was aware of the consequences of failure.

Heinrich Müller stayed in the shadows to survey the swiftly unfolding scene. His brief was clear. He had been instructed to accompany a unit of *SS* troops and help co-ordinate their movements. He trusted the *Walter P38,* at his belt, would prove unnecessary. It seemed inconceivable that the carefully planned operation, executed under curfew, was likely to run into much opposition.

'Müller?'

A sharp voice from across the yard. Heinrich looked round to find a helmeted trooper striding towards him.

'I'm Lamm. You're assigned to me. Since you want to see the fireworks, get into the back of the truck!'

Soldiers ran over to the transport vehicles. A whistle blew. Clouds of blue fumes filled the air as the convoy rumbled out into the street. Heinrich's truck followed third in line, ahead of a small armoured car with two SS staff officers. As the military procession passed under the lights of street lamps, he made out the thin, bespectacled face of Schneider. Lamm peered out over the rear of the truck.

'Whatever you do, don't light up! We got over a hundred litres of kerosene on board. One spark and we'll be toast!'

Heinrich smiled wanly at the poor attempt at humour. *SS-Sturmmann* Lamm settled down for the short journey.

'Don't suppose you're going to need your weapon. But never know your luck. Them old Jews ain't going to be thrilled when they see what we're up to. The sensible ones will stay in their rat runs. We don't expect no trouble!'

The convoy continued through the deserted streets before heading for the river embankment. In minutes, a gaunt, brick building got picked out in the glaring headlights. Heinrich recognised it as the synagogue. The vehicles ground to a halt. Shouted orders filled the night air as the driver ran round to release the tailgate. Lamm leapt off the vehicle with Heinrich letting himself down more gingerly.

'Our job's to keep guard on this kerosene 'til after the building's been searched.'

A small group of uniformed men ran up steps and began attacking the great door with long-handled axes. Sounds of their heavy blows echoed around the square. One or two lights went on in upstairs windows and Heinrich spotted anxious faces behind hurriedly parted curtains. A second detachment of soldiers charged round to the rear of the synagogue. Moments later, Heinrich detected sharper sounds of splintering glass. It appeared the building was being broken into at various points. The young *Wehrmacht grenadier* thought of the Rabbi he had met that morning.

'It's all my fault. This could have been avoided.'

He hid his guilt in the shadow of the bulky fuel carrier. *SS-Sturmmann* Lamm admired the ruthless determination of the troopers who resumed their physical assault on the entrance.

'Look! The door's giving way. They'll be in, any minute. Lucky sods. Never mind, we'll get our chance when the time comes. Give us a hand with these cans.'

For the first time, Lamm noticed Heinrich's slung arm.

'Oh! You're injured. My fault. I forgot. They did say something about it. These cans are bloody heavy so I'll get bodies. We need two fellers to each one.'

The *SS-Sturmmann* ran over to a group of soldiers idly surveying the scene. Two came back with him, disappointed at not being selected for the main activity. Lamm took charge.

'Give us a hand getting these cans out, lads! Müller's done his arm in so he's not much use. Take it steady. Remember…no smoking!'

The reluctant helpers got to work with Heinrich looking on. Their task was onerous, indeed hazardous, but they soon succeeded in standing four kerosene cans on the cobbles. Two troopers staggered out of the synagogue bearing a heavy metal filing cabinet. They lurched over to Heinrich's truck and begged for help to heave it onto the back.

'There's a couple more of these,' one shouted. 'Don't go away!'

They leapt off the back of the truck and returned to the building, now illuminated by its own internal lamps. Three more soldiers appeared at the smashed front door. They staggered down the steps. Each bore an armful of gold and silver ornaments.

'Lots more of this stuff in there! We've been told to stick it in your truck. Like to know what's going to happen to it. Do we get a cut?'

Over the next few minutes, a succession of loot found its way onto the covered transport vehicle. Heinrich stayed mute, recognising the synagogue furniture he had admired on his visit, stashed on board. His only consolation was that no-one asked him to give them a hand. It appeared he was regarded as a semi-invalided and unnecessary guard. To his dismay, *Standartenführer* Schneider appeared on the scene. From his facial expression he was apparently delighted with the night's haul. He surveyed his booty with studied satisfaction.

'Well, Müller, a successful operation!'

Heinrich made no reply. Schneider pointed at the sacred rolls of the *Torah* that were in the process of being loaded.

'Keep a special eye on them for me,' he ordered. 'Make sure they don't get damaged. Those embroidered covers are worth a fortune.'

He paused and glanced round, slyly.

'We shan't bother with a detailed inventory, tonight. That's your task, first thing in the morning. For now, make it your job to look after these covers. Have them taken up to my office when we get back. No questions asked. Understand?'

Heinrich felt bemused but mumbled an affirmative. Schneider's attention was taken by the neat dump of large fuel cans.

'I want those containers carried up the steps, at once. Lamm will find the labour. Two are to be taken inside. We'll stand one by the main entrance. The other, somewhere down the side. Is that clear?'

The *Standartenführer* walked off to bark orders at the troopers resting from their axe work on the resistant door. A minute later, Lamm arrived with a wheeled trolley and organised the loading of the kerosene cans. Heinrich was under no illusion. The multi-purpose aim of the night's mission was obvious. Office records had been located and possessed. Following that, the building had been systematically stripped of its valuables. He was only too aware he was participating in an organised looting spree with vandalism to follow.

Five *SS* militia dashed past carrying unlit incendiary torches. They darted around the building as Lamm organised the troops carrying kerosene cans round the synagogue entrance. Heinrich's eyes grew wider as he saw one soldier unscrew the cap of one of the containers. His companions lifted it and staggered into the building to spread a trail of flammable fuel over the wooden floor. In less than two minutes, they re-appeared at the damaged doorway and hurled the empty can back into the sanctuary. An officer shouted an order. Men bearing torches held lighted matches to the tips and each one burst into flame. The fire-lighters split up, two running down the sides whilst the others ploughed straight into the vulnerable interior.

Heinrich detected muffled explosions. A fire-lighter charged out. He stopped to hurl his incendiary back into the synagogue. His companion was not so fortunate. Silhouetted in the red glow of the gathering inferno, the soldier stumbled out of the building. Yellow flames licked at his tunic. Two *SS* guards rushed forward, hurled him to the ground, and rolled him over on the pavement. A third soldier sprang forward with a fire bucket at the ready. Heinrich heard the man's screams. Within seconds, the burning fire-raiser was given a second dousing. Two medics ran forward carrying a stretcher. They lifted the victim carefully before hurrying away towards a military ambulance, on stand-by.

'*Himmel und blitzen!* The people are out!'

SS-Sturmmann Lamm pointed in the direction of the main town.

'Heading straight for us!'

Heinrich glanced anxiously up the hill. Despite the limited light of the street lamps, he made out a crowd of angry civilians bearing down on the blazing synagogue. Men, women; even children. Some only half-dressed, they waved their arms and howled *en masse*. A sudden gush of flames burst through the gaping side windows of the building. The glowing internal furnace illuminated the distraught faces of the people. But they slowed their advance when they became aware of the presence of armed *SS* storm troopers. *Standartenführer*

Schneider rallied his forces, ordering them to get in line and raise their weapons. Each man took aim, awaiting his final order. The angered townsfolk stopped only metres in front of their potential executioners. A bloodbath seemed inevitable.

At that moment, a small man in a long, black coat stepped in front of the gesticulating crowd. He raised his hands and faced the grimly set Germans. With clouds of black smoke bellowing from the windows of his synagogue, Rabbi Wallenstein dropped to his knees to appeal to the *Standartenführer*. Schneider drew out his pistol, coolly measured his aim, and shot the Rabbi, point blank. The Jewish spiritual leader groaned and turned his face to the sky before collapsing in a crumpled heap. The determined German troopers took a unified step forward. A young woman, with uncombed long hair, inched forward to confront the raised guns.

'Let us pass. Stand aside. We must rescue our sacred relics!'

Schneider strode forward, struck her across the face with his gloves and pushed her to the ground. She backed off, tears welling in her eyes, as the sacred building burned even more fiercely. A dumbstruck Heinrich spotted a second wave of townsfolk approaching from the direction of the river embankment. Within seconds they would reach the truck. *SS-Sturmmann* Lamm yanked his pistol from its holster and held it aloft as a warning.

'Get back! You're breaking the curfew. I'll shoot!'

The second wave of protestors halted within shouting distance. A middle-aged man thrust himself through the gathering.

'You criminals!'

He spotted the synagogue's treasures heaped under the truck's awning.

'Thieves! Vandals!'

He attempted to mount the duckboard but Lamm panicked and took close aim with his pistol. Heinrich heard the sharp crack even above the increasing roar of the nearby inferno. The man clasped his hands to his chest and tumbled under the wheels of the vehicle. Lamm panicked and shot blindly into the crowd. He was joined by two troopers who fired over the heads of the retreating protestors. A small boy and girl remained, riveted to the spot. They stared uncomprehendingly under the truck where their father lay bleeding to death. Judging from their dark eyes and hair, Heinrich suspected they had to be Jewish. Lamm, out of his mind with fear, threatened the brother and sister with his weapon.

'Get away!'

The children ignored him and knelt by the twisted body of their fallen father.

'Can't you see? He's dead! Clear off, you vermin!'

Heinrich leapt out of the shadows. Ignoring his damaged shoulder, he tried to thrust Lamm aside but the burly *SS* man was too strong for him. Heinrich lost his footing and crashed headlong onto the cobbles. Lamm levelled his weapon at the boy's head and fired. The child's face disappeared in a mask of blood. Heinrich struggled desperately to get up to discover the sister was now under threat. Lamm fired…but nothing happened.

'God damn it! My gun's jammed!'

Lamm tossed his weapon into the truck.

'Müller...shoot her with your *Walther*!'

Heinrich tugged his pistol out of the holster and levelled it at Lamm's temple. The *SS* bully blanched. Heinrich saw the whites of his eyes as he begged for mercy.

'No, Müller! Don't do it. Don't kill me!'

Heinrich released the safety catch.

'Please, Müller! I was doing my duty!'

The young *Wehrmacht* soldier fought to control his impulse.

'Get into the truck, you bastard,' he snarled. 'Stick your hands on your head and keep them there. One false move and I'll fire!'

He heard Lamm whimper.

'Don't move a muscle or I'll blow you away. I've fired in action. Proper battle. Not your kind of war. I'm not an *SS* murderer!'

Lamm backed into the truck, cowering under a purloined table. Heinrich turned his attention to the shocked child. She knelt in blood on the cobbles. He spoke urgently.

'I'm so sorry! You can't stay here. You must find your mother. Quickly now!'

It was clear the child spoke no German.

Heinrich lifted her gently to her feet and pointed towards the town. He watched the stricken child stumble away in an unsteady trance. Meanwhile, glowing timbers of the razed synagogue gave out intense heat in the conflagration. Wicked flames illuminated a horrifying scene of human slaughter and wanton destruction.

viii

'I've interviewed Lamm. It's all very unsatisfactory.'

Standartenführer Schneider eyed Heinrich, nastily, through his steel-rimmed glasses.

'You had no right to undertake responsibility for any action you were involved in. You were there to carry out orders. Pointing a loaded gun at an *SS* trooper and threatening to kill him is a serious offence. If tried and found guilty, I've no doubt you'll be shot.'

Schneider suspected his words were not penetrating the confused mind of the *Wehrmacht* recruit.

'You do understand, don't you, Müller?'

Heinrich remained at attention.

'Yes, sir. Only too well. I was given no information on the aim of last night's mission. Earlier in the morning you sent me to talk to the Rabbi. My instructions were to gain his co-operation.'

He had nothing to lose. In fact, Heinrich no longer cared. He was heartily sick of the invasion and revolted by the *Schutzstaffel*'s behaviour. If he was put up before a firing squad, he was ready to accept his fate.

'I never asked to be sent to this unit. You told me my role would be Army liaison. So why was I selected for the synagogue raid? As for killing innocent civilians, that's not in our *Wehrmacht* code.'

The *Standartenführer* shifted uneasily in his seat.

'Sit down, Müller, for God's sake. You're too hasty!'

Heinrich reluctantly lowered himself onto the bare wooden chair to face his inquisitor. Schneider's invitation seemed out of keeping with the tone of the conversation, thus far.

'You're young…naïve, even. Look…you don't appreciate the embarrassing position you place me in. I phoned *Hauptmann* Kempff, at 28th Infantry, only half an hour ago. You'll be interested to hear he'll oppose any action we might wish to take against you.'

Schneider picked up a fountain pen and played with it in his fingers.

'Are you aware that you've been put up for a gallantry medal?' he asked coyly, already knowing the answer. Heinrich blinked, uncertain of the direction of the conversation.

'This places us in an impossible situation,' Schneider continued. 'We value liaison with the *Wehrmacht*. You're extremely fortunate. None of my own men would get away with your disgraceful act. That said, although I really shouldn't disclose this to you, I'm furious with Lamm. I'd issued orders that the dissolution of the synagogue was to be carried out without loss of life. Not that the Poles in this town have much sympathy for the Jews. But the shooting of a child is about the most reckless act a soldier can commit. Particularly in front of witnesses. Embarrassing…be they Jews or non-Jews. We were fortunate that our swift armed response forced the mob to back off. All morning, the town's been awash with rumour. But given time, the accidental destruction of the synagogue will wash over. However, the *SS* can't permit a situation where the killing of children is encouraged. We've enough difficulties subjecting the Poles to our ways. That sort of action only compounds our difficulties.'

Schneider placed the pen carefully on the ink blotter before him. Heinrich's brain worked overtime in the attempt to take in what he was hearing. By now, he had lost all fear of the *Standartenführer*. Deep in his heart he felt revulsion, almost to the point of openly despising the *SS* leader. He chose not to challenge the use of the term 'accidental'. Although feeling bolder, he fought down the temptation to reveal his true response to the previous night's actions.

'So what happens to me now, sir?'

It was a blunt question. Schneider raised his eyebrows.

'The situation's delicate, Müller. Your *Wehrmacht* commander isn't so keen to have you back, despite the proposed medal. He tells me he doesn't know what to do with you. And you certainly don't fit in with us. The sooner the *SS* sees the back of you, the better. However…'

Schneider paused, pushing his spectacles back over the bridge of his thin nose.

'…I think I may have come up with a solution that suits us all. I've checked your records and noticed you studied in Salzburg before you joined up? Is that so?'

Heinrich could hardly conceal his surprise at the conversation's turn.

'Music,' Schneider continued. 'Violin studies, I understand?'

Schneider looked critically at Heinrich's damaged side.

'Don't suppose there'll be much future in that direction, young man. If you want a future, you'll need to think of something else.'

It was an uncomfortable moment for both protagonists.

'I have a well-placed contact in Salzburg,' Schneider went on. 'My second cousin, who's based at the Schloss Leopoldskron. A grand palace, so he tells me. Never been there, myself. D'you know it?'

Heinrich looked startled.

'Well, just a little, sir. On the edge of the city. By the lake.'

Schneider nodded. Heinrich's confidence was rising.

'I went there once or twice, maybe. We were invited to perform. No fees but they fed us well. We gave a couple of student concerts.'

The *Standartenführer* relaxed.

'Most interesting! My cousin's involved in the running of the place. Cultural matters of some kind. I understand he organises entertainment for distinguished guests.'

He smiled.

'A pleasant job. He wouldn't wish to swap places with *me*! Although he's not native to Salzburg, he's Austrian, nonetheless. We've always got on well. It might be that a quiet word in his ear might guide you in his direction. You could forget all about the war. Perhaps offer your services to something artistic.' There was the faintest trace of a sneer in Schneider's voice.

'Would you be interested?'

Schneider congratulated himself in conjuring up a practicable ruse to remove the *Wehrmacht* man from a potentially explosive situation.

'Of course, Müller, there's been no time for me to make detailed enquiries. But once the current fuss dies down, I'll be able to fix up some kind of arrangement. We'll get you…'

He paused.

'The English have an expression for it…"*out of harm's way*". It seems to me a perfect solution for all parties.'

The young German found his head in a spin. Schneider's shock proposal caught him unawares. Minutes before, he had entered the room fearing he was potentially facing execution. Suddenly, he felt a touch of gratitude towards Schneider.

'Of course,' the *Standartenführer* continued, 'the SS would insist you sign an undertaking not to disclose last night's events. You do understand, Müller? Bad things can happen in war. We're all caught up in it. Innocent in our different ways. Fortunately, this conflict won't last much longer. The *Führer* has all but gained what he set out to do. The German *Reich* can now expand to find new living space for its people. After that, we can arrange a deal with the West. And our friends, the Russians, are honour-bound to keep their part of the Non-Aggression Pact.'

Schneider appeared to have the future course and duration of the war mapped out.

'When this nonsense is over, we can all go home. I'll contact my cousin, in Salzburg, and arrange to visit the famous *Schloss*.'

He laughed out loud.

'So you and I may meet again under different circumstances! If I have it right, we turfed out the original owner after the *Anschluss*. Reinhardt? Was that his name?'

Schneider scoffed.

'Some kind of theatre producer…a Jew, of course! With sleazy contacts in high places. He managed, somehow, to get himself and his wife out to America.'

Heinrich kept his silence. He did not enlighten the *Standartenführer* of his previous acquaintance with the rococo palace adorning the placid Salzburg lakeside. And he could not help bringing to mind the memory of the extraordinary woman who ran the *Schloss*. A Princess, he remembered, with top society contacts in Vienna and Berlin. Would she still be there?

ix

Retrospective. Paris, early 1938

When Vienna-born Stephanie Richter received a cable message from her Berlin lover, she was startled at its tersely-stated contents. She tottered over to a chair in her hotel room and sank into it. Her heart raced. Faster even than at the high points of climatic moments involving prestigious men amongst the European elite. Stephanie reached to a side table for a thin, gold case, embossed with the initials of a disposed lover of some months before. With shaking hands, she took out a *Gitanes* cigarette and applied it to an elegant holder. It took a minute or two of soothing nicotine to help steady her nerves. Then she stood up and walked over to the window facing the elegant Parisian boulevard.

'Blessed Fritz,' she exclaimed out loud. There was no-one to hear her, not even her maid. 'You are the *most* incredible man!'

Stephanie drew slowly on her cigarette.

'This is the moment I have worked for. Slaved, even!'

Glancing again at the short cable message, she conjured up in her mind the handsome face of Captain Fritz Wiedemann; tall, dark-haired, with distinguished military bearing. Wiedemann, married in his mid-forties, had gained influence at the very apex of the Berlin *Reich*. Stephanie recalled the sacrifices she had made for the cause. By craft and guile, the low-born Viennese had writhed her way into the uppermost echelons of the ruling hierarchy. She then turned her attentions to the Germans. Von Ribbentrop and Goebbels were close friends as was Hitler's favourite, Hermann Goering. Stephanie's ultimate ambition was to target the *Führer*, himself. But the German despot remained aloof, surrounded by impenetrable rings of *SS* security and a web of sycophantic underlings. She calculated that it was through Wiedemann she could wangle the priceless opportunity of an audience with Adolf Hitler. Wiedemann's terse cable read:

'You are summoned to Berlin. The Chief wishes to meet you.'

Breathless with excitement, Stephanie recalled the strenuous efforts she had made to infiltrate key elements of the British Establishment. Foremost amongst these was press baron Lord Rothermere, apologist for the *Nazis* and co-founder of the London-based *Daily Mail*. Intent upon appeasing the German government, Rothermere had come to rely on the exotic, quick-silvered Viennese libertine. She had hinted she had secret channels to the *Führer*, himself. This, in keeping with so many of her dealings, was not wholly accurate. Nothing Stephanie ever uttered or imagined could be construed as for truth. But now that she had succeeded in seducing Hitler's trusted Wiedemann, she sensed achieving her final goal would only be a matter of time.

Stephanie Richter opened the hotel window to get rid of the *Gitanes* smoke. A slow smile of satisfaction spread over her cunning little face.

'Dear Fritz. How smart he is!'

As a captain in the German trenches in the Great War, Captain Wiedemann had served as former Lance Corporal Hitler's senior officer. Now, twenty years on, the former colleagues' roles were reversed, although intertwined. Upon succeeding to power, the *Führer* had selected his old Captain to act as his Personal Adjutant and confidante. Stephanie understood the curious relationship, perfectly.

'Nothing reaches our great leader without my Fritz's say-so. Through him I shall channel the missives entrusted to me by my London contacts.'

Stephanie Richter was only too aware of the significance of allying elements of the British Establishment with the *Nazi* rulers. The British Right feared the perceived threat of Bolshevists spreading from the East. A signed German-British alliance was high on Hitler's priority list. He envisaged two great nations remaining at peace and respecting each other's empires. Germany hoped to expand east into the limitless plains of Slav-dominated territory. First, Czechoslovakia. Then Poland. And after…?

'I mustn't run away with myself,' Stephanie thought. 'Remain calm. One move at a time.'

The cable from Hitler's adjutant to the Princess' Paris hotel was the final piece to fit into the duplicitous jig-saw. She held it close to her delicate-boned face and looked again at its contents.

'The Chief!'

Stephanie drew heavily on her *Gitanes* and took in the enormity of the message. Despite her beating heart she felt no fear. After all, similar to her own rise, had not Hitler also climbed the ladder from obscure social origins? She felt a close bond to her fellow Austrian upstart; an empathy stemming from her lower middle-class background. Born in Vienna and raised within a mundane family, Stephanie had suddenly and unexpectedly inherited money from a distant relative. Using this newly acquired fortune in the 1930s, she had manipulated entry into fashionable aristocratic Viennese drawing rooms. At a hunt dinner, a bold military attaché had asked the twenty three year-old to play the piano. On hearing her play, Prince Friedrich Franz von Hohenlohe-Waldenburg-Schillingsfürst went further. He invited her to join him in a duet at the keyboard. Stephanie chuckled at the distant memory.

'Foolish man! He was taken in when I passed myself off as a seventeen year-old. That rather suited his tastes.'

Stephanie Richter, rising star of Viennese society, soon announced herself pregnant by the Prince. In order to contain a society scandal, her aristocratic lover married Stephanie, abroad, at a low key ceremony. The former Stephanie Richter's first ambition had been achieved. She was now a 'royal' related to the Hapsburgs…Princess Stephanie von Hohenlohe-Waldenburg-Schillingsfürst. An ironical triumph considering that the child in her womb had, in all likelihood, not been sired by her new husband. In fact, the pregnancy was almost certainly the result of an overnight affair with another man!

This was the moment she had planned for. It had involved selling body and soul; her social triumphs earned by lies and flattery. Stephanie's personal wealth increased, too, as handsome money favours came her way, consummate with the relative wealth of her celebrity lovers.

On receiving Captain Wiedemann's cable, Princess Stephanie immediately took the Paris express to Berlin. Upon arrival, she was met at the station by Hitler's aide in a chauffeured limousine. He wasted no time advising her how to conduct the fortuitous encounter with the rising man of Europe.

'The *Führer* will see you for only a few minutes,' Wiedemann told her. 'He's impatient and has weighty matters on his mind – the forthcoming meeting with the British Prime Minister being only one. Hitler's not known to be intimate with women. He was taunted in the trenches. I told my troopers to back off and leave him alone. Never even known to go with women who offered their professional services. But Corporal Hitler could always be relied upon to carry out his messenger duties, even under fire. So we got on. That's why he sent for me after all these years.'

Princess Stephanie stole a glance at her influential lover from under her dark, seductive eye lashes.

'I require only ten minutes. I have a letter to hand personally to the *Führer*. It was given to me by Lord Rothermere. He told me the British Foreign Secretary was involved in its compilation. Many elements in the British Government are seeking peaceful relations with us. They're desperate to prevent hostilities breaking out again, in Europe.'

She glanced at the hurrying pedestrians on the street.

'Unlike the warmonger Churchill, they want a discreet arrangement. Rothermere's convinced that Churchill will oppose Hitler at every turn. But he's out in the political wilderness so the British Establishment takes no notice of him. That includes their Government so we can ignore his drunken ramblings!'

As ever, Captain Wiedemann was impressed by the socialite's astute political mind. Her contacts were immaculate. He felt the gentle application of brakes as the government limousine slowed to a halt outside the Berlin Chancellery. A stern *SS* guard opened the rear door and stood expressionless as the Princess and her lover vacated the vehicle to make their way into Hitler's headquarters. Under escort, they advanced along high-ceiling corridors, stopping only briefly before being waved through various check-points. At last, the pair reached a pair of ornate, carved doors set in a polished marble surround. Here, they were asked to be seated on comfortable chairs and await the *Führer*'s command.

Two helmeted armed *SS* guards stood rigidly to attention at the imposing entrance to Hitler's office. After a short while, an official spoke quietly to Wiedemann who rose from his seat and explained to the Princess he had been requested to enter the inner sanctum, alone. After waiting with nail-biting uncertainty, Princess Stephanie was then ushered into the presence of her *Führer*. She took in the room flecked with marble wall panelling. Shaded standard lamps and wall lights shone pools of light into the most recessive corners.

A pink-purple Persian carpet ran from the door to the far end that featured Hitler's desk. On his worktop were a simple blotting pad, ink well and telephone. A small potted plant softened its otherwise austere appearance. Stephanie made every attempt to compose herself as Adolf Hitler rose from an armchair in front of a dark marble fireplace. He wore a light-coloured, double-breasted suit.

The Princess held her breath.

'My dear Princess…how kind of you to come and see me.'

Hitler stepped forward to offer his hand. He took hers and kissed it graciously. Then, cupping her own small, white hand in both of his, Hitler pierced his guest with steely, pale blue eyes. He smiled and continued to grip her, warmly.

'I've heard so much about you. I know you've worked tirelessly for our cause. Your former husband, the Prince, has also carried out important work in Switzerland. But we're more impressed with your personal diplomatic contacts with the British. I can't begin to tell you how essential it is to be friends with influential individuals who are sympathetic to our aims.'

Hitler released the Princess' hand. She was taken aback by the warmth of the friendly greeting. It contradicted all she had been told. Nervously, she stammered out her first words.

'My *Führer*, you flatter me. I'm a mere woman. My work is of little consequence. The complexities of international relations are far beyond my reach. I would give anything to be able to establish further contacts on your behalf. But I don't flatter myself that I possess the skills.'

She smiled nervously. Hitler bowed graciously and invited her to take a seat.

'My revered Princess,' he continued, 'you under estimate yourself!'

He turned and half-smiled to his Adjutant who stood quietly in attendance.

'Wiedemann…you've arranged this meeting with your usual skill. Did you explain to Her Royal Highness that we have a little gift for her?'

Fritz Wiedemann stepped forward and handed his leader a small, lidded black box. Hitler opened it to reveal its interior lined with white satin. He invited the Princess to stand.

'Dear lady, in recognition of your outstanding services to our *Reich*, I have decided to award you something granted to only the very few.'

In his hand he held a gleaming medal.

'Please accept this, Princess…a rarely offered award. Our *Gold Medal of Honour*. It admits you to the highest levels of The Party.'

Adolf Hitler stepped forward and pinned the medal on the Princess' coat lapel.

'Wear this medal with pride. You've given great service to the National Socialist Movement. Although I would ask you not to wear it in the presence of the British. I want them to see you as a *neutral* go-between. It would be unfortunate should they ever suspect you work for us!'

He nearly smiled.

'You're the only person we can entrust with such delicate tasks.'

For once in her life, Princess Stephanie was dumbfounded. She caught Wiedemann's relaxed grin, realising he had been party to the surprise award. Hitler walked a bell pull to order tea and gateaux.

'I see I've over-whelmed you, Princess. I understand, absolutely. But now…to business!'

The *Führer* motioned his guest to return to her seat. He strode to a side table to pick up a leather-bound folder. Then returned to his place and opened the folder at the first page.

'We share a common heritage, you and I,' he said earnestly. 'Both proud Austrians. Of course, you're from the sophisticated metropolis and I come from the rural north west…Linz. I don't know if you've visited my part of the country? Well, no matter. I have a particular fondness for nearby Salzburg…and that's what I wish to consult you about.'

Recovering her composure, Princess Stephanie relaxed but failed to see where the *Führer* was leading.

'Indeed,' Hitler continued, 'I've visited that city on a number of occasions. But only fleeting visits. Mostly to attend concerts at the *Festspielhaus*. I assume you're aware of my love for the music of our revered Wagner?'

Adolf Hitler pulled out a piece of paper from the folder and handed it to the Princess.

'This is a picture of the Schloss Leopoldskron, on the edge of the city by the lake. Curiously, I haven't yet visited the Schloss. I must correct that in the near future.'

Hitler looked sharply at his new-found companion.

'You'll be aware that I've built my private country retreat just over the Austrian border. The Berghof above

Berchtesgaden. I spend much of my time there. It's wonderful to escape the noise and bureaucracy of Berlin. In the remoteness of the mountains, I can think. The pure air clears my head so I find it possible to plan the future.'

He paused.

'I don't refer to my own future or even that of our German people, but of the world as a whole. It's at the Berghof where I dream my dreams and issue my orders.'

The Princess detected a slight stiffening in the *Führer*'s posture coupled with a rise in tension in his voice. The brief smile with which she had initially been rewarded had vanished.

'Schloss Leopoldskron was originally constructed in the early eighteenth century by a Prince Archbishop. It was he who had the great lake excavated.'

Princess Stephanie felt obliged to offer a contribution to what was becoming a one-way conversation.

'I recall, sir. I walked briefly around part of the lake with a friend. Some years ago. Such a wonderful view of the palace. Rococo…very spectacular. Does the current Archbishop of Salzburg reside there?'

It was an innocent question. Hitler flashed the Princess a sharp look.

'Certainly not!' he snorted. 'A few years ago the palace was acquired by the Jew, Reinhardt. Have you heard of the fellow? Filthy rich from ill-gotten gains!'

Princess Stephanie felt unsure. Was this a trap? She shook her head before demurely raising a tea cup to her delicate mouth. Hitler was in full spate.

'The Jew took over the place and ruined it with barbaric alterations, so I'm told. Just what one would expect from his kind. He also organised the Salzburg International Festival from the Schloss. Theatre, dance…that sort of thing. The *Berliner Philharmoniker* pays a visit at the time of the Summer Festival. My personal preference is opera.'

The Princess was acquainted with a number of Viennese socialites who routinely attended the annual international arts gathering at Salzburg. The pitch of Hitler's voice rose higher and he gripped his folder more tightly.

'I've given orders for the Schloss to be handed over to the German State,' he went on. 'Reinhardt fled the country. He's now in America with his fellow money-grubbing Jews. There's no way he'll ever set foot inside that palace, again. That I'll guarantee!'

The *Führer* paused for breath and the Princess seized the opportunity to get in a brief word.

'I'm sorry, sir, but I'm not fully understanding. May I ask why you're telling me all this? Fascinating as it is,' she added hurriedly.

Adolf Hitler got up from his chair and stood with his back to the fireplace, his hands folded behind his back.

'You must forgive me, madam. My mind flies so fast that even I can't keep up with it. Come and see me at the Berghof. I invite notable people there as guests. Currently, I'm working on the recently abdicated King of England and his lady partner. The American…'

He hesitated and the Princess dared to interrupt.

'I think you refer to Wallis Simpson, *mein Führer?* I'm acquainted with her and her royal husband. Charming… both extremely sympathetic to our cause.'

Adolf Hitler was impressed.

'Exactly, dear Princess. You read my mind. This is why I intend inviting the distinguished couple to my mountain retreat. The former King retains some influence in the British capital. I'm directing you to execute a difficult task. With your contacts, I wish you to engineer an unofficial visit of the royal couple. Both will be welcome guests!' His mood lightened.

'That'll annoy the British!'

Princess Stephanie's razor-sharp mind was already piecing together the ambitious span of Hitler's proposal. Once again, he interrupted her thoughts.

'I'm commanding you to go to Salzburg where you'll take control of the Schloss Leopoldskron. I want you to run it as a retreat for the foreign politicians and aristocrats we wish to attract to our cause. They'll spend time with you and indulge their interests…cultural pursuits, arts, hunting… whatever. At some point, I'll send down for them from the Berghof. The relaxing days spent in your company will soften them up for the business to come!'

To Princess Stephanie, Hitler's cunning ploy was now crystal clear. It could not be argued that his expansive mind did not fly at great pace. It was almost impossible keeping up with him but Stephanie's electric mind was more than up to it. Adolf Hitler turned to his Personal Adjutant.

'Well, Wiedemann, the deed is done! We have the right person in place. Now, our task is to persuade the people who influence matters in Europe to join us. Our dear Princess is the perfect choice for such a responsible role.'

Far from a minimal appointment of a mere ten minutes, it was more than two hours before Princess Stephanie and Captain Wiedemann returned down the formidable Chancellery corridor. They kept their silence all the way back to the hotel booked for the Princess' convenience. In the privacy of her room, the Princess removed her coat and examined her medal. She turned to Wiedemann.

'Fritz…I don't wish to sound negative and I'm certainly not ungrateful to our *Führer*…but I've never carried out anything remotely like the demanding task he's set me. I hardly know Salzburg. How would I be expected to manage a historical palace and estate? Am I dreaming this?'

Fritz Wiedemann slipped off his jacket and tie. He kicked his shoes away and lay back on the king-sized bed.

'Come here, my little sorceress! I haven't kissed you, all day. I can only spend a few minutes more.'

Princess Stephanie somewhat reluctantly joined him on the bed but did not object when he slipped his arm round her slender shoulder.

'I haven't told you everything, my darling,' he told her. 'In your new role, you'll work directly to me. I'll install you in the Schloss. Hitler's told me you're to regard the palace as your own *home*. And we're talking about the finest building outside Vienna. I'll settle all your bills and help with the initial setting up. We'll appoint suitable staff, including security. The palace is already geared up for high-powered visitors as it offers sumptuous accommodation. I'm also briefed to pay you a considerable personal retainer. This will come directly out of the *Führer*'s private funds. Your function is to act as hostess to the distinguished guests who will go on to Hitler's Berghof for confidential meetings. You'll also be expected to invite the finest artists to stay at Leopoldskron. Europe's cultural elite. Have no fear. We believe in you!'

Fritz Wiedemann slipped his hand over the Princess' pert breast. Minutes later, they made love as they had never loved before. It did not take long. A satisfied Wiedemann levered himself off the bed to dress. He glanced at his watch.

'You must forgive me, my dear. It's getting late. I must get home to my wife and family. Tonight, we'll be eating *apfelstrudel!*'

He smiled, tied his shoe laces, and departed. Princess Stephanie von Hohenlohe-Waldenburg-Schillingsfürst lit her final cigarette of an auspicious day. She lay back on her pillow and watched the blue smoke curl slowly up to the ceiling. It did not occur to her to wonder what her princely former husband might be doing at that precise moment. Nor was she especially bothered.

X

Salzburg, late 1938.

'Maestro, you're very welcome! We're delighted to receive you as our special guest even though your stay will be so short. Of course, we understand such a busy concert schedule doesn't permit too much time in Salzburg.'

Princess Stephanie Hohenlohe's command of the English language was competent and she permitted her hand to be taken by Leopold Stokowski, the famed orchestral conductor. He was a catch. A big fish. Admittedly not a political fish but one more celebrity for the Princess to chalk up against her ever-increasing list of distinguished house guests.

Maestro Stokowski bowed graciously. Not, however, as low as he might have offered his audience in Philadelphia.

'Your Highness,' he said graciously. 'A great pleasure. As you know, I have business with the Festival Committee. My professional engagements are planned well in advance,' he added. 'We work three or four years ahead.'

Stephanie Hohenlohe raised her dark eyebrows,

quizzically, flashing her ever-ready smile to show off her pearl teeth. No man could fail to be impressed.

'I plan to take you around the Schloss, Maestro. We're beginning to improve things. But first, permit me to show you the terrace. After your tiring journey you must be in need of refreshment. I've organised a light tea and trust you'll join us, later, for dinner?'

She turned smartly on her fashionable heels and escorted Stokowski through the great entrance hall with its polished black and white squared marbled floor. The celebrated musician took in the gilt-framed paintings on the walls and the opulence of the 18th century gilded stucco plasterwork. Stokowski courteously held back to permit the Princess to step outside onto a terrace. He joined her to admire the immaculately tended gardens and symmetrical, low manicured box borders. Stephanie indicated the distant mountains.

'You see the summit of our beloved Untersberg. It towers over the border between my own country and Germany. Of course,' she added hastily, 'since the *Anschluss* we Austrians regard ourselves as part of a single Germanic nation, led by our inspired leader.'

Stokowski nodded politely but made no comment. His immediate interest was in the lake beyond the terrace.

'I had no idea,' he told his hostess, 'your lake was so impressive. How still it is. Reflecting the light.'

He followed the stately progress of a pair of mute swans and their reflections. The Princess explained the lake's origins.

'It was excavated when the palace was built, nearly two hundred years ago. The Prince Archbishop at the time wanted to make a statement of his wealth and power. Along with his commitment to culture and the arts.'

She showed Leopold Stokowski to a cushioned wrought iron chair by a table decorated with the finest china.

'Anna!'

Stephanie's sharp voice rang out to summon her trusted maid. Anna Stoffl appeared as if from nowhere. The Princess ordered her to bring out refreshments for her prize guest. Stokowski remained enchanted by the idyllic scene.

'I have to say, Your Highness, I've rarely witnessed such a peaceful setting. The house is perfect. Far grander than I'd imagined. And you've made it so beautiful. Do you entertain guests throughout the year?'

Stephanie feigned to look modest.

'I've only been here a few months, Maestro, but in that time a good number of influential people have graced our home. I like to think we offer a dynamic experience for dignitaries across the arts to meet and mix. Tonight, we're to be joined by important Party dignitaries from Berlin. The Schloss acts as a retreat for a lively exchange of views.'

Leopold Stokowski frowned.

'I'm sorry,' he said, 'you must forgive me. You mentioned "Party dignitaries". Who exactly would they be?'

His hostess hesitated before responding. She was unsure of the political affiliations the American-based musician might hold.

'Oh…just high officials in the Reich government. Mind you, I try to make it a rule, as far as possible, for my guests to avoid *political* conversation. I'm not in the slightest political, myself, preferring to inculcate a cultural atmosphere. My dinner table simply vibrates with contributions. Personally, I have little to offer. Yet it's such a privilege to sit back and listen to finer intellects than mine.'

The Princess imagined her studied attempt at humility was beguiling.

'I see myself as a catalyst,' she added. 'Aiding cross-fertilisation of ideas between great minds!'

After tea, Stephanie von Hohenlohe escorted her guest around the gardens already beginning to show signs of new life, following a severe winter. Stokowski was taken to see the latest state of construction of an open air swimming pool. It represented one of Stephanie's many innovations for her visitors. The cost of works on the house and gardens rose by the month but Adolf Hitler's direct financing ensured all expenses were easily met.

A manservant showed Leopold Stokowski to his room. The conductor welcomed the opportunity to take a short nap before dinner. His hostess had hinted a musical entertainment would be offered. A student string quartet from the *Mozarteum* would play for the guests at table. Stokowski was intrigued by the Princess' parting comment as he was about to ascend the great stairway to his room.

'Maestro, I hope to show you something very special. I've discovered that just under two hundred years ago the Mozart children performed here for the Prince Archbishop. Isn't that extraordinary? Of course, you'll be aware their father was Deputy *Kappelmeister* in the Archbishop's court orchestra. So I've had the idea to invite a currently talented brother and sister from the town. Remarkable child musicians. The little girl plays the piano with her younger brother. He's also a promising violinist. Of course, I make no claim they equal the unique talents of their Mozart predecessors. However, I'm reliably informed these children possess precocious gifts!'

Lying on his bed in his sumptuous room, the international conductor drifted into energy-reviving sleep. He had not been taken in by the Princess' blatant display of false modesty. Indeed he was relieved that, at dinner, he would be able to concentrate on the musical entertainment. Leopold Stokowski had no intention of indulging in chit-chat with jumped up politicos from Berlin.

Student violinist Heinrich Müller carefully placed his instrument into its case. He was pleased with the new bow purchased by his comfortably-off father. He and his friends had practised all afternoon. Lotte on her viola along with Dieter on cello and second violinist, Ingrid. Heinrich led the newly formed group.

'We must think of a name!' laughed Lotte. 'I know we've only played together for a few weeks but I think we're something special.'

Dieter Gramlisch agreed.

'I've been searching my brain,' he said, 'I thought of the "*Amadeus Quartet*" but it sounds a bit formal. No matter! As far as the Schloss concert's concerned, we're just four penniless students from the Mozarteum.'

Heinrich, however, was a little concerned. He clamped the catches on his violin case.

'Our prof. told me there's someone special there, tonight. A big international conductor. We'd better be on top form!'

Ingrid, Heinrich's closest friend and fellow string player, made light of the prospect.

'We'll busk it,' she said, confidently. 'But stay focussed. No-one can be as critical as Prof. Schwarz. Thank God he won't be there!'

The friends left the old building and turned into the street. They elected to walk to the out of town palace by the lake. Dieter hitched his cello onto his back and the four set off for the old bridge crossing the Salzach. Ten minutes later, they had passed through the outskirts of the historical quarter of the city. The quartet walked alongside a grass meadow that led up to the wrought iron gates of Schloss Leopoldskron. On reaching the palace they were in for a shock. A sentry box stood by the great stone gate post, its red and white barrier barring entry into the short drive, leading to the grand entrance.

'Your passes? Identification?'

A grim black-uniformed guard stood in their way. The students were at a loss. Placing their instrument cases on the ground, they searched their pockets for identity papers. A second guard appeared and insisted on double-checking the documents. Heinrich felt uneasy. It took a few moments before the soldier convinced himself the papers were genuine.

'Everything seems in order. What are you doing here?'

It seemed a stupid question given that four musical instruments lay in their cases, at the students' feet. Heinrich fished inside his jacket pocket for the official invitation and offered it to the sentries.

'We've been invited to play for Princess Stephanie von Hohenlohe,' he told the soldier. 'I'm sure we're expected.'

The guard glanced at his companion.

'I'll ring through,' he said, tersely. Then, turning to the nervous music students, he ordered them to wait. Stepping inside the box, he spoke harshly into a receiver and after a silence nodded unsmilingly. He jerked his thumb in the direction of the grand entrance to the Schloss.

'You'll be met at the door,' he said. 'Just follow orders. You'll be escorted into the presence of the Princess.'

Excitement and aspiration gave way to anxiety in the minds of the young musicians. They trudged along the short driveway of the surprising shallow front garden with increasing apprehension. The great door opened and two more *SS* men appeared.

'Security!' one announced. 'Open your cases!'

The students obeyed and were relieved when their inquisitors seemed satisfied.

'Good evening!'

A suave-sounding civilian appeared at the entrance.

'Please follow me. Her Royal Highness regrets she's unable to meet you, right now. You'll understand she's busy with tonight's arrangements.'

The performers picked up their cases and entered the great marble hall of the palace.

'The concert begins in just over an hour,' the official told them. 'I'll take you to the adjoining chapel where you can settle and rehearse, if you wish. Light refreshments will be provided in about fifteen minutes' time. Please ensure you remain within the confines of the chapel until sent for. Tonight, you'll be joined by two other performers who'll share the concert with you. They're young so they'll go on first as their parents insist they must leave before nine o'clock.'

The four students were ushered into the chapel built into the interior of the palace. Brought up in the Lutheran church, they gazed in awe at the sumptuousness of the Baroque décor of the small yet high-ceilinged room.

'It's amazing,' Constanze gasped, trying to take in the almost brazen rococo opulence.

The finest artists and craftsmen of their time had been employed to produce a private chapel for the royal archbishop. At the far end, above a small altar with the Host, stood an enormous canvas of the Madonna and Child with tending shepherds. Heinrich's plainer Lutheran tastes reacted against the excess of flecked pink marble and gilt, framing the holy scene. Likewise, the gilt sculptures of a pair of guardian angels, each side of the altar. A number of other sacred pictures hung from the side walls.

'Great acoustic!' Dieter announced cheerfully. 'I wouldn't mind playing in this. Better than in some great dining room with boring old people chatting away over their food. I bet they'll not even bother listening to us…'

He stopped short in response to Lotte's frantic signals.

'That's where you're wrong, young man!'

Out of nowhere, a high, haughty voice. Dieter spun round. To his embarrassment, the Princess had entered the chapel. Stephanie von Hohenlohe looked at him up and down.

'You'll be playing to distinguished people of culture. Amongst them will be Maestro Leopold Stokowski, no less.'

The Princess' voice hardened.

'I suppose even someone as young as you *may* have stumbled across the name?'

The student cellist choked out a rapid apology. His friends prayed for the ground to open beneath their feet.

'Never mind!'

The Princess reverted to her normal, measured charm. She turned and beckoned to two young children hovering nervously by the threshold of the doorway.

'Come inside, my dears. Meet your fellow performers in tonight's concert.'

The brother and sister formally shook hands with each member of the quartet.

'Meet Sura and Johan,' the Princess continued. 'Their parents are out in the gardens. You'll have noticed we've moved a small grand piano into the chapel and you'll find music stands over in the corner. Before we arrange refreshments for you all, we thought you might like to share your music, prior to the concert.'

Princess Stephanie flashed her glitzy smile and turned to leave. The four late-teenagers and two children looked at each other, nervously. Lotte broke the silence.

'Please,' she gestured to the piano. 'Play for us. What have you been working on?'

Eleven year-old Sura in a pretty white dress, decorated with lace and tied with a golden bow at the back, stepped forward shyly.

'We don't know very much,' she said. 'But we like Mozart because he was born in the city.'

Lotte offered encouragement.

'And Johan? What will you give us?'

The diminutive, but self-assured, eight year-old opened his violin case.

'Oh, we're only doing Mozart, tonight,' he said. 'That's what the lady asked for.'

Heinrich wondered where they kept their music for the performance.

'May we see which editions you work from?'

He was startled when the boy told him he and his sister did not require music to perform.

'It's up in our heads,' Johan said confidently. 'I'm pretty good at remembering!'

The older students were impressed as they would not have dreamt of performing without their heavily marked scores. Ingrid invited the children to play. Sura made her way to the piano. She twiddled with the adjustment knobs on the side of the stool raising it high enough to reach the keys. Her toes only just touched the pedals.

'This is one Mozart's sonatas,' she informed her ad hoc audience. 'I'm not sure which one but I know it's in C Major. I like the first movement best because it's jolly!'

For the next few minutes the students from the Salzburg Mozarteum stood entranced. The little girl completed the piece with a flourish and got up from her stool. Heinrich and his friends applauded lightly.

'I think that's the C Major sonata K. 309,' Dieter offered. 'The *Allegro con spirito*. Well done! And you, Johan...what have you got for us?'

The children sensed the warmth generated by the admiring students. Johan took out his less than full sized violin and tuned it with the piano.

'Sura will accompany me,' he said. 'I'll play Violin Sonata No. 17. It's the only one I've learned so far.'

Brother and sister composed themselves before launching into a lively first movement. When they had finished, they asked their new friends to play for them.

'If you'll forgive us,' Lotte said, 'we'd prefer just to go over the tricky bits we're not so good at. There won't be time to play the whole thing. We've offered two quartets that your friend Mozart wrote for Joseph Haydn. They were good friends even though Haydn was much older.'

Sura laughed.

'A bit like you and us!'

The students enjoyed the innocent remark, appreciating that nineteen year-olds probably appeared very mature, if not ancient, to children not yet in their teens.

Lotte explained they were playing a quartet nicknamed '*The Hunt*'.

'And our other Mozart piece is a challenging one…with dissonance. It's in C Major, too,' she went on to explain. 'But it might sound a bit weird at the beginning. Wolfgang Amadeus was trying something special.'

The youthful quartet pulled up seats and arranged their stands so they could see each another. After a brief tuning, Heinrich directed them into Mozart's dissonant gift to his older composer-admirer. Sura and Johan expressed surprise when the first movement fell apart in the middle.

'We told you it was difficult!' Dieter explained from behind his cello. 'I always miss that second subject entry but I'll get it right, tonight.'

Heinrich grimaced. The door opened as a cook from the kitchens wheeled in a trolley of sandwiches, pastries and drinks.

'We hope there's enough for you all,' she said cheerfully. 'I'll be back in a few minutes to find out.'

The six musicians, by now firm friends despite the age-gap, tucked in with relish. They were joined by the children's parents, *Herr* and *Frau* Steaffel.

It was time to be escorted to the Dining Room where the princess' guests assembled beneath the glittering chandeliers. A single, large round table had been laid for a dozen diners and the magnificent meal had been enjoyed by all. Now it was the moment for coffee and spirits, with cigars for the gentlemen. The guests relaxed and politely applauded the nervous gaggle of young people appearing before them. Stephanie von Hohenlohe rose from her seat to greet the newcomers.

'We're very proud,' she told her select audience, 'to present our musical talents here in the city where Mozart was born. From the Mozarteum, we have first year students who've formed their own quartet. They'll play for us a little later. But to begin, let me welcome two very young musicians whose gifts have been brought to my attention.'

She gestured for the brother and sister to come forward. They smiled shyly at the august assembly.

'Sura and Johan Steaffel live only ten minutes away and are already tutored by Salzburg's best teachers. They'll start together at the piano, Johan playing the upper part and Sura the lower.'

She smiled gracefully at the diminutive performers.

'Will you tell us what we're about to hear?'

Sura announced in a shaky voice they would play the opening movement of a Mozart Sonata for four hands. She sat down demurely and gave her brother a little nod. Without further hesitation, the child prodigies launched into their duet. Leopold Stokowski sat back in his chair appreciating the musical and technical excellence of the juvenile duo. He was further impressed when the boy played the violin, his sister accompanying.

The Princess was in her element. Even the least musical of her guests were semi-impressed. An encore was enthusiastically demanded. This time, the boy pulled off a party trick that was clearly pre-arranged with his hostess.

'I have a silken handkerchief here,' Stephanie announced. 'And I understand little Johan is able to play without looking at his hands. Is this really so, my dear?'

The eight year-old confirmed as the Princess covered his small hands.

'I've made up my own little piece,' he announced. 'I wrote it the day before yesterday!'

Whereupon, he dazzled his amazed audience not only by his keyboard wizardry but also the quality of his instant composition. Leopold Stokowski sat bolt upright at the dinner table. Even he had never witnessed such pianistic mastery by one so young. On completion of the little piece, the audience expressed its appreciation and the children took their bows before hurrying back to the chapel. Stokowski turned to his nearest dining companion, a curator of Fine Arts in a prestigious Viennese museum.

'Remarkable! Does he remind you of someone from the

past?' he enquired incredulously. His companion, equally impressed, comprehended his line of thought.

'Of course, Maestro Stokowski. You refer to the boy Mozart? Was he not able to perform such feats at a similar age? What a curious co-incidence. Here in Salzburg of all places!'

The diners broke up to relax on sofas and easy chairs. Further drinks were pressed on them before Princess Stephanie begged their attention.

'Ladies and gentlemen…now, the second part of our concert. We invite you to enjoy chamber music provided by a newly formed student group from the Mozarteum. Please make them welcome.'

At least half of her guests would have preferred to retire for the night but politely applauded the appearance of Heinrich's unnamed quartet. The concert went off well. The great orchestral conductor was delighted with the freshness of the performances.

'Bravo! I congratulate you.'

As the rest of the audience burst into applause, Leopold Stokowski voiced his appreciation. After the concert, he asked to meet with the Mozarteum undergraduates and praised them generously. By then, the Steaffel children had long returned home to be tucked up in their beds. The four students walked out into the chill of the night to return to the distant lights of the city. Extrovert Dieter was beside himself.

'We did it! Wait 'til old Prof. Schwarz hears about this. We've met the great Stokowski and he even praised us!'

His voice filled with emotion.

'Let me tell you something. We're on our way!'

Dieter could not have been more wrong. He was not to know that within a matter of months he and Heinrich would be called up for military service whilst the girls returned, separately, to their distant homes. The quartet of so much promise was fated to break up forever and enjoy only a few more concerts together. Oddly enough, it would not be long before Princess Stephanie was ordered to vacate the Schloss and fled to Britain seeking the patronage of the *Daily Mail* proprietor. Adolf Hitler expressed his fury when he discovered his trusted Liedemann was enjoying a long-standing affair with the woman. There were hints from Gestapo links that she was actually a Viennese Jewess. Given the circumstances, she was fortunate to get away with her life. The Gestapo also informed the *Führer* that Stephanie had, in all likelihood, been acting as a double agent receiving favours from both the Germans and British alike!

xi

June 1940. The Berghof, Adolf Hitler's mountain retreat above Berchtesgaden in the Obersalzberg.

'My dear young fellow!'

Hermann Goering strode across the paved terrace of the *Nazis'* high retreat in the German Alps. He presented his formidable form and figure before Heinrich, blotting out his view of the nearest mountain. Despite the social occasion, Goering's expansive uniform glittered with medals. Heinrich noted the Iron Cross and a sparkling *Pour Le Merite,* the blue enamelled cross otherwise known as the Blue Max.

'Müller, isn't it? I've heard interesting things about you.'

Since the Fall of France, the commander of the *Luftwaffe* had been appointed *Reichsmarschall,* increasing his status amongst the German commanders. Although he did not carry it with him on the Berghof terrace, he was particularly pleased with his bejewelled baton, a personal award from Adolf Hitler. Goering beamed his charismatic smile at the former army private who felt embarrassingly out of sorts in such high company.

'You acted bravely in Poland, young man. Wounded under fire whilst rescuing a comrade? That's why you were specially selected by the *Führer* for your presentation. It's not often we get to meet the lower ranks. But it's good to be reminded of the sacrifices young people are prepared to make for the *Reich*. Feel very proud of yourself!'

Heinrich found himself at a loss for words. He had never anticipated he would come face to face with the top echelons of the *Nazi* regime. He struggled to put on an appearance of respect and humility, hoping the unexpected experience would not last long. Heinrich's ambition was to return to obscurity, sitting out the war and doing no damage to humanity. The *Reichsmarschall* enveloped the unguarded former soldier with his fleshy right arm. Heinrich gritted his teeth.

'I understand, Müller,' Goering spoke intimately, 'you're a bit of a scholar? In Poland, you were set the task of making out an inventory of the treasures of some synagogue or other?'

His bright blue eyes pierced Heinrich like daggers.

'Well…I tried, sir. But things got a bit out of hand. Before I could start, the synagogue was raided. I don't think many treasures survived.'

Hermann Goering let loose his iron grip and waved his hand, airily.

'No matter! Third rate Jewish junk. Wouldn't fetch a *pfennig* on the open market!'

His tone became conspiratorial.

'As it happens, I'm a bit of an art fan, myself. My family loved good things so I came to value the culture in our civilised society. My country house, outside Berlin, is bursting with my collection. One of the advantages of high position, young man. It keeps one ahead of the game!'

Heinrich wondered what game Goering referred to. Uninvited, the *Reichsmarschall* was happy to expand.

'The *Führer* and I are happy to secure artworks and treasures from the occupied territories. What use have the likes of the Poles with high culture?' he snorted. 'Pigs in the gutter. Art's wasted on their snouts!'

Goering beamed with pride over his instant metaphor.

'Come over to the corner,' Goering suggested. 'We can speak, quietly. Some of the people here are charlatans with no appreciation of high art. Can't recognise a Renoir from a Matisse!'

He turned suddenly on Heinrich, thrusting out his prominent jaw.

'Can you?'

The *Reichsmarschall's* sudden challenge demanded an instant answer.

'Oh…yes, sir,' Heinrich stumbled. 'I think so. My main subject's music. Art's something I studied on the side.'

He was not sure where the conversation was leading. Goering took in the glories of the distant mountain peaks. Once more, his hypnotic eyes turned on his unhappy captive audience.

'You'll be aware,' Goering boasted, 'that we're enjoying immense success on the Western Front. My *Luftwaffe* leads the assault. Paris is about to fall at any moment and we'll soon be marching down the *Champs Elysees*. I shall attend, personally. There's still a bit of mopping up to do in the rest of France.'

His bull face glowered.

'The wretched British prick us with their tin pot warplanes. No matter! It'll all be over within the month.'

The young musician was unsure he should be hearing such information from one so high in the *Nazi* ranking. Goering stared the wilting Heinrich in the face.

'I intend taking advantage.'

The *Reichmarschall's* expression turned from grim determination to relaxed charm.

'As fellow art connoisseurs, the *Führer* and I are anxious about the Paris treasures,' he smiled. 'No city in the world boasts such diversity. As a talented painter, himself, he's interested in pictures. So am I but I have the greater knowledge of furniture and books…precious manuscripts…that sort of thing.'

He paused, gazing at the wispy clouds gathering on the summits.

'Our leader's concerned that many valuable works may be smuggled out of the city. It's even rumoured the British are trying to get their thieving hands on them.'

His brow puckered.

'For some reason, the French seem determined to prevent us from viewing such wonders.'

Heinrich remained dumb, permitting the *Reichmarschall* full flow.

'So we're hatching up an emergency plan. German culture will never forgive us if these treasures get stolen or damaged. I've offered to set up a rescue mission and need to get to the French capital as soon as possible. You may not know this but I have my own private train. A *sonderzug* named *Asien.*'

Heinrich looked flummoxed. Goering paused to check the young man was paying full attention.

'My *sonderzug*'s rather special. When I travel through the *Reich*, I use *Asien* as my mobile headquarters. It's in full radio communication with Berlin and my *Luftwaffe* commanders. Very shortly, I'll venture into the newly occupied territories.'

Heinrich at last plucked up the courage to interrupt the flow of the former air ace's ramblings.

'I'm sorry, sir. I'm a little bewildered. It's just that I'm not sure I should be hearing any of this. It must be high grade military intelligence?'

Hermann Goering slapped the young man on his wounded shoulder, Heinrich biting his lip to conceal the pain.

'Integrity, Müller! Good man. *Of course*, I shouldn't be telling you any of this. So I'm swearing you to secrecy. You're a smart fellow and it seems to me you're wasting your talents at that fancy *Schloss* down in Salzburg. It's a luxury venture of little consequence.'

Heinrich caught a whiff of perfume as the *Reichmarschall*'s corpulent face challenged him from centimetres' distance.

'It's time for you to step up. I want you to come and work for me,' Goering continued expansively. 'You can remain a civilian. That'll have its advantages. And I can get round any objections the bureaucrats are bound to put in the way. Müller...you're the fellow I want to entrust with the cataloguing of the treasures of *Le Louvre*. Once identified, we can transport them back from Paris for public display. We may also add a few world-class works acquired from our Jewish friends. Of course, we hold the advantage that these treasures are no longer at risk from war damage. The French Air Force is already defeated and the RAF are locked up inside their own island.'

He turned disdainful.

'In the coming battle with the Royal Air Force, we'll knock every one of their aircraft out of the sky. Once a Treaty's signed, life will settle down again. Berlin and Germany will be enriched with some of the world's finest art treasures!'

Hermann Goering beamed his vulpine grin from ear to ear.

'Our capital will be recognised as the artistic centre of the world!'

He raised his eyebrows and nearly winked then held out his pudgy hand.

'Are you with me?'

Heinrich shook it out of courtesy, wincing as the *Reichsmarschall* crushed his delicate violin-playing fingers. Goering pointed to a rustic house on the nearby hillside.

'*Landhaus Goering*, Müller. The Party awarded me that simple farmhouse for services rendered. Of course, it's not as fine as our Leader's home. And never will be. That said, I have development plans and intend adding an outdoor swimming pool.'

He guffawed.

'No expenses spared!'

Goering paused to give time for Heinrich to be impressed.

'Müller,' he went on, 'I want you to visit me, there, later this afternoon. Report to the gatehouse. They'll be briefed. I'm picky and choosy about people I invite in.'

Goering lifted his head and took in the spectacular scene surrounding him. Two hundred metres away, slave workers toiled on the construction of a new *SS* barracks.

'There's so much riff-raff round here, Müller. *SS* thugs with small minds crazed with ridiculous notions. Blind obedience. But extremely valuable to the cause.'

He grew more confidential.

'You and I,' he intimated, 'are two of a kind. A cut above the rest. Tells in the breeding. With your cultural background, I know my special mission is in safe hands. And,' he added, 'you'll get the chance to go to Paris!'

The *Reichmarschall* turned on his heels and bore his corpulent form down the winding path.

'Four thirty, sharp!' he called back.

Heinrich remained still. How was it that he was continually getting caught up in things that were alien to him? What did people see in him that he had not discovered for himself? Or was it simply that he was too reticent and timid to speak out? Whatever his deficiencies, Heinrich sensed he was embarking on a challenging new chapter of his young life.

As the agreed time approached, Heinrich felt increasingly nervous. He knew he was out of his depth but recognised that refusal to co-operate would go down badly. Yet there was also the exciting opportunity to visit Paris; the chance of a lifetime. He felt unsure about Goering's keenness to acquire and preserve foreign artworks and treasures but rationalised this would happen whatever the circumstances.

Heinrich walked up to the large two-floored dwelling and took in the apparent domestic alpine scene. A wild flower meadow surrounded the frontage whilst behind rose a slope with trees. Red-and-white-painted shutters had been thrown back at the windows to let in light. An upper floor veranda ran around the front and sides. Above this, a large and gently-sloping Tyrolean roof.

He nervously mounted the short flight of steps to the front door. Heinrich's imminent arrival had been forwarded by the guard at the small gatehouse, lower down. To his surprise, Hermann Goering's gargantuan figure awaited him at the top of the steps.

'On time, Müller!' he beamed. 'That's my man. Step inside. Can I offer you coffee…or a cold drink?'

Goering was clad in a rustic outfit. A huge pair of *lederhosen* stretched to the knees, supported by braces crossing over his ample shoulders. He wore a long-sleeved white blouse and woollen socks up to the knee. In his hand he grasped a long bow. With some amusement, he noted Heinrich's look of surprise.

'A little rural pastime of mine!' Goering explained, cheerfully. 'Archery keeps me in touch with country ways.'

He carefully placed the bow by the door and ushered Heinrich into his *landhaus*. The young man followed in Goering's wake, taking in the sumptuous furnishings. They passed swiftly through a lounge offering a sumptuous, patterned sofa and matching chairs. A metal chandelier hung from the ceiling. He was then beckoned into the *Reichmarschall*'s office dominated by an enormous porcelain heater, garishly tiled in green, yellow and white. Family photographs topped the filled bookshelves.

Goering waddled behind his stout wooden desk and invited Heinrich to pull up a chair.

'This is where I plan the war!' he jested. 'Our Leader has his own ideas, of course. Mostly fantasy. But of little value if they can't be put to practical purpose. As Commander-in-Chief, I'm granted freedom to deal with major tactics and strategy. My principle interest, naturally, is in our noble *Luftwaffe*.'

He looked up sharply at his nervous former *Wehrmacht* companion.

'Not everyone is up to date with the brand of warfare we propose. Too many of our generals remain rooted in their 1914 trenches. *Blitzkrieg* is the only way to fight modern combat. Tanks and armoured columns supported by fighter-bomber squadrons. Then, it's up to the Infantry. I've the devil of a job to convince the old diehards!'

As was now his custom, Heinrich kept his silence. He had never expected to hear a top military man put down senior colleagues in front of a nonentity such as himself. To put it mildly, it seemed seriously indiscreet. Hermann Goering turned to other matters.

'From now on, you work directly to me, Müller. Take no orders from any other person. If you run into trouble refer back, immediately. I brook no argument with those who oppose me. Make yourself ready to move, next week. Thursday or Friday, at the latest. There's no more time to waste. I'll fix things with your *Schloss* employers.'

The puffed up military commander heaved himself out of his seat.

'Get things packed and be ready to go as soon as you can. You'll travel on my personal *sonderzug* and have a compartment to yourself. I've already arranged for catalogues of the stuff we're looking for to be sent to me.'

He strode over to the arched window and gazed out on the blue-grey mountains.

'I'll also arrange travel documentation and all necessary military passes and visas. On the journey, you'll have time to study the catalogues to compile an inventory. No-one is to see this and everything you do must be regarded as confidential.'

Goering turned swiftly from the window. Despite his ludicrously out-sized Tyrolean dress, he made a forbidding and threatening figure.

'And when I say no-one, Müller, I mean exactly what I say. You'll work under my full authority and those working with you will be told not to ask questions. Only help you in your quest. Snooping on their part will be noted and they'll answer to me.'

He looked grim and menacing.

'Of course, you know what that implies. Our new *Reich* tolerates no opposition or back-sliders. And the same rule applies to *you*. In this new era, we're unforgiving and intolerant of failure.'

Hermann Goering completed his tirade and brusquely showed Heinrich the door. The previous offer of coffee or a cold drink had long flown out of his power-crazed mind.

xii

Heinrich returned to the Schloss with much on his mind. His accommodation was not housed in the main building but in the adjacent and less spectacular Meierhof complex. Here, the permanent staff was granted bedrooms according to status. Low down the pecking order, Heinrich slipped up the back stairs to his small attic room. It was plainly furnished and unheated. He was relieved to think he was no longer likely to spend the winter in it. A heavy oak wardrobe took up most of the space left by the single bed. He walked over to the window and looked out on the trees now in full leaf. He then turned back to the bed and tumbled onto it. Gazing at the ceiling he permitted his mind to float through the extraordinary turn of the day's events.

Despite the Nazi presence in the small city, Salzburg still retained the atmosphere of a cultured backwater sheltered from atrocities played out on faraway foreign war fronts. Heinrich thought about his former colleagues in Poland. Where were they now? Had they survived? Where would they go next? Just as he had imagined he had found a safe niche away from the realities of conflict it seemed he was about to be thrust into a new venture.

There was nothing about the personality and demeanour of the *Reichsmarschall* that impressed him. Despite the outwardly bluff and easy manner the man was terrifying. Heinrich hardly dared consider the possibility of failure in his new mission. Getting on the wrong side of Hermann Goering was something not to be contemplated. He turned over on the ill sprung bed and tried to get some sleep.

Was that a knock on the door? Half-drifted into unconsciousness, Heinrich roused himself and rubbed his eyes. There it was again…soft yet percussive…urgent. He rose slowly and stepped over to the door, turning the handle to create an opening just wide enough for him to see who was calling.

'Yes?'

'Heinrich?'

A young feminine voice. It jolted him to his senses.

'Oh! Sorry. Who are you?'

He half-opened the door. In the narrow, dusty corridor stood a young woman perhaps two years younger than himself. He thought he might have seen her before.

'I apologise. May I come in? It's very important.'

The young clerk stood back, flustered.

'Of course,' he said. 'I think I was nearly asleep…please.'

His visitor in white lace long-sleeved blouse and black skirt entered timidly.

'You must forgive me,' she half-whispered. 'I know I shouldn't be up here.'

Heinrich could offer only the basic hospitality of a bare, wooden chair. He crossed to the window. Now he recalled where he had seen the girl before. Her pretty, black ringlets and soft brown eyes had previously caught his attention.

'I think you work at Reception?' he asked awkwardly.

The girl blushed.

'I do,' she replied. 'Nothing very special. My job's to make our guests comfortable.'

Her eyebrows puckered.

'They're not so easy to please. I get told off for the least thing.'

Heinrich relaxed. In his short time at the Schloss he had not managed to get to know anyone beyond the demands of his work.

'D'you mind if I sit on the bed?' he said. 'I've had a tiring day. Hardly know if I'm coming or going.'

He remembered his manners.

'Look, I'm really sorry but I don't know your name.'

The two young people shyly avoided each other's eyes.

'Maria-Anna,' she responded. 'My family's Catholic. I'm local. We live on the other side of the river. That's why I'm not resident.'

She smiled laconically.

'I have to be here by six in the morning. Whatever the weather.'

Heinrich warmed to her gentle manner.

'I was here as a student,' he told her. 'Just before the war. Late last year. I love your city. You must be proud to live here.'

Maria-Anna pushed back hair falling over her eyes.

'I found out you studied at the Mozarteum,' she said. 'Like me, you love music!'

They were on common ground yet Heinrich felt confused by the girl's unexpected visit. She stood up, moved over to the door, and closed it quietly.

'They say you're a brilliant violinist.'

The young man looked up, startled.

'I'm not so sure. That's all in the past. I can hardly hold an instrument any longer.'

The girl looked down at her feet. Then she tilted her head. Heinrich saw how pretty she was.

'I stayed on for the concert you arranged for the guests,' Maria-Anna continued. 'Of course, I couldn't join the audience but I managed to squeeze behind a pillar. I don't think anyone spotted me!'

Heinrich laughed.

'Well, I didn't! But I'm glad you were there. Did you enjoy it?'

They were growing comfortable in each other's company.

'Those children…Sura and Johan,' she said. 'So talented. I always wanted to play something. Piano, mostly, but my parents couldn't afford one. I do a bit of singing…our local girls' choir.'

Heinrich smiled his appreciation. Maria-Anna sighed.

'They're very special.'

He agreed but, suddenly, the girl's face darkened. She glanced anxiously at Heinrich.

'I don't know why I'm telling you this.'

He detected tension underlying her apparent calm exterior.

'You'll promise not to tell anyone, won't you?' she implored.

Heinrich looked up sharply.

'Tell who?' he said. 'About what?'

From her expression, he could see she was upset.

'It's very bad,' she said softly. 'Those children…they don't live far from me. I know a little bit about them.'

She paused. A cloud passed over the sun.

'They're Jewish!'

The two young people shared a silence that lasted more than a minute. Heinrich felt faint, supporting himself on the wardrobe, aware of the serious implication of Maria-Anna's revelation. The Salzburg maid sat still on her seat, hands clasped in her lap. She struggled to regain composure.

'It's even worse,' she said. 'I understand the Steaffel family has been marked down for deportation. A labour camp somewhere across the border. Close to Munich…I think it's called Dachau.'

Heinrich felt as if his head was about to burst. Like most Austrians he had heard rumours of the growing numbers of alleged labour camps in Germany and the occupied countries. Being powerless to intervene, it was the sort of thing he tried to put out of his mind. There was little point in having an opinion on such matters. If expressed openly it could lead to repercussions. Of late, his sole concentration had been centred upon his personal survival whatever the final outcome of hostilities. It represented the dark side of existence. Survival even. And he had no idea as to where it might lead. Best not to worry. Easier to sweep it under the carpet.

In her undemonstrative way, Maria-Anna had succeeded in bringing Heinrich up short. All of a sudden he was faced with reality and a matter that directly affected him. This was personal. He could not conceive of the children, with whom he had developed a warm relationship, forced out of their city into a grim unknown. Of course, he was aware of surreptitious rumours sweeping through Germany and Austria. Heinrich pulled himself together. His voice broke as he broached the subject with the young woman sitting demurely in his room.

'Maria-Anna…why are you telling me this?'

He felt immediate guilt.

'I'm nobody,' he continued. 'I've no authority. No influence.'

Maria-Anna looked up and spoke with surprising conviction.

'I know that, Heinrich. We're pawns in a horrible game. I hate these Nazis. Even feel ashamed to be working here. But what can I do? I have to support my parents. The money supports my younger brothers.'

She cast her eyes down, ashamed. Heinrich tried to reassure her.

'I understand,' he said. 'Not that my parents need any help. They're sympathisers to the new ways, anyway. But…you and me…we're caught up in something we don't understand. And don't like.'

He paused and took in a deep breath.

'I hate the *Nazis*, too,' he declared.

Almost immediately, he regretted the admission. Had he gone too far?

'It's hardly my fault but everything I've done in the last few months has turned out wrong. I've seen and heard terrible things. Somehow, I've got tangled up in events. First serving in the *Wehrmacht*, in Poland, and then with the *SS*. Because I got wounded I ended up here and serve the very monsters who've taken over our nation.'

He recalled his brief moments with Goering and other high-flying *Nazis*.

'I've even met some of them. Been in the same room if only for a short time.'

Heinrich shook his head.

'It's like a bad dream. A nightmare…and I'm getting sucked in further. Can't see the way out. Am I going to end up like one of them?'

Heinrich realised his voice was rising. This was unwise in the Meierhof where walls might have ears.

'Sorry…we must speak quietly,' he said. 'I need time to think. In a few days, I accompany the *Reichmarschall* to France. I'm not sure what he wants of me although I'm beginning to piece it together.'

His young face painted a picture of misery.

'All I know is I'm getting drawn into the web of a poisonous spider. What does it mean? Either I get caught as a fly or end up a minor spider. Where's it all leading?'

He choked on his words.

'Will I become a monster, too?'

Maria-Anna rose slowly from her seat, stepped towards the young man, and took his hand gently in hers.

'Of course you won't, Heinrich,' she said. 'You're too good for that. But there's something we must do. I've no idea how but those children have got to be saved. And the whole of the family, too…if it's possible. I've nearly driven myself crazy but I think there's a way.'

She gripped Heinrich's hands firmly.

'There's a priest in Salzburg. A Pastor. I heard from a friend that he helps Jewish families in peril. I'd go to him, myself, but I get nervous. I don't expect he'd take me seriously. Also, it's risky as I don't want to get my family into trouble. I wondered if you might come with me?'

She looked up at him, pleadingly.

'I know it's a big thing to ask.'

Without thinking, Heinrich placed his arms gently around the girl's shoulders. He detected the beating of her heart.

'A priest?' he said. 'A Catholic…here in Salzburg?'

It seemed like fantasy.

'Why would a Pastor get involved in helping people not of his own religion? Besides…it's madness. Helping Jews is a crime. We all know that. If your priest's reported to the authorities he'll be arrested by the *Gestapo*. Their Headquarters are in the main square. You know what they're like. People disappear. Never seen again. No explanations.'

He felt her soft hands on his upper arms. A sudden thought exploded in his mind.

'Listen, Maria-Anna!' he said urgently. 'You mustn't get involved. It's too dangerous.'

The girl looked at him, perplexed.

'It's something *I* should do,' Heinrich insisted. 'I've got nothing to lose. I hate what I do…what I've done even. So it's time to make up. Let me have the name of this Priest and I'll try to contact him. I'll think up an excuse.'

xiii

Hermann Goering was in bullish mood. Reports from the Western Front indicated his air force, which he regarded as his own personal property, had succeeded in devastating his British opponents, over France. Before his resignation from office, the French Prime Minister had implored his allies across the Channel to send more fighter squadrons to counter-attack German advances. He was aware that the French military had put up a poor showing in battle. The British, from the German perspective, had performed little better. By the skin of their teeth, they had managed to evacuate most of their Expeditionary Force that had been stranded at the port of Dunkerque. Prior to that, they had adamantly refused to respond to the French demand for increased air cover. From Goering's point of view, the reason was starkly obvious. The RAF had suffered such catastrophic losses they were down to their last reserves. There was no chance they could send their few remaining aircraft to hold up the unstoppable German *blitzkrieg*. He stomped around his office employing Heinrich as an involuntary captive audience.

'The English are finished!' he announced. 'They'll be forced to sue for peace. That fool Churchill will be thrown out of office and the government will come to its senses.'

He swivelled round to confront the clerk sent up from the Schloss.

'Now it's the turn of my bombers,' he added with enthusiasm. 'Imagine…three hundred *Heinkels* and *Dorniers* flying in tight formations across the Channel. We can threaten their capital! They've no resistance left. God knows how many Hurricanes and Spitfires they wasted in France. We shan't even have to drop a bomb. Quite simply, a show of force is all that's needed. They'll soon get the message and come running. The British have deserted their allies in their hour of need and soon they'll be on their knees seeking surrender.'

Heinrich pretended to look interested. He was incredulous to be present at the very heart of German strategic planning. There seemed no stopping the expansive ambitions of the *Nazi* war machine. Did they intend taking over the whole of Europe? Goering picked up his jewelled Marshal's baton and continued to parade around the room. He dropped his voice slightly. His mind raced ahead to greater things.

'The English have three choices. Fight, die or surrender. What they choose makes no difference to us. If they fight… they die. But if they decide to surrender without further contest we may show them magnanimity. The *Führer* has a sneaking regard for the island race. Including their Empire. If they see reason we can do a deal. We'd leave them alone, pretty well, so they can continue as normal. All we seek is peace…a Non-Aggression Pact…but on our terms. The British can stay in their island and run their Dominions whilst we expand across Europe into *Lebensraum.*'

The *Reichmarschall* collapsed into a comfortable, well-upholstered chair.

'Fix me a drink, Müller. The French dry white is in the ice bucket. Excellent vintage and a good year.'

He smiled, confirming his exuberant mood.

'Help yourself to a beer!'

Heinrich sensed he was regarded as an obedient dog. The way things were going it appeared Goering would soon be his master. The *Luftwaffe* chief enjoyed his first sip.

'Excellent!'

'Chablis!' he announced. 'I had it sent direct from the chateau.'

He glanced at the label.

'They tell me it's a very good year…although still young!'

He motioned to Heinrich to take a seat.

'I, too, hold the British in high regard. In the First War they were stout opponents. Nearly had me a number of times in aerial combat. I had over ten fighters on my tail during one operation. They hit my aircraft and punctured the fuel tank but I managed to make it across our lines.'

He sneaked a glance at his Blue Max.

'Touch and go,' he said. 'Crash-landed with a bullet in my thigh and ended up in a field hospital.'

Heinrich listened impassively. His new master looked at him almost kindly.

'I know what it's like to be wounded, young man. I understand. We're birds of a feather. I've checked up on you.

Bit of a rebel so they tell me. And lucky to escape the firing squad in Poland.'

He guffawed.

'That's what I like about you. I was always getting into scrapes with my commanding officers. Got into serious disciplinary trouble more than once! Following orders is one thing but using your own initiative is another. This is why I want you to work for me, Müller.'

Heinrich blinked, bewildered.

'Sir?'

Goering was in full stride.

'I've arranged for you to take a look at my pride and joy,' he said. 'My *sonderzug*. It'll be steamed up in the next two days. You'll never guess where it is!'

The young clerk felt at a loss for a response.

'I suppose Salzburg's the nearest station, sir. In the sidings?'

Goering laughed.

'Oh, much better than that. You'd be surprised at what goes on round here. Of course, I'm not the only one to have a *sonderzug*. The *Führer* has one for himself and I have to admit it outranks mine in luxurious fittings. Right now, his is in Berlin but part of mine is stationed in the aborted Berchtesgaden tunnel. From there, it's a good hour to Salzburg as the line isn't that direct. After that…the world! I want you to see the set-up. I'll show you round, myself, and already arranged a pass for you at the tunnel guard house. Come!'

The *Reichmarschall* steamed out of his study. He shouted orders at a secretary in the adjoining room, demanding the instant ordering of a car. After five minutes' impatient waiting, a chauffeur-driven black Mercedes appeared bearing a small swastika flag on the bonnet. It bore the unlikely duo down the winding road from the relative height of the Obersalzberg to the small village nestling in the valley, below.

Twenty minutes later, the limousine crossed the fast flowing river coursing down from the mountains and parked at the nearby terminus station. This was unusually grand for a small country village. Recently constructed for the arrival of prestigious *Nazi* officials and generals summoned to the Berghof, the handsome white building with red roof tiles dazzled in the afternoon sunshine. Long red, black and white banners with swastika designs fell from on high. On the right of the brand new entrance hall stood a tall round tower, reflecting local Bavarian architecture.

It was clear that the high-ranking staff Mercedes was expected. A small posse of armed guards at the station saluted and ushered the *Reichmarschall* through. He and Heinrich entered the grand hall decorated with massive coloured murals of country scenes. Stepping through an arched doorway, Goering strode along the end of the otherwise deserted platform.

'Normally, I board the train, here,' he said. 'But right now they're working on the *sonderzug* so it's tucked away at the end of the sidings.'

At first glance, it appeared to Heinrich that the line terminated about two hundred metres away, below a vertical cliff. But, shielding his eyes from the sun, he spotted an abandoned dark tunnel bored into the rock face. It was faced with a grand stone archway. *SS* men bearing automatic weapons came out of cover on both sides. On recognising their superior officer they snapped rapidly to attention and presented the full *Nazi* salute. A soldier ran out of the cover of the guard house adjacent to the tunnel. He handed Goering a set of papers.

'Special pass, sir, in the name of…'

He glanced nervously at the paperwork.

'…Herr Heinrich Müller. Is this the gentleman?'

Goering snatched the papers from him.

'Of course it is, you oaf! I trust they're in order?'

The man blanched.

'I believe so, sir. They arrived this morning.'

Goering looked over his ample shoulder and jerked his thumb in Heinrich's direction.

'Come on, Müller. You're not claustrophobic are you?'

The tunnel originally started to take the line further down the valley smelt of smoke, coal dust and heavy machine oil. Heinrich hurried after his master who stomped along the tracks and disappeared into the gloom. In the limited artificial lighting, Heinrich made out the monstrous boiler of a steam locomotive. It was silent and unmanned.

'I always wanted to drive one of these!' Goering joked. 'Maybe I'll get a ride on the footplate. They can hardly say "no"!'

His enthusiasm echoed off the tunnel walls. They passed the enormous tender full of coal and found the first carriage. An *SS* guard awaited them.

'I've arranged for the lights to be on, sir.'

Goering nodded gruffly.

'Good man! Stay where you are. Are there other personnel on the train?'

The guard affirmed that the radio unit was checking equipment and that cleaners were hard at work, making the carriages ready. Goering signalled for Heinrich to follow. To his astonishment, the unwilling traveller found himself squeezing past a long, heavily armoured truck housing a pair of anti-aircraft guns.

'I see the *sonderzug*'s well-defended, sir. In case of aerial attack?'

Hermann Goering slapped his fat hand on the thick plating.

'Correct, Müller! This train's been to Poland and now we go to France. Can't take unnecessary risks. We'll have an additional locomotive running several hundred metres ahead of us. If there's disruption to the line it's the crew's job to spot it and communicate back.'

He laughed out loud.

'If they fail, they're in trouble...but at least *we* get advanced warning!'

Hermann Goering selected a carriage and heaved himself up the high double steps from the ground. He indicated Heinrich to follow. They plunged into a long, dimly lit corridor.

'I haven't time to give you a full guided tour,' Goering joked. 'This is only half the train. The other half will be brought in from the side valley. There'll be plenty of opportunity for you to look around when you come aboard.'

He pushed his way down the corridor to the next carriage.

'The boring stuff's in the other half,' he said. 'Troop accommodation wagons, dining wagon for staff; light maintenance truck for electricity supply to the refrigerators. Radio and luggage cars.'

They ploughed on. Goering opened a door leading to the next carriage.

'Ah, I'd forgotten,' he said. 'We have to go through my private quarters to get to your accommodation.'

He glanced at his watch.

'Oh, who cares? I'll show you, anyway.'

Heinrich gawped like an awestruck schoolboy at the rich interior of Hermann Goering's private carriage. A soft grey velour carpet covered the floor area with red leather sofas and seats neatly arranged along the length of the vehicle. He spotted a writing desk with telephones and brass table lamp. Bookshelves lined the sides below the windows. But before he could take it all in the *Reichmarschall* encouraged him on.

'See this!'

He pushed his way through to the next carriage and flung open a varnished, panelled door. A dumbfounded Heinrich gazed upon a luxury bath tub with gold-plated hot and cold taps.

'Personal bath!' Goering jested. 'They stop the train when I decide to bathe otherwise water slops all over the floor!'

Heinrich was impressed. Here was a man who knew exactly what he wanted and how to get it. Two carriages on, they stopped at what was clearly a sleeping car with a side corridor.

'This one's yours!'

Goering flung open a door to reveal a narrow but liveable compartment. Two bunks, one on top of the other, lined one side whilst opposite had been mounted a metal desk with a shaded lamp. Angled into the far corner by the window stood a tiny basin with hot and cold taps.

'You're lucky, Müller! I don't want others nosing around trying to find out what you're up to. You're under strict orders not to reveal a thing. The crew will be ordered not to ask. Remind anyone who dares defy.'

The *Reichmarschall* turned serious.

'I mean it. Not a word! You're to say you're my administrative assistant dealing with security matters. And you're not allowed to speak about them. Don't let *anyone* in here. That's why I've provided you with First Class accommodation. You'll have it to yourself. I don't mind you mixing but don't get too friendly with people you don't know.'

He snorted.

'They're not your type, anyway. Keep yourself to yourself, Müller. Any questions?'

Heinrich felt a pang of excitement well up within him.

'No, sir,' he replied. 'It seems fine. Thank you! I prefer to stick to my own company.'

He shrugged.

'I suppose it's the way I am.'

Goering swung round and headed back. His massive bulk filled the narrow corridor. It was clear the brief guided tour was over. They made their way back to the formidable locomotive whose silhouette was caught in the bright light at the tunnel entrance. His master spoke briefly to the guards.

'Now you've met Herr Müller, I want you to remember his face. He has my full permission to access this train as he sees fit. Is that clear?'

The uniformed guards shot to attention as the *Reichmarschall* departed with an exchange of Nazi salutes. The chauffeured car was ready at the station to drive them up the hill to Hermann Goering's house up at the Obersalzberg.

'I've a spare office in my annex,' Goering explained on the way. 'You can use it to gen up on the Paris art world. I've got plenty of stuff for you to sift through. Have a word with my cook about meals. She'll be willing to rustle something up. I recommend her pork *schnitzel!* The finest in Austria!'

He beamed.

'You're in for a cultural treat!'

XIV

Maria-Anna Weber was not easily cowed. On her way home to the *Linzergasse*, across the river from the domed cathedral, she had time to reflect on her earlier conversation with the unusual clerk whose musical promise had been blighted by war. She already sensed his high intelligence and sensitivity. This was why she dared risk the wrath of her bosses by visiting him in his tiny room. But could she trust Heinrich? She was placing herself at risk by revealing her sympathy with the potential plight of the Jewish children and their family. After all, he was caught up in the arachnid web of a Baroque palace that had become a seething *Nazi* nest.

She was also aware that the recently appointed *gauleiter* of the Salzburg District was Franz Rainer, a hard, unrelenting persecutor of dissidents perceived to be enemies of the State. After the sudden and unexplained disappearance of the Princess, Rainer had taken up residence at the Schloss and indulged in lavish hospitality. She had spotted him once or twice at the concerts when she had volunteered to boost the staff serving at table. Rainer had even attempted to flirt with her but she had given him no encouragement.

Having taken the risk, Maria-Anna still found Heinrich mystifying. He was gentle and sensitive but also highly thought of by the awesome Hermann Goering whose bombastic behaviour was the antithesis of the Mozarteum music student. Already, she felt close to him and hoped he might have feelings for her. But she was only from humble origins whereas he came from a professional Viennese family. Heinrich had been adamant that Maria-Anna must not risk herself, or those close to her, on a venture that might end in tragedy.

She admired his bravery and willingness to get involved with her brainchild, the scheme to save the Steaffel family. But he had under-estimated her stubbornness and unwillingness to play second fiddle. She smiled quietly at the thought of the metaphor that summed up her dilemma.

'I'll go with him, myself, to see the Priest,' she thought to herself. 'Whether Heinrich agrees or not.'

Meanwhile, Heinrich pondered over the curious conversation between himself and Maria-Anna. It was clear she was brave. Perhaps too much for her own good but he felt honoured she had thought to contact him. He also knew she had destabilised his feelings and found it impossible to get her out of his mind. From the first moment he had set eyes on Maria-Anna he knew she was special. Already he was thinking of her protection and the hope they might get to know each other better, on his return from France.

Next morning, he sought out Maria-Anna. She asked her Reception partner to cover whilst she slipped into the garden with Heinrich.

'I have the afternoon off,' she told him. 'Why don't we meet in the Schloss Mirabell gardens not far from where I live? The Pastor's church is close by. St Andra. I expect you know it. We can work out what to say to him.'

Heinrich reminded her that he preferred to see the priest, alone. But Maria-Anna's strong will won the day and he conceded. It presented an ideal opportunity to see her again, this time off the premises. They arranged to meet in the afternoon sunshine by the fountain of one of the city's prize jewels. Schloss Mirabell shone in the bright light, its beauty almost excelled by the glory of the public gardens. Gravel paths separated extensive flowerbeds. The expert gardeners arranged an array of colours; blues and bright yellows of bedding plants punctuated by ground-hugging red and white begonias. Every bloom seemed to have been planted precisely in its own place. The young couple headed for the shelter of the parallel avenue of linden trees.

The young clerk slipped his hand in hers as they walked down the shaded grove. A wooden bench looked onto the gardens and, beyond, the impressive symmetry of the grand Mirabell building. Heinrich opened the conversation.

'I still think you're crazy, Maria-Anna, but I shan't go on. I left a message for Father Wesenaeuer. He finishes Confession at three o'clock and his assistant told me to wait by the box. I said the matter was urgent and confidential. They probably think I'm in some kind of trouble and need advice. Still, it's good of the Priest to agree to see me.'

Maria-Anna let her head fall softly on Heinrich's shoulder and he slipped an arm around her.

'I really don't want anything happening to you, you know,' he said softly. 'We've only just met.'

Maria-Anna smiled. She was in Seventh Heaven and had hardly slept.

'Don't worry,' she replied. 'Me and you. We're not the problem. Nothing can happen to us. It's the Jewish family that matters but I don't have the answers. That's why I'm hoping the Pastor can help. We're just pawns in a bigger game. But I don't like the way things are going. I'm not sure who I can trust in this city, any longer.'

She looked up at him, cheekily.

'Except you, of course!'

Time seemed to fly by. Heinrich consulted his watch.

'Good Lord! We're nearly due at St Andra's.'

They jumped up from their bench and hurried towards the far end of the long, rectangular gardens. Beyond the far corner, rising above the trees, stood a white stone building flanked by two square towers with steeples. The young couple ran over a small *platz* to the main entrance. Their hurrying footsteps echoed in the nave as they sought the confession boxes. A serious-looking young priest in white robes stood beneath a window, hands clasped before him. Heinrich approached with respect.

'Father…I am Heinrich Müller. You must forgive us for arriving a little late.'

The priest interrupted him.

'Ah yes. Heinrich Müller? We haven't met.'

He glanced at Maria-Anna.

'I understood I would be talking to only one person. This is most unusual.'

The Pastor seemed almost suspicious. Certainly there was little warmth in his welcome. Heinrich felt flustered and tried to explain.

'As I say, Father, please forgive us. But we do need to talk.'

He glanced round, nervously. The church appeared empty. Pastor Wesenaeuer remained solemn.

'Follow me.'

He turned and led the two young people up a side aisle and towards a door close to the altar. They passed down a narrow corridor to be invited into a small, gloomy room. It was bare except for a small wooden table with chairs. A wooden crucifix stood on a small window ledge.

'Please!'

The Pastor invited them to sit and looked at them sternly.

'I meet many young couples such as yourselves. It's my duty. I take it you're in some kind of trouble? Are you Catholics?'

They confirmed they were and Heinrich attempted to rescue the conversation.

'With respect, Father, we're not in trouble. In fact, we've only recently met. I'm sorry I gave you to understand that only I would be coming. But…'

He glanced at Maria-Anna.

'My friend insisted on being here. Her name's Maria-Anna.'

The priest softened a little.

'Maria-Anna? A holy name, my child. You must do your best to honour it.'

Maria-Anna smiled nervously and promised. The three sat in silence.

'Well?'

He was surprised that it was she who responded.

'Father, it's a family that's in trouble. They live close by. The mother and father are good parents and have two children.'

The Pastor nodded sagely.

'The little boy and his older sister are gifted. Musically. They play the violin and piano.'

Maria-Anna looked to Heinrich for support.

'I came across them where I work,' he said. 'The other side of The Festung. Schloss Leopoldskron.'

He shrugged his shoulders.

'I'm a lowly employee, there.'

Father Wesenaeuer frowned and shifted uneasily in his robes.

'Leopoldskron? Max Reinhardt's old place? I know it but have never been inside. Has it not been taken over by the *Reich*?'

Heinrich confirmed but did nothing to allay the priest's fears.

'We live in difficult times,' the priest went on. 'The Church keeps out of politics. In so doing, we have little contact with the authorities who now run our nation's affairs.'

His tone stiffened.

'You say you work there so you're implicated in matters unknown to us. I find it hard to understand why you would wish to consult me.'

Heinrich summoned up his courage. He took the Pastor briefly through his military record even mentioning his brief encounter with the *SS*. It was clear that the anxious Father Wesenaeuer remained sceptical especially when he learned the young man worked directly to Hermann Goering.

'Father,' Heinrich implored, 'I'm asking so much of you. But I, too, know the children Maria-Anna mentioned. I was horrified to find they're Jewish and therefore under threat. Everyone knows people are disappearing. There's open talk of rounding up families and sending them to labour camps.'

He got up from his seat and paced the room.

'Most people shrug their shoulders. They pretend not to notice and look the other way. Don't want to know the truth about what's going on around them. I'll put it to you straight, Father. Maria-Anna has heard rumours that you and another Pastor, Father Zeiss, sometimes offer help to families in danger. We don't know how…'

The priest leapt angrily to his feet.

'Where have you heard such nonsense? We don't get involved, I tell you!'

He turned on Heinrich, pointing an accusing finger.

'You've been sent here. It's a deliberate trick. What are you trying to get me to do? Confess to a crime I haven't committed?'

He stormed over to the small leaded window.

'You're a spy. You're both spies…working for the Germans at the Schloss! They sent you here!'

He turned on Heinrich who thought he was about to be attacked. Maria-Anna swiftly intervened.

'No Father! It's not true. Yes…we both work at the Schloss but we're patriots. We're Austrian through and through. We hate the *Nazis* and what they stand for. I'm a good Catholic and attend Mass at the church of St Sebastian. We're taught to love and not to hate. You know that. It's what you must preach every Sunday!'

The Pastor paced nervously around the small room, turning every few steps. His anguished expression betrayed his nervousness. Heinrich spoke softly.

'Father, Maria-Anna and I want to help this family. They're innocent of any crime. But we're helpless. We've no contacts and no-one to turn to.'

He paused and faced the Pastor.

'This is why we came to you.'

The priest asked the young people to sit down and resumed his own seat. He cupped his head in his hands.

'There is something I must tell you,' he said quietly. 'My colleague Father Zeiss has been taken into custody by the authorities for questioning. He's accused of helping persecuted families by finding safe homes for them in the countryside. He's also been accused of falsifying documents.'

Maria-Anna went over and touched the Pastor on his shoulder.

'I'm so sorry. We didn't know that. It was Father Zeiss we were first advised to talk to. He sounds a brave man.'

The three remained silent for a while. Father Wesenaeuer's voice rose in pitch.

'My Brother is a fool to himself,' he said. 'As I am. We've both falsified the Parish Registers when certain Jews come to us in the name of Christian conversion. We omitted to include details of their original ethnic origin. The authorities have no evidence of intention but I expect to be sent for at any moment.'

A pin dropped in the room could have been detected in the sudden silence. The Pastor had admitted he was involved in treasonable activities. There was no need to speculate about the penalties. He got up slowly, looking older than his relatively young years.

'Well, there it is. You can go back to your Schloss and tell your masters. I shall take the inevitable consequences with God's grace.'

Maria-Anna rested her hand on his wrist.

'You know we won't do that, Father. Your secret is safe with us.'

She turned to her friend.

'Isn't that right, Heinrich?'

The young man nodded humbly.

'Of course…of course!'

Father Wesenaeuer got up slowly.

'Then I believe you,' he said. 'You're good young people but don't meddle in affairs far beyond your remit.'

He sighed.

'Sometimes, we have to leave things well alone. It's impossible to cure all the world's ills in a hurry. We have to be patient. The Lord works in his mysterious way. I am very, very sorry but, in the present circumstances, I can offer no aid. Nor comfort. All I can do is pray.'

Maria-Anna and Heinrich bade their regretful farewells to the Pastor who had placed his trust in them. In effect, his life. He saw them off into the sunshine of the small *platz* opposite the Mirabell Gardens. They walked, once more, past perfectly tended flowerbeds shaped as linked sickles, forever curving, within the carefully maintained lawns. It was impossible to work out how these designs led into one another. The dazzling begonia beds represented the national colours of Austria. The Mirabell gardens lay close to Heinrich's beloved Mozarteum. Out on the street, Heinrich spotted a small shop on the far corner and guided his friend over the crossing.

'I want to buy you flowers,' he said awkwardly. 'Even if we can't help the family, we still have each other.'

Maria-Anna was touched.

'But you've no money!' she said.

Heinrich thrust his hand into his pocket and pulled out a few *schillings*.

'Not a lot! I'd like to get you roses. This time,' his tone was insistent, 'I'm getting my own way!'

Arm in arm, the couple proceeded up the old *Linzergasse*, Maria-Anna's own street. Suddenly, she stopped.

'I've had a brainwave,' she said. 'There's this friend of mine. She lived a long time ago but sometimes I go and talk to her.'

Heinrich looked mystified.

'She must be very old?'

Maria-Anna laughed.

'She would be if she was still alive. Come on!'

Bewildered, her young man followed obediently. Continuing up the narrow street, they passed an impressive Baroque church.

'Saint Sebastian,' she said. 'It's where my family worships. I was confirmed here. But I'm taking you to the cemetery, next door.'

After the afternoon's failed mission Heinrich found it hard to raise much enthusiasm. Nevertheless, he followed Maria-Anna through the wrought iron gates. He was in for a surprise.

'Oh…it's beautiful…peaceful!'

Each grave was neat and well-tended. Running round the sides was a stone mausoleum with shaded arches supported on pillars. Maria-Anna took his hand as they approached a vertical memorial, more prominent than its near neighbours. It stood quite high, mounted by a stone cross. A small clump of begonias, again red and white and lovingly cared for, nestled at the foot.

'D'you see?'

Maria-Anna could see Heinrich looked puzzled.

'Try reading the inscription.'

He took in the major lettering.

'Constantia von Nissen?' he read slowly. 'Sounds important. Is she a relative?'

His new friend tossed her black ringlets in the sunshine. 'I'd like to think so but not really!' she smiled. 'Read on!'

Heinrich did as commanded.

'Constantia von Nissen
Wittwe
Mozart
Geborne v. Weber'

His eyes moved down to the finer details
 'Died 6th March 1842. Sorry…am I being slow?'

Maria-Anna giggled.

'Yes…very! What kind of musician are you? Look again!'

He did as recommended but paused at the name of Mozart.

'Oh, my goodness! You mean…surely not?'

He examined the inscription again.

"Constantia von Nissen"…"widow"…"Mozart?"

It made contradictory sense. Maria-Anna interrupted his puzzlement and pointed to a plain, engraved stone set in the ground close to that of Constanze. Heinrich's head swam with confusion.

'*Leopold* Mozart?' he asked.

'Yes,' she replied. 'Mozart's father. He's remembered here but they say his body lies under the stones in one of the cloisters.'

It all came back to Heinrich.

'Of course! Now I remember. Wolfgang died in Vienna, owing money. His young wife was left with a little boy. And I think there was a baby just a few weeks old.'

He looked at Maria-Anna querulously.

'Are you suggesting she married again?'

The Salzburg girl laughed.

'Yes…many years later. She married a Danish diplomat who later got posted to Salzburg. What a co-incidence. Salzburg had never been Constanze's city. In her heart, she always loved her first husband but I'm glad she found happiness again.'

Heinrich turned serious.

'So she died in the city?'

Maria-Anna slipped her arm round his waist. With her free hand she gently teased out a single pink rose from the small bunch he had given her. Then she took a step towards the grave and bent down to lay the bloom at the foot of Constanze's memorial.

'I've read lots about her,' she said. 'She was a lovely person. Kind and good to her boys. After her second husband died, Constanze cared for Mozart's widowed sister and nursed her to her death. Bless her…she lived to a grand old age!'

Maria-Anna looked lovingly at the rose.

'Constanze's always been my inspiration,' she continued. 'I feel she guides me. Somehow, she'll tell me how to help the Steaffels.'

The young couple turned to go, walking respectfully past silent rows of graves. Soon they found themselves back in the bustling *Linzergasse*. Maria-Anna stopped outside her front door.

'Number 51,' she said. 'This is where I live. Perhaps one day you'll come and visit me, Heinrich?'

He gave her a loving hug.

'Of course I will,' he said. With some reluctance he glanced at his watch.

'Must go. I've got to pack up at the Schloss and get ready for the Paris trip. Not long now.'

He kissed her softly on the cheek.

'Make sure we meet, tomorrow,' he said.

He turned and made his way towards the river. As he crossed the *Staatsbrücke* a curious thought entered his head. Regarding Constanze Mozart…what could Maria-Anna mean? Was it possible a person who died long ago might inspire the solution to their dilemma?

XV

Next afternoon, after work, Maria-Anna and Heinrich arranged to meet on the paved path leading to the lakeside. They gazed out over the still expanse of water and inverted reflections of trees lining the banks. The craggy peak of the Untersberg mountain frowned down from the distance. The couple walked together through the box hedge gardens to a less tended area of wet grasses, bog and trees. Crossing a small wooden bridge they discovered a hidden moated garden embellished with cherubic stone statues. They embraced in the shadows of the trees that obscured them from the Schloss. Maria-Anna spoke first.

'Last night, I called on Herr and Frau Steaffel. They were surprised by my call but welcomed me into their home. Sura and Johan were there. Just for once, they weren't practising. Johan has a model railway. He's crazy about trains!'

She sat down on a stone bench of some antiquity that overlooked the lake.

'It was difficult at first as the Steaffels had no idea I knew their ethnic origins.'

She turned more thoughtful.

'I explained my connection with you, Heinrich. They think the world of you and are grateful for all you've done for the children.'

Heinrich was content to listen.

'They're desperate!' Maria-Anna continued. 'They told me they've already received papers from Gauleiter Rainer. Orders to get ready to leave home. And their residence will become property of the *Reich*. I think that means a German family will move in. Possibly an official and his family from over the border. The Steaffels have been told they'll be redirected to work for the *Reich*…whatever that means. No date's been fixed but they fear it could happen, any time.'

Maria-Anna held back her tears.

'The Steaffels curse themselves for not getting out of the country, before now. They simply didn't think things would get this bad. It's all happened so suddenly. Last year, they had an opportunity to leave for Holland. But it wouldn't have done them any good as that country's been occupied since.'

Heinrich appreciated how such families were trapped with no valid possibility of escape. Maria-Anna gripped Heinrich's arm. Hot tears ran down her cheeks.

'The awful thing is that they had a chance to get the children out. There's a distant cousin in England and she agreed to take Sura and Johan, in any emergency. But the parents were too slow so they were caught out. Even now, they're trying to come up with some scheme to smuggle the children out of Austria.'

Heinrich looked grave.

'That's impossible,' he said. 'Our borders are closed and tightly guarded. Everyone travelling is searched and has to show identity documents on demand. I don't think Jews qualify any longer for such paperwork. They're stuck…with no safe place to go.'

A dark cloud obscured the sun.

'It's so ironical!' Heinrich went on. 'Sura and Johan have been commanded to perform up at the Berghof, tomorrow evening. Before the *Führer*, himself. I've been told to act as chaperone. Can you imagine? It'll be my last duty for a while because I'm on stand-by for Paris. Just two hours' notice. When I return, the family may have already been detained.'

It was difficult to live with such gnawing helplessness.

'I'd never forgive myself if all we can do is watch things happen from the safety of the wings. And never raised a finger to help,' he added miserably.

Maria-Anna gave his arm an extra squeeze. Then she took out a handkerchief and dabbed her eyes.

'Unless…'

Heinrich waited for her to complete the sentence.

'Unless what, Maria-Anna?'

She lifted her pretty head and stared out over the calm waters.

'You'll think I've gone mad. Maybe I have. But I went back to Constanze Mozart's grave, last night. The rose you gave me is still there. I knelt and prayed. When I'd finished, I got up and found my head spinning. Really weird. I had to sit down on the nearest bench. That's when it came to me.'

Heinrich narrowed his eyes.

'Came to you…meaning?'

'The idea!' she replied, brightly. 'Out of nowhere. Like a blinding light!'

Maria-Anna was aware of Heinrich's confusion.

'I know it sounds crazy...and I haven't figured out how to help their parents. But I think there's a way out for Sura and Johan. I'm sure we can smuggle them out of Austria.'

Heinrich pulled a face.

'Out of Austria?' he responded, almost contemptuously. 'To where? The Germans have already taken over half of Europe. And Italy's no good. There's no place for them to go. Nowhere's safe!'

Maria-Anna disagreed.

'There's one country left,' she said. 'And that's England. It's their only hope. Remember...they have a relative there so they could be looked after.'

Her young man raised his eyebrows and shuffled, uneasily, in his position on the stone seat. This was embarrassing. Much as he admired Maria-Anna, he was aware she had not benefitted from his level of education. But he did not wish to upset or patronise her. She caught his expression and interrupted his thoughts.

'If we can get Sura and Johan to France...then it's only a short step to England!'

She made it sound simple. Heinrich fought to control his emotions.

'Look, Maria-Anna, it looks simple on maps, like in a school atlas. You can get half Europe on a double page spread. But real distances are huge. I know. I fought in Poland. It took us hours to get there. France is impossible, anyway. The country's already half occupied and England's a whole step further. Across the sea!'

He tried not to sound too mocking.

'There's a channel in the way. The *Pas de Calais*.'

Heinrich sat tight-lipped, unable to understand why Maria-Anna had not foreseen the hurdles to her scatter-brained idea. But she was not ready to give in.

'You're so slow, Heinrich! *You're* the one going to France, aren't you? I can keep a secret. You told me Goering's train is going all the way to the coast. And you'll be on it in your own private compartment. Don't you see? Sura and Johan can travel with you!'

Heinrich looked up, startled. He was beginning to see where the Leopoldskron receptionist was coming from. It was farcical.

'Listen, Maria-Anna,' he said firmly but not unkindly. 'I'm not travelling on any old peacetime passenger service. The *sonderzug*'s a private military train teeming with armed troops and security guards. Everyone setting foot on it is searched. We're fully vetted with passes signed personally by the *Reichmarschall*. Normal citizens aren't allowed within a hundred metres of the thing. It's guarded day and night.'

He had no wish to upset the girl he loved.

'It's a great idea,' he said. 'I know, in theory, it sounds like it might work. But in practice…there's no chance!'

Maria-Anna looked crestfallen. She felt foolish having come up with an unworkable plan. Heinrich was all but ridiculing it. She almost wished she had not raised the subject. Then her eyes flashed. The humble Salzburg maiden was not beaten and fired her final shot.

'So you think I'm stupid, do you?' she snapped. 'I know I'm not half as smart as you but at least I've come up with something.'

She got up, tossed her head angrily.

'Which is more than you have!'

She darted swiftly through the trees for the Schloss. Heinrich hurried after her.

'Hold on, Maria-Anna! I didn't mean to upset you!'

The palace receptionist did not look back. She picked up her skirt and ran towards a side entrance. Heinrich stopped. He knew he had blundered. The couple had suffered their first tiff.

*

Next day, preparations were made for the evening's entertainment up at the Berghof. A professional pianist and two singers had been booked for the main concert. Piano arrangements of well-known arias from Wagner dominated a varied programme. Sura and Johan were to make brief appearances before the interval. In his role of chaperone, Heinrich had been drafted in to supervise the afternoon rehearsal.

Adolf Hitler was in a particularly jovial mood. His advances in the West were nearly complete. British capitulation was only a matter of time. On a personal level, he had recently received the generous gift of a Steinway grand piano from the makers, in Hamburg. It had been installed in his private sitting room, adding an air of culture and sophistication. A tuner had been sent with the instrument to prepare it for its auspicious debut. Hitler looked forward to the evening's entertainment. It made a change from Hollywood movies, his particular passion.

Heinrich packed up at the Schloss to settle in at the small annex offered by Hermann Goering. To his surprise, a smiling *Reichmarschall* appeared unannounced at his door. His fat arms bulged with new catalogues of Parisian artworks.

'We're nearly ready for the off, Müller. Let's get this wretched concert over then head for France within the next two days!'

He dumped the brochures on Heinrich's desk.

'Are you all prepared? Set to go?'

Heinrich confirmed arrangements were in place. He had compiled a growing list of the French capital's top museums and galleries. Also the names and contact details of curators and owners. Goering seemed pleased with his progress.

'So! You'll put these Salzburg children through their paces when they arrive? They'd better be good. How old are they?'

His new clerk explained Sura and Johan's background, omitting the crucial facts of their Jewishness. Goering slapped him on the back.

'Come on, Müller! I want to see these so-called geniuses at work. Let's run over to the *Führer*'s house.'

There was no way Heinrich could prevent his master from inviting himself to what he had assumed was to be a private rehearsal. Together, they strode up to the imposing mansion on which Adolf Hitler had indulged his rapacious appetite for luxury. The former farmhouse had been enlarged and improved, with an imposing, terraced veranda looking onto the nearby Alpine peaks. Heinrich's stomach churned as he accompanied the *Reichmarschall* up the front steps of the Berghof.

Security appeared to be slight. Although a newly-completed *SS* barracks stood within sight, there was only a minimum of armed guards on the approach. Nevertheless, upon Goering's appearance, two hand-picked troopers on sentry detail snapped to attention. He breezed past them with a casual salute and entered the building as though it was his own. Then he guided Heinrich to an imposing room with soft furnishings. At one end, the Steinway had already been assembled and positioned. Goering, never one for discretion, chose to drop a piece of inside information on the curious habits of his leader. He glanced at his watch.

'Hmph! The *Führer* will be taking his afternoon nap,' he muttered. 'The man has to rest his brain so he can handle his mighty responsibilities! He has a great mind that thinks in Wagnerian proportions. Here, at the Berghof, by looking up to the peaks of the mountains, his thinking is inspired. No-one but he is capable of such glorious insight.'

The *Reichmarschall* turned confidential.

'Keep this to yourself, Müller. Our great Leader is currently changing his mind about the Soviets. Last year, he and von Ribbentrop manoeuvred them into a Non-Aggression Pact. Molotov thought he was smart. Even Stalin bought it. But believe me…the Ruskies are on borrowed time. One day we shall strike further East than they imagine. It could even be this year!'

The door opened and the Steaffel children entered, clutching their music. They were accompanied by two unarmed soldiers. In the imposing surroundings, Sura and Johan appeared nervous and ill at ease. Despite their callow age, they had been made sufficiently aware of the significance of the occasion. Performing in front of the *Führer* was a high honour. At the same time, it was an unnerving prospect for the inexperienced children.

'Ha!'

Goering displayed his good humour.

'I'll sit here and listen. Take no notice of me!'

Sura and Johan edged nervously away from him. Heinrich went over to the corner of the room to fetch a stiff-backed chair. He placed this by the side of the piano stool. When Johan sat on it, it was clear he needed a cushion in order to reach the keys, comfortably.

Sura placed their music on the stand and Heinrich explained to the *Reichmarschall* they would play a duet. The children had worked on Ravel's *Mother Goose Suite*. To his relief, Goering listened with rapt attention and applauded with enthusiasm. The work was followed by two lively Haydn duets. Only now and again did the young pianists break down and repeat a tricky passage that had thrown up difficulties. It was a relief to Heinrich when the short session drew to an end. He had arranged an afternoon tea for the children and was expecting them to stay at the annex with him until the time came for their evening appearance. Hermann Goering was in expansive mood.

'Excellent!' he informed the performers. 'A fine example of Aryan youth. No nation in the world, except Austria and Germany, could produce such talent!'

He slapped his ample thigh and addressed Johan.

'Tell me, young man. How many hours a day d'you practise?'

The boy hesitated before replying.

'Maybe two, sir. We've only one piano so I share the time with my sister.'

The *Reichmarschall* sounded impressed.

'Only two hours, hey? Of course, you must go to school and that takes up most of the day. What d'you do in your spare time?'

Johan thought carefully before replying.

'My sister likes reading, sir. Me…I like playing with my train set!'

Hermann Goering's fleshy ears pricked up. He grinned at Heinrich.

'Train set, did he say? I expect the boy would like to see my "train set", as he calls it. Over at my hunting lodge, outside Berlin. I have a whole room devoted to one of the finest model railway lay-outs in Europe. Been adding to it since I was this boy's age.'

He glanced at a wooden Bavarian clock on the wall.

'There's plenty of time before the concert starts. Why don't you take these two to see my *sonderzug*? I can phone down permission and arrange transport for you.' He faced the children who clearly had little idea of what he was talking about. Sura piped up to ask the key question.

'Please, what's a *sonderzug*?'

Amused, Goering ordered Heinrich not to tell them. It added to the mystery.

'Herr Müller will take you into a dark tunnel and show you!!'

He heaved himself out of his armchair and asked the children to excuse him.

'Come! I'll show you to the front door.'

Shaking hands with the young musicians, he begged his leave and strode away.

'I'll fix it with the guards at the Berchtesgaden terminus!' he called back. 'Get down there as soon as you can. No time to waste. I'll order a car. But don't be late for the concert. Good luck!'

The two astonished children watched him disappear before turning to Heinrich.

'We don't understand,' Sura said. 'I don't want to go into a tunnel!'

Heinrich laughed, relieved.

'Oh, it's just the *Reichmarschall*'s way of talking. I didn't know about his model railway. Or his hunting lodge. He's talking about a real train. Nothing to be scared of. We'd better go and see it else he'll be angry with me!'

Johan leapt for joy.

'He's got his own train?' he laughed. 'I want to see it!'

Sura pouted, unimpressed.

The previous day's car ride down from the flat heights of the Obersalzberg was repeated. On reaching the station, the small party was escorted to the tunnel. Johan sprang forward.

'Look! A loco! Can we go and see it?'

Heinrich called him back. As the three visitors drew nearer, they saw that the tunnel housed a double track that disappeared into the interior. On one line, the end of a passenger coach could be made out, a few metres from the entrance. A powerful locomotive reversed slowly on the adjacent track. Johan's eyes went round with wonder.

'The loco…it's so BIG!'

The young boy stood entranced as the intimidating behemoth belched forth large plumes of grey smoke. Hot jets of high-pressure steam shot out from outlet pipes. The great driving wheels, rotated by churning pistons, ground towards the tunnel entrance.

Heinrich shielded his eyes from the sun. He took both children by the hand and approached the semi-concealed train with a degree of trepidation. Sura gripped him, tightly, trying her best to overcome her fear of menacing machines. Unlike Heinrich's previous visit, this was a hive of noise and activity. The black, gleaming metal monster breathed fire and pulled up just inside the high-arched entrance.

'I'm scared!'

Sura shrank back and turned to run away. An eerie red glow from the firebox furnace danced on the sooty walls and rounded ceiling. Heinrich held out his hand to Sura.

'Stay this side of me. It's not alive. It's not going to eat you!'

The little girl pressed close, hanging onto his arm. Conversely, her younger brother was out of his mind with excitement.

'It's fantastic!' Johan shouted over the cacophony, breathing in a lungful of smoke from the funnel on top of the enormous boiler.

'Um! Lovely!' he coughed. 'Look at those smoke deflectors. I'm going to count the driving wheels!'

He ran alongside the steaming behemoth.

'It's a DRG Class 01!' he called back. 'I've only seen

them in pictures. This one looks quite new and it's got Pacific wheel arrangements!'

His chaperone had no idea what Johan was talking about. A helmeted guard stepped out of the gloom and onto the side of the track, barring their way. He pointed his rifle aggressively at Heinrich who reached inside his pocket for his papers.

'Here,' he said. 'Boarding Permission from the *Reichsmarschall*, himself.'

He thrust the documents forward.

'Take a look!'

The guard, a lad of about his age, flashed a torch and scrutinised the contents. He looked up from the small, attached photograph. Then shone the torch directly into Heinrich's face.

'Hold on! Don't I know you? You were at my school in Vienna…*Academisches Gymnasium.* I was in the year ahead of you. Were you in the fencing team?'

Heinrich peered more closely at the stern young soldier. He could just make out his chiselled features in the poorly lit tunnel. The fact that the guard wore a steel helmet did not help matters.

'I'm sorry,' he responded, 'it's difficult to see in this light. But you're right. I did a bit of fencing at the *Academisches* in the *Beethovenplatz.*'

He was being modest as he had excelled at the sport. The guard relaxed a little and lowered his weapon, pointing the long barrel at the oily floor.

'I'm Fischer,' he said. 'Carl Fischer. I was in the Athletics team…high jump and javelin.'

He handed back the papers.

'Good! Your pass is in order, Müller.'

He turned to the children; reluctant Sura and eager beaver Johan.

'Who are these?' he asked. 'What are they doing here? Kids! I can't allow them any further. Orders!'

Heinrich sought to reassure him.

'They're playing in the *Führer*'s special concert, tonight, up at the Berghof. I'm working directly to the *Reichmarschall* who gave them special permission to see his train. He said he'd phone down.'

Fischer looked doubtful.

'Not to us, he hasn't. What are you doing here, anyway? Even you shouldn't have got past the guards, never mind these kids.'

Heinrich tried to explain.

'I promise you,' he responded, 'the *Reichmarschall* insisted they took a look at his *sonderzug*. He met them, earlier, up at the Berghof. I've been put in charge. I was going to show them my private compartment. It's about two carriages down.'

Fischer could not hide his confusion and turned suspicious.

'Your private compartment? On the *sonderzug*? What d'you take me for, Müller? If you want my advice you'd better get out quick before I summon the security police.'

He reached for his whistle. Heinrich turned to Johan.

'I'm sorry. This is as far as we get!'

The boy pianist looked crestfallen. Heinrich addressed the security guard.

'Look, Fischer…I can't say any more. I'm not allowed to

divulge my business. Let's just say I've got reason to travel abroad on secret work for the *Reichmarschall*. And I've got papers to prove it.'

Fischer began to back down.

'Sounds strange to me but we're fellow *Academisches*. Maybe I can trust you,' he added reluctantly. 'If you're under orders not to divulge, I shan't enquire.'

He glanced hurriedly at his watch in the meagre light.

'Listen…I'll give you five minutes,' he said. 'Not a second longer. Then report back here!'

Fischer placed his foot on the bottom step of the nearest carriage and opened the door.

'Quick…get in! I don't think there's anyone aboard. It's all outside maintenance work, right now. And they're coaling up.'

He slammed the door behind the three entrants as they clambered into the first car. Heinrich signalled his appreciation. Without a further word, he slipped the youngsters along the gloomy corridor.

'This is my compartment,' he announced when they reached his berth. He opened the door and switched on the light.

'I'm getting my own special key, soon,' he added.

The children gazed in awe at the simple but efficient layout of the confined space. Even Sura was impressed.

'Two bunk beds!' she cried. 'I like your desk Heinrich. It's got a lamp. You must be very important but didn't tell us. Where are you going?'

The civilian clerk was about to answer but held himself back.

'It's a secret,' he responded. 'Not for your ears!'

Johan was more interested in climbing onto the recently made up bunk.

'It's quite comfortable!' he jested. 'Can *we* come? You can sleep on the floor, Heinrich!'

Sura and Heinrich caught each other's eye.

'Definitely not!' Heinrich laughed. 'What would your parents say? We couldn't tell them where you'd gone. They'd be furious...not just with you but with me!'

Johan was not defeated.

'We could be stowaways!' he suggested. 'Hide away like in stories. No-one would ever see us if you have the key.'

He looked at Johan, imploringly.

'If we play well at the concert and please the *Führer*, will you let us come with you? I could have the top bunk and Sura can sleep underneath!'

It all seemed so simple but it was already time to leave. Heinrich did not want to get his former school colleague in hot water.

'Come on,' he said. 'Out you get, both of you. You haven't had your tea, yet. Then you've got to change into your concert togs. We can't be late for the *Führer*. It wouldn't go down well!'

They hurried back along the train and jumped down to the trackside close to the tunnel entrance. Fischer seemed edgy and relieved to see them again.

'We got the call from the *Reichmarschall*'s office, in the end,' he informed them, 'so I guess there won't be any comeback.'

He looked sharply at the children.

'Don't *dare* to tell anyone about this. Keep it a secret. If news gets out, I'll be for the high jump but it won't be over a bar like when I was at school!'

They giggled and made a solemn promise not to get him into trouble. Heinrich thanked Fischer and turned to go. Then he was struck by a sudden thought.

'Are you travelling with us, Fischer?' he asked. 'Or d'you have to remain in Berchtesgaden?'

Fischer drew Heinrich aside in the gloomy light.

'I'll be on the train,' he said, concealing his mouth with his hand. 'We make a brief stop at München where we take on more water and extra coal. They've given me a pretty nasty job to do. I've got to supervise the loading of a special piece of apparatus.'

He made sure the children were out of ear shot, even with the deafening noise.

'It's my duty to guard it. All the way to Paris, so I believe.'

'Special?' Heinrich asked.

The whites of Fischer's eyes showed, even in the darkened surroundings.

'Don't breathe a word. I've been told it's a guillotine. German design but based on models the French used in their revolution. We're transporting this one to Paris. My senior officer thinks it's an excellent joke. Claims it's turning things back on the French!'

His tone took on a more serious note.

'He's weird. "We'll see French heads roll," he told me. I pretended to be amused.'

Heinrich did not know how to respond, detecting a tremor in Fischer's voice.

'The executioner's travelling with us on the train. It's macabre!'

His expression darkened.

'We've been told he'll have two assistants with him. Just hope I don't have to meet them. They must be ghouls. The very thought of it makes me squirm! But…'

Carl Fischer fell silent for a moment.

'…what can I do? Orders are orders.'

The two young men solemnly shook hands but Heinrich had the parting shot.

'Maybe I'll see you on the *sonderzug*?' he called back. 'We can chat about old times!'

It was a relief to break out of the noisy, smoke-ridden tunnel and step into bright daylight. Heinrich's eyes adjusted to the sudden dazzle as they trooped back to the railway station. A car to take the children back up to the Obersalzberg drew up. On the journey, Johan babbled on about DRG Class 01 locomotives and their wheel arrangements. Sura shut herself off, gazing out on the trees. Likewise, their chaperone remained curiously quiet. He knew he had to focus on the evening's auspicious event but battled with wild ideas spinning in other directions.

'Maria-Anna's mad plan,' he thought. 'It's hopeless! Even if I did take Sura and Johan with me what would I do with them? I could hardly hand them over to the French authorities. They'll soon be toeing the line and obeying orders.'

Suddenly, he sat up straight in the front seat of the Mercedes. The chauffeur, concentrating on the difficult bends leading to the Obersalzberg, gave him a sharp glance.

'I can see a way,' Heinrich thought. 'And it's every bit as crazy as Maria-Anna's mad scheme. Ridiculous, even. And yet…and yet…it might just work!'

Having successfully negotiated the road up to the Nazi hideaway on the high plateau, the sullen chauffeur dropped them off at the Goering *landhaus* where Heinrich had arranged a late tea for his gifted companions.

XVI

The concert was a stunning success. Adolf Hitler, who claimed to like children, personally congratulated Sura and Johan on their sparkling performances. He smiled and pinched their cheeks as a sign of affection. Heinrich tried to contain his embarrassment as Sura appeared to cringe away from the *Führer*. But she charmed the applauding throng when she showed affection towards Blondie, Hitler's Alsatian. Hitler had called for silence to inform the gathering he had a medal to present to a brave soldier. A special, new award instituted on the first day of the Polish campaign. An astonished Heinrich was summoned to stand, erect, before his leader. High-ranking *Nazi* officials in the room applauded as the young civilian received the *Ritterkreuze*, Knight's Cross, Second Class. Hitler stood before him and pinned onto his lapel an iron cross whose arms were narrower at the centre than the perimeter. It was framed with silver and contained the *swastika* at its heart.

Shaking Heinrich's hand, the *Führer* also presented the former lowly *grenadier* with a ribbon flash sporting red, black and white stripes for occasions when wearing the medal was not appropriate. Heinrich mumbled his thanks to a smiling Hitler who enquired courteously about his wound.

After the concert interval, in which various high-ranking party members paid their compliments to Heinrich, he and the children were chauffeured home. An anxious Herr and Frau Steaffel were relieved to see their children again and plied them with questions.

'We're so grateful to you, Herr Müller,' Frau Steaffel told him. 'Such a big occasion and you helped put the children at their ease.'

Heinrich assured the parents that the children would have performed perfectly well without him. Johan informed them that the best part of the visit was the cream tea.

'We could have had as many pastries as we wanted,' he said. 'Except Heinrich stopped me eating any more after three!'

As they said their goodbyes on the doorstep, Heinrich detected a sudden stiffening in Frau Steaffel's manner as she spotted the military award decorating his lapel. Slightly embarrassed, he ran down the steps to the car and stepped round to the driver's door. The man wound down his window.

'Sorry,' Heinrich told him, 'but my girlfriend's house is just a few doors down. D'you mind if I pop a note into her box? I won't disturb her so it won't take a minute.'

The chauffeur grunted some kind of acknowledgement and agreed to wait. Heinrich looked for No. 51 and was relieved to find a postbox outside the door. He slipped his note through the slit and walked back to the car.

'Thanks! I'm grateful.'

The driver started the powerful engine and the dark saloon purred across the Salzach to enter the old city. Dusk fell as they reached the outskirts of Berchtesgaden where lights twinkled in farmhouse windows. The Mercedes turned off the main road to drive up to the guarded entrance of the *Nazi* leaders' complex hovering over the town. Once back at the Goering *landhaus*, Heinrich thanked the chauffeur and walked round to his humble quarters at the back of the building. Turning on the light, he slumped down on the makeshift bed and gazed at the ceiling. Tomorrow, he would meet Maria-Anna at an arranged time. He just hoped that the call to board the train would not coincide with this but that was out of his power.

In the morning, he learned that the *sonderzug* departure had been delayed and it would leave for France at eleven o'clock, the following day. With more time on his hands than he had anticipated, Heinrich cycled down to the small tourist town nestling in the mountain valley. There he took a bus for the half hour ride into Salzburg, passing through Anif. Maria-Anna had finished work early in the afternoon and sat waiting for Heinrich at a table in Tomacelli's coffee house in the Altmarkt. She chose to sit downstairs amongst the earnest coffee drinkers perusing newspapers on sticks provided by the proprietors.

Thursday was the day of the week when many of the women and teenage girls of the area chose to dress in traditional costume. Maria-Anna wore her *dirndl*, a dress of two halves. The apple green top was buttoned quite high to the neck, whilst the lower half was chequered in delicate pink and white. Beneath the top, she chose her *dirndlbluse,* a white blouse puckered at the shoulders with short sleeves and lace. Tied round her slender middle Maria-Anna wore her *schürze*, a matching green apron, tied at the waist on her left-hand side. This informed the young men of Salzburg she was not spoken for.

From a street window she looked out on the Altmarkt, a busy, wide thoroughfare thronged with pedestrians. A tourist carriage pulled by two smart, brown horses bore an elderly holidaying couple through the square. The driver sat perched at the front, sporting his brimmed felt hat. Near to hand, a long-handled whip projected vertically although it was never used.

'Hello!'

Heinrich kissed Maria-Anna softly on her cheek.

'Glad you could make it.'

They exchanged loving pleasantries before issuing their order to the formally-attired waiter in attendance. Heinrich spoke for the two of them.

'*Eiscaffe*…coffee ice cream for two, please. Oh…and with extra cream! We'll take our coffees at the same time.'

The waiter checked if each required a small glass of water to accompany the coffees. There was no time to waste. Heinrich turned to Maria-Anna, his hand cupped over his mouth.

'I had to see you,' he said. 'I can't get Sura and Johan out of my mind. You're right, Maria-Anna. I have to apologise. The *sonderzug*'s the only way of escape. I'm sure I can keep them hidden. God knows what I do when we reach the French coast.'

He pulled a face.

'Guess I'll just have to think of something on the way.'

Maria-Anna cautioned him to lower his voice.

'Ssh!' she warned. 'Tomacelli's is no longer safe. I've wracked my brain but can't come up with anything better.'

She pursed her lips.

'I feel really bad but there's nothing we can do for the parents. They'll just have to take their chances.'

Heinrich had to agree.

'Look!' he said. 'There's a faint chance we can smuggle Sura and Johan onto the train. I've learned that Goering will be boarding his *sonderzug* at Berchtesgaden. It won't stop long and it's hardly on enemy territory. So I'm guessing security won't be that tight. An old school colleague, Fischer, will be on guard duty.'

He paused to sip his coffee and enjoy the first spoonful of ice cream. The two lovers tackled their desserts as if they had not a care in the world. All of a sudden, Maria-Anna grasped his arm. Heinrich detected repressed excitement in her tremulous voice.

'Heinrich…I think I've got it! Goering's already met the children, hasn't he? You said he was very taken with them. How about…how about…'

She turned back to the ice cream but her silver spoon slipped from her hand to the floor.

'I know how to do it!'

People at adjacent tables noticed her increased animation. She bent down to retrieve the spoon.

'Would the *Reichmarschall* be charmed,' she whispered, 'if Sura and Johan came to the station to wave him off?

Perhaps they could each present him with a small bunch of flowers to wish him a speedy journey.'

Heinrich nearly choked on his coffee. Maria-Anna glanced round, fearful of drawing attention.

'You know what Goering's like,' she continued. 'I bet he's easily flattered so it would appeal to his ego. You could work on this Fischer friend…then…'

Heinrich waited before interrupting and spoke slowly.

'You mean…if the children appeared at the station…I could invite them onto the platform with their flowers? You're right! With all the fuss around the *Reichmarschall*, I could easily open a carriage door and slip them into my compartment!'

He giggled, nervously.

'If anyone spots what I'm doing I'll just say Sura and Johan were curious to see what the *sonderzug* looked like inside. So I invited them in…for just a minute. I can always grovel and plead stupidity. I've done that often enough!'

Maria-Anna looked at him with admiration. She, too, cupped her hand over her mouth.

'You're nearly as crazy as I am!' she responded. 'Perhaps that's why I like you. All that education doesn't seem to have done you much good!'

They sat in a quandary looking out on the comings and goings of the bustling crowd in the square. Heinrich's quick mind raced on.

'It's you who'll have to make contact with the parents, Maria-Anna. I can't do that. I'm so caught up with the *Nazis*, the Steaffels are bound to be suspicious of me.'

He did not mention the display of his bravery award.

'I expect you're right,' she agreed. 'Of course, they might refuse our scheme. After all, Sura and Johan are their children and not ours, so it's their right. The Steaffels might even think we're as mad as we think we are!'

Her lovely brown eyes danced in the sunlight.

'I'm coming with you!' she whispered. 'The children will need me. Being just a boy, you'll never cope!'

Heinrich narrowed his eyes and looked at her, seriously. After they had finished their coffees he signalled to the waiter. He took her small hand.

'You're special,' he told her. 'I really admire you. You're the bravest person I know.'

Maria-Anna looked startled.

'But,' Heinrich went on, 'there's not a chance of you coming with us on the *sonderzug*. And don't try to persuade me. You're to wait here until I get back, Maria-Anna. *I absolutely forbid you to step on that train!*'

It was clear he was not to be argued with. Maria-Anna seethed inwardly but Heinrich did not give her the chance to challenge.

'If you try pushing me,' he said determinedly, 'the whole thing's off!'

Sensing her rising frustration, Heinrich tightened his grip.

'Listen, Maria-Anna, I don't think you've caught on. There's something I have to tell you. Something very important.'

He glanced shyly down at the table.

'I love you,' he said simply. 'I love you with all my heart. I won't risk placing your life in peril. So I beg you to do as I ask. This crazy scheme's full of risks and might go wrong at any moment.'

From the serious expression in his blue eyes, the young Salzburg maid detected Heinrich's sincerity. Her own eyes filled with tears as she sneaked a small handkerchief from the laced sleeve of her *dirndlbluse*. It was a sign she was prepared to concede. Heinrich slipped his good arm around her shoulder.

'Thank you, Maria-Anna.'

He settled his bill and indicated they should leave. Hand in hand, the young couple left the dark confines of the celebrated coffee house. Maria-Anna smiled to herself.

'I knew you'd see sense,' she said lightly, taking Heinrich by the arm. I told you. Constanze Mozart is very powerful!'

He shot her a cynical look. She indicated back to the café.

'You know she lived in this very building?' she continued unabashed. 'The von Nissens had rooms in Tomacelli's. I bet you didn't know that!'

They threaded their way through the shoppers in the narrow streets to reach the river. Crossing over, they strolled along a footpath bordering the broad Salzach and selected a spot on the sloping bank where they could sit on the grass. Maria-Anna's practical mind began planning ahead for the children's adventure.

'On our way back,' she said, 'we'll call in at a shop where they sell children's clothes. Sura and Johan will need a change of underwear and other stuff to keep them warm. I can guess their sizes. And they'll need toothpaste and toothbrushes. I'll think of other things, as we go.'

Heinrich regarded her practicality with admiration.

'By the way,' she continued, 'you'll have to pay. I've hardly got a *schilling*!'

He, himself, was hardly flush with money but suspected he had just enough to pay for the articles she might choose.

'This will be the first time we've been seriously shopping, together,' Maria-Anna told the young man who had gained her heart. She tossed her freckled face to the sky and giggled.

'You'll have to get used to it, Heinrich. It's what men are for! Oh, and by the way,' she added, 'we'll have to purchase a chamber pot.'

Heinrich blinked.

'What for?'

Maria-Anna punched him lightly on his good arm.

'What d'you think?' she laughed.

Giving Heinrich a playful look, she untied the green bow positioned on the left hip of her *schürze*. Then, with a knowing smile, she re-tied it, this time on the opposite hip. Heinrich could not contain his blushes. In true Salzburg fashion, Maria-Anna was telling the world she had met someone about whom she felt passionate.

xvii

'I want you with me, Müller!'

Hermann Goering, resplendent in white, belted uniform, *Reichmarschall's* cap and an array of boastful medals ranged across his chest, lumbered down the steps of the Obersalzberg mansion. His new wife stood at the top of the steps to wave him off. Heinrich followed behind clutching two bags, one with his clothes for the journey and the other apparently stuffed with gallery catalogues and his fastidious notes. Beneath these were the children's things. In the car, his boss was in buoyant mood.

'I've ordered the German and French railway authorities to give us priority and clear the line ahead. We should arrive in Calais before some time the day after tomorrow. There are bound to be delays, possibly diversions. Then…off to Cap Gris Nez, as the Frenchies call it, to take a look at England!'

Heinrich was rather shaken.

'England, *Reichmarschall*? Have we won the war?'

Goering shook with laughter.

'Excellent, young man! The right attitude. No...that comes later. I thought we'd take a little peek at the enemy, first. Cap Gris Nez's a cliff top looking out over the *Pas de Calais*. Amusingly, the English call the same stretch of water the Strait of Dover. Well, they won't need to argue over that, any more. I can't wait to get a good sight of the white cliffs of Dover through my Zeiss binoculars. Soon, I'll be giving the order for my brave boys to set out on their bombing missions. Concentrate on their southern airfields and take out what's left of their fighters, on the ground. They'll soon cave in. No need to blitz their cities!'

The Mercedes wound its way carefully down to the village where the outlandishly designed railway station hove into view. Security traffic police indicated a parking spot by the round tower and Goering leapt out of the vehicle before a minion could be found to open his door for him. A small crowd had gathered, lightly policed by security guards. The admirers smiled warmly at the important man in their midst and offered straight-armed salutes. Goering returned the compliment and was about to enter the main entrance when a young woman stepped forward. She curtsied then gestured to two children who each carried a small posy of flowers. They came forward nervously to present the posies to the *Luftwaffe* chief. Hermann Goering stopped short and beamed.

'Well, well! Don't I know you two?'

He turned back to Heinrich who struggled with his luggage.

'Look who's come to see me off, Müller! Your little musician pals.'

He bent down to Johan and spoke quietly.

'Did you get to see my *sonderzug*, boy? What did you think of the locomotive?'

Johan grinned.

'Great, sir! It's a DRG-01 Pacific. The driving wheels are bigger than me and I liked the lamp on the front of the boiler!'

Goering was impressed.

'Spot on, young man!'

He bowed graciously to Sura.

'And thank you, both, for my flowers. Now, if you speak to Herr Müller very politely he might let you *onto* my train for a couple of minutes. Is that all right with you, Müller?'

Heinrich swiftly agreed.

'Of course, sir. Whatever you say. I'll make sure they're off in good time!'

The *Reichmarschall* strode on as officials crowded round to escort him to his private coach. At the top of the platform, pointing in the Salzburg direction, the dazzling black loco puffed and panted as if desperate to be unleashed. Heinrich gathered the children and told them to keep close to him. There was a brief moment when he caught a glance of a pretty girl in the crowd. He also caught sight of a stressed-looking couple, close to tears, who looked longingly over the pressed crowd at their beloved children. With no time for sentimentality, Heinrich found his sleeping coach and invited the children in. As he had hoped, all the attention was directed at the *Reichmarschall* who was being directed to his luxury compartment. Further along the platform, a smart military band struck up *Deutschsland Über Alles*, before moving on to music of a more relaxed nature.

'Quick! In you go!'

He glanced down the platform to find a uniformed soldier staring at him with intent. His heart missed a beat when he realised it was Carl Fischer. But there was no going back. The children clambered up the steps into the corridor where Heinrich identified his berth and ushered them inside. Sura stopped at the door.

'We didn't say goodbye to Mummy and Daddy. There wasn't time to kiss them.'

Their travelling companion shook his head.

'I know,' he said, gently. 'I spotted your parents amongst the crowd and they were sending you their love. In my pocket is a letter for you both. Maria-Anna gave it to me, yesterday.'

Johan frowned.

'They said they couldn't come with us because no-one would let them. Will they take the next train?'

Heinrich hardly knew what to say. Maria-Anna would have found the appropriate words but she, too, was not on the *sonderzug*. It suddenly dawned on the young man that all three individuals closeted in the compartment might never see their loved ones again. Although Heinrich hoped to return to see his girl, he knew he could not make false promises to the two runaways. He stumbled over his words.

'Maybe they'll be able to join you after the war's over,' he suggested, his throat tightening. 'The *Reichmarschall* says it can't last long so I guess it'll soon be finished. For now, we'll have to be brave. I'm going to miss my Maria-Anna so we must look after each other.'

Sura looked grave but Johan's less mature mind was turning to the excitement of the rail journey with the acrid smell of coal fumes exciting his nostrils.

'Where we're going,' Sura said, 'will they have a piano?'

Heinrich struggled to control his emotions and foresaw the journey was not going to be as simple as he had hoped. He locked the door, from the inside, with the external key issued to him.

'Listen!' he said, urgently. 'I know this has all happened very suddenly but your mummy and daddy are certain it's for the best. They're doing it for you. That's why they trusted me and Maria-Anna. You know you're going to stay with your great aunt in England. But I can't tell you for how long.'

Johan frowned.

'It's my birthday on Sunday. I'll be nine and they promised to take me to the zoo at Munich. I wanted to see the polar bears!'

Heinrich went over to the window and pulled the curtains.

'Your journey's a secret, remember. We don't want anyone seeing you through the window.'

He reached into his travelling bag and ferreted around inside.

'Look! I've got a change of clothes for you both and… guess what?'

He pulled out a small white and black spotted cuddly toy dog. Sura's face lit up with joy.

'Bimperl!' she cried.

Heinrich handed it to her.

'Mummy and Daddy insisted he came with you. And guess what?'

He rummaged in the bag again. This time he pulled out a well-worn bear with a missing ear. Johan grabbed it from his grasp.

'It's Ludwig!' he cried, holding the bear close to his cheek.

The children clambered onto their respective beds, feeling a little happier and more comforted. Suddenly, there was a sharp knock on the door. Heinrich froze.

'Quick…hide…under there!'

There was room only for suitcases beneath the lower bunk but he managed to conceal the brother and sister by placing his bags on the floor, alongside them. A second knock and a harsh demand.

'Open up! Papers!'

The young fugitive fumbled for his documents and unlocked the door. A grim, square-jawed policeman confronted him.

'Why have you locked this door?'

Heinrich hesitated for a fraction of a second. He felt his heart race and tried to control the shaking starting in his hands.

'I'm sorry. I didn't think. Please…!'

He handed over his identity card and various permits.

The policeman wore a soft cap and black uniform, heavily belted, with a pistol holster at his hip. He stared past Heinrich.

'Why are the curtains closed?'

He took his time scrutinising the documents in his possession then gruffly returned them to their owner.

'So! You're working directly to the *Reichmarschall*. In what capacity?'

He made it clear he required an instant answer. Heinrich asked permission to put his hand into the inside breast pocket of his civilian jacket. He pulled out his *Ritterkreuze* and revealed it to his inquisitor.

'Our *Führer* presented me with this only two days ago up at the Berghof,' he responded. 'I'm entrusted with a confidential mission.'

The man looked startled and Heinrich's confidence rose.

'I'm not prepared to answer prying questions as I'm under the strictest instructions not to do so. If you wish to challenge me then the matter is simple. Take me to my master. His name is Hermann Goering.'

He stared the man hard in the eye.

'You may like to know,' Heinrich went on, 'that I won this medal on the Polish battlefield whilst you were keeping the peace on market day, in some Bavarian village. So make up your mind. What are you going to do?'

The policeman blanched, attempting to conceal his sudden discomfort, and stepped back into the corridor. He blurted out a flustered apology.

'I'm sorry! I wasn't fully briefed on all passengers. Please continue with your activities. We'll not bother you further... sir!'

Highly bemused, he headed down the corridor in deep embarrassment. Heinrich slammed the door shut and sat on the edge of the bed. Two young heads peered out from underneath.

'I said you must be important,' Sura said brightly. 'He sounded a horrible man. I could only see the toes of his black boots!'

Heinrich stood up, very shaken. His false bravado was a masquerade and he knew it. How long could he last out and get away with this outrageous deception, right under the *Reichmarschall*'s nose? His attention was taken by something on the lower bunk. To his horror, Sura's Bimperl sat demurely on the clean white pillow. The policeman, thrown off course for vital seconds, had failed to spot it.

The muffled shriek of the locomotive whistle penetrated the interior of the cramped compartment. Instinctively, Johan rushed to the window to open the curtains. Fortunately, it was not on the platform side of the train but Heinrich swiftly pulled him back and sat him down on the lower bunk.

'You mustn't be seen!' he warned. 'It's vital. It could ruin everything.'

The DRG 01 Class let out a second, short shriek. Dull, staccato thumps of smoke-release from the chimney echoed back from the nearby cliff faces. They were accompanied by snakelike hissings of high-pressure steam escaping from convoluted pipes. The coach groaned as its bogie wheels responded to the piston rods commanding the driving wheels. In the small crowd that hung about, a young woman stood watching the final carriage enter the tunnel in the München direction. She felt desperately anxious about the three people who were being borne away from her. Only metres away and not daring to make contact, the Steaffels held each other closely and wiped smudged tears from their cheeks. The bus journey back to the city would be agony; two empty seats where previously Sura and Johan had sat. The parents were starkly aware of the likelihood they would never again see their precious children who had brought them so much joy.

A long plume of grey smoke streamed behind the *sonderzug* as it picked up speed through flat, grass plains. It presented a formidable sight; a combination of dull green functional coaches and the *Reichmarschall*'s exotic luxury carriage. Towards the rear, the defence truck bristled with anti-aircraft weapons, alert helmeted gunners in attendance. Security precautions were strictly enforced even on the peaceful German-Austrian border.

Inside the locked compartment, Heinrich and his young companions settled the issue of sleeping arrangements. Johan lost the battle for the top bunk to his older sister and Heinrich nobly offered to make his bed on the floor.

'It was far worse than this, in Poland,' he told them. 'Sometimes we had to sleep in the forest in pouring rain with only oilskins to protect us. I'll cope!'

As the prestigious train headed towards the border town of Freilassing, Heinrich took the early opportunity to explain to the children the seriousness of their situation.

'I don't know how much Mummy and Daddy told you,' he said, 'but you must understand if we're caught we'll all be in big trouble. Neither of you have tickets so they'll send you back to Salzburg. As for me…'

He felt his chin and looked grave.

'I'll be arrested. Goodness knows what they'd do to me. I expect I'd be sent to prison for a very long time.'

He smiled grimly.

'If I was lucky!'

The children struggled to understand. With the greatest tact, he went on to reassure them that their parents had made the right decision and it was in their interest.

'It isn't going to be easy,' he continued. 'Three of us cooped up like this. The journey's going to take hours so we might get a bit fed up with each other. I guess we'll just have to get along. Look…I'm really sorry but I can't let you out of the compartment, even to go to the toilet.'

The children grimaced.

'Ugh!' Sura responded. 'I'm not very good at holding it in so what are we supposed to do?'

It was a fair question. Heinrich produced a tin chamber pot out of his luggage.

'This is all I can offer,' he said. 'I'll go out but neither of you are allowed to pass through that door. I'll just have to be careful emptying the pot in the toilet at the end of the corridor. Make sure no-one's around, you understand?'

The brother and sister nodded, glumly. Mixed emotions of fear and excitement welled up inside them.

'Will we be able to write to Mummy and Daddy?' Sura asked. 'I mean…when we get to England.'

Heinrich hesitated.

'We'll have to see,' he said. 'It depends if Britain and Germany can make peace. Let's hope they can. That would make things a lot easier.'

The children settled down to the routine of the journey. Sura lay in her top bunk trying to read a book whilst Johan gazed out at the passing fields and forests, forbidden to wave to occasional, admiring agricultural workers. Picturesque, red-roofed Bavarian farmsteads flashed by in undulating meadows where contented cows had learned to ignore trains. Issued with an itinerary for the journey, Heinrich knew the first stop would be at München. He had been issued with a pass that entitled him to attend the second lunch sitting in the restaurant car, when clear of the city. Heinrich had already prepared for the children's needs by secreting two bottles of apple juice and several packets of biscuits.

Shortly after two o'clock in the afternoon, the impressive train snaked slowly into the complexity of sidings outside the München *hauptbahnhof*. Johan was disappointed they were not able to get a glimpse of the magnificent station terminus. To his joy he found, in the compartment, a *Deutsch Bahn* map of railway connections. With Heinrich's help, he concocted a list of continental cities he speculated they might pass through.

'Mannheim,' he announced, 'then I reckon we'll see Augsburg, Ulm, Stuttgart, Mannheim, Mainz, Köln and Aachen.'

Heinrich was impressed.

'After we cross the border,' he interrupted, 'I suspect we'll avoid Paris and head for Lille. There may be delays and re-routing.'

He had heard resistance was beginning to spring up.

Around seventy metal wheels screeched to a halt once the *sonderzug* had wound its way to its appointed slot. Heinrich half-closed the curtains and warned the children not to peek through.

'I'm going to leave you, for a while. Shan't be long. It's time I made contact with one or two people I know on the train.'

He was hoping he might bump into Carl Fischer as meeting up with him might lighten the journey. He locked the door behind him then threaded his way along the corridor to the exit door. Pushing down the window he stuck his head out and was astonished at the sight of parallel rows of freight trucks lined up along the tracks. Each was loaded with an ominous-looking *panzer* tank, or large artillery piece. Clearly, preparations were underway to reinforce the Western Front troops. Tough-looking police officers with sniffer dogs patrolled the tracks whilst impassive armed soldiers watched on.

Heinrich's attention was taken by movements further along the *sonderzug* where a canvas-topped military truck drew up alongside a luggage car. Soldiers leapt off the back and fixed a wooden ramp before rolling out a sturdy-looking trolley built to take a heavy load. Heinrich looked idly on as the men struggled with a machine from the back of the truck. Some joked and made faces as they toiled with it, pushing the contraption over to the train. In a flash, he recalled Fischer's remark in the Berchtesgaden railway tunnel. A *fallschwertmaschine*...a transportable guillotine!

Two civilians in dark suits supervised the transition. Heinrich recoiled in horror. The steel blade, secured by a winching wheel at the side, glinted in the afternoon sun. The guillotine was nowhere near as tall as he had seen in history books on the French Revolution. His imagination ran riot as he gawped at the solid wooden platform that had already borne the prostrate bodies of past victims. With a great deal of pushing and pulling, the cumbersome machine was successfully transferred into a freight wagon. A policeman slid the heavy door bolts into place and the civilian supervisors turned to board the train.

Heinrich debated if he could face a meal after such a horrendous revelation. However, he knew he had to secure scraps from the table for his young companions. With a heavy heart, he approached the dining car. A waiter in dark Deutsche Reichsbahn uniform approached him and asked to see his reservation. He showed Heinrich to a seat at the window who, as he settled, was startled by a cheerful greeting.

'Müller! May I join you?!'

Carl Fischer, trim in his *Wehrmacht* uniform, slid into the opposite seat. He grinned and shook hands before turning round to check for listening ears.

'You won't believe this,' he said. 'I've just helped load that creepy *fallschwertmaschine* on the train. They told me it's already done a few jobs. Doesn't bear thinking about.'

Fischer picked up a menu and approved the courses on offer.

'Vegetable soup followed by dumplings or *schnitzel*… what better? With new potatoes and cabbage. I expect the *schnitzel* comes with a sauce.'

Heinrich felt no hunger but knew he had to fill the large paper bag he had carefully folded and slipped into his jacket pocket.

'For dessert,' Fischer continued, 'a choice of fresh fruit or cheese. No *apfelstrudel*…never mind! Perhaps they'll offer that for supper.'

He looked up sharply as two middle-aged men approached, directed to the table by the head waiter. Heinrich swallowed hard. They were the civilians he had seen supervising the loading of the guillotine. Fischer forced a smile as he had already worked with them and moved up to allow the older one in next to him. Both newcomers wore hard, unsmiling faces. Heinrich, pinned in at his window seat, curtly acknowledged his unwanted dining companions before gazing out on the passing scenery.

'My name is Reikhart,' the older man announced in a curt voice. He turned to Fischer. 'I must thank you for your efforts in getting our guillotine aboard. I trust it's secure. We don't want it damaged in any way.'

Carl Fischer felt flummoxed, hardly able to think of a suitable response.

'Of course not, sir,' he said. 'We made sure the ropes were secure. I understand it's being taken to Paris.'

The man confirmed the destination.

'There'll be much work to do. We're reliably informed that the French have put up more resistance in Paris than anticipated. Communists as always. Most unfortunate. We'll offload at Köln to make the connection to the French capital. Naturally, we regret the necessity of our work but orders are orders and criminal dissidents can't be tolerated. Previously, I worked as State Executioner for Bavaria. My brother, here, worked with me.'

The waiter came to their shared table bearing a large ladle and silver soup bowl. The four diners sipped their soup in silence, sharing bread, and waited for the main course. Fischer could not help but vent his curiosity.

'You must forgive me. I have not seen such an instrument before. Was it manufactured in Germany?'

The man looked up solemnly whilst his gloomy brother remained silent.

'Of course! My family's been in the business for three generations. This *fallswertmaschine* is very much of our own design and based on experience. It's better than the French originals. In one hour, we can push through more executions. That's why we've been invited by the newly-appointed *Gauleiter* for Paris to speed the process along.'

Heinrich's stomach churned but he fought back the urge to push past his morbid companion and return to his compartment. He held on, determined to take back a decent amount of food for the young stowaways.

'We did a lot of work at Standelheim Prison, in München,' continued Reikhart in his matter-of-fact manner. 'People think we hood the prisoner but we've abandoned that. My brothers restrain the condemned and position him under the blade.'

It was clear Herr Reikhart took pride in his profession and warmed to his theme.

'One of us places his fingers over the condemned's eyelids. I usually do the cranking up, myself. And…'

Sensing his friend's unease, Fischer interrupted the morbid executioner and skilfully turned the conversation.

'We're going on beyond Köln,' he interpolated. 'Heading for the French coast, so we've been told. Goodness knows what time we'll reach it. There are bound to be hold-ups and diversions even though the *sonderzug*'s requested priority. I spent a few minutes in the radio car and they're worried there may be trouble when we get to Northern France. Reports are coming in of resistance but I suppose that's to be expected. There's a lot of foreign workers up there.'

Forced to dine together, the four men sat out the rest of the meal in glum silence. To Heinrich's relief, the German executioners were keen to get back to their machine. Fischer excused himself with a cheery excuse.

'I must get back, too,' he said brightly. 'I'm helping the radio boys and fancy having a go at their transmission job, one day.'

He paused and gave Heinrich a curious look.

'I saw you let those wretched kids on the train, again,' he said. 'What on earth for? I assume they got off before we left Berchtesgaden?'

There was something in his voice that disturbed Heinrich. Was the question as innocent-sounding as it appeared?

'Of course I did!' he whispered. 'Sura and Johan's parents were waiting for them. I'd obtained a small present for their thoughtfulness to my master but left it in my compartment.'

Fischer seemed satisfied.

'You'll excuse me?' he said. 'I've been asked to double up on radio communications so can't hang about.'

Left to himself, Heinrich peered out of the window as the train steamed through a dense forest. But his thoughts were elsewhere. Fischer's remark worried him. Was he hinting at something? Heinrich could not be sure but tried to brush the matter aside. Then he reflected on the previous conversation with the professional executioners, vowing to avoid them for the rest of the journey. Settling down, he took the opportunity to sneak a couple of apples into his bag and used a napkin to conceal dumplings he had saved on the side of the plate. He got up from his seat, carefully concealing his acquisitions under his jacket, and returned to his carriage. Letting himself into the private compartment, he was relieved to find Sura and Johan lying quietly on their respective bunks.

'We counted cows,' Johan told him. 'I reckon there've been sixty seven since München but Sura says I'm exaggerating!'

Sura pulled a face.

'He always exaggerates,' she explained. 'I only counted forty eight.'

All three saw the funny side.

'Not to worry,' Heinrich announced. 'I managed to snaffle a napkin to wrap dumplings in. You must eat them, now, as they're going cold. And I sneaked a couple of rolls but no butter. After that, there's fruit. Just hope you eat apples?'

The children smiled.

'Mummy tells us to,' Sura said.

A shadow fell over her delicate face.

'I wonder what she's doing now?'

XVIII

The hours passed slowly. Cooped up in their crowded box of a sleeping compartment the young travellers ached to be allowed into the corridor. Heinrich was aware that one small slip or error could bring down the whole scheme. It was becoming increasingly difficult trying to explain the situation to the children.

'Just for a minute, Heinrich!' Johan pleaded. 'Please! I need to get my legs going again. How long will it be before we get off?'

Sura was more patient and understanding and invented games to play. But these soon palled against the backdrop of the pedestrian passing of time. Given their unasked for confinement, the children bore their ordeal well. However, Heinrich sensed that the key question behind the adventure would have to be tackled. He worried that, when it was asked, he would not be able to provide a convincing answer. Swinging her legs from the top bunk, Sura's deep brown eyes betrayed the anxiety she fought so hard to suppress.

'It would've been much easier if Mummy and Daddy were with us.'

She blushed, not meaning to hurt Heinrich.

'Daddy's a teacher so we're not rich or anything. He said he had only enough money to afford the fare just for us two. And he'd try to save more and come after us.'

Sitting at his desk, her chaperone felt at a loss to explain. The last thing he wanted to do was undermine the good intentions of the parents who were complicit in the deception.

'I hope that's right,' he replied. 'Also, they told me your great aunt, in England, doesn't have a large house so maybe it's best to get you two settled first?'

The thought took time to sink in before Johan broke the silence.

'But how will we talk to her? I think her name is Christine. I wonder what she's like?'

Again a short silence; this time broken by Sura.

'I hope she's nice. Does she speak German?'

Heinrich wanted to sound positive.

'I think she left Austria, only a few years ago to get married, so she's bound to remember lots. The practice will be good for her. You can help her and she'll teach you English!'

Johan was distinctly unimpressed.

'I don't want to speak English,' he said, grumpily. 'What's the point?'

Heinrich smiled.

'I speak a bit, myself,' he responded. 'It's quite useful. We were taught it at school.'

An idea struck him.

'How about…' he ventured, '…how about…me teaching you a few English words? Then you could surprise your aunt when you meet her.'

Sura was intrigued.

'So what's English for "*Wie geht es ihnen?*"'

Heinrich laughed.

'*How are you?*' he replied.

The children looked doubtful.

'It's too difficult,' Johnan complained but his sister was more prepared to give it a go.

'*How…are…you?*' she struggled. '*How are…you?*'

She giggled.

'How do you say *guten morgen*?'

Heinrich was quick to respond.

'Easy…*good morning*. It's like the German.'

Johan began to show interest.

'*Good…morning*,' he spoke slowly. 'Yes, it's like our language!'

Heinrich explained as best he could that English contained many words that had come from Saxony, hundreds of years before.

'*Good morning*,' Johan tried. '*How…are…you?*'

His sister got in on the act. She wanted to learn the response to the question. Heinrich came to her aid.

'So for "*Danke, gut*" you say, "*Thanks, that's good!*"'

Again the children were astonished to discover a connection between their own language and that spoken in their country of destination. Heinrich was astonished at their children's-ability to pick up things quickly. He got out a paper and pencil and wrote the words down. For the next hour or so, the brother and sister practised, writing down new words and phrases. Outside the carriage, trees threw dark shadows. It was getting dark and Heinrich consulted his watch.

'Goodness! Look at the time! I'm booked in for Dinner in five minutes.'

He got up and refreshed himself at the tiny wash basin.

'With any luck, I'll come back with some good stuff!' he continued. 'You've both been brilliant so I'll do what I can. It'll be easier, this time. I can ask if I can take a few things back for the night. Don't expect they'll mind as there's always food over.'

He made the children promise not to venture out into the corridor and was only too aware he was asking a great deal of them. But his trust in Sura's good sense was well-founded.

'I'll be as quick as I can,' he continued. 'Your next English lesson will be on food. Not the worst idea when you think about it!'

Turning the key in the door, he raised a warning finger to the stowaways.

'*Be good!*'

Johan blinked but Sura got the message.

'You've got to be good, Johan. In English!'

Heinrich's dinner passed off uneventfully except that he was able to extract key information from Carl Fischer. Because of his friend's contacts in the radio car, he learned that the *sonderzug* was expecting a delayed journey to *France Nord*.

'We've been getting reports of sabotage in the Bethune district. There's an immigrant community there of different nationalities. Some of them work in the coal fields. They escaped their own countries as they were being occupied. Now, they're trapped in France and can't get away from us. So they've decided to try to resist our efforts!'

This was news to Heinrich. He had no idea that tens of thousands of foreign nationals had streamed into France in the months before the war had started. It sounded like bad news. If they were enemies of the *Reich* they might be capable of causing all sorts of problems.

'News coming in,' said Fischer, 'tells us that these foreign workers are doing stupid things. Not stuff that's going to win the war or hold up our advance. Things like trying to blow up lock gates on canals or cutting telegraph wires. What worries me is we got a report on one or two groups trying to derail trains. Troop trains, obviously. And units supplying ammunition and heavy armour to the Front. I don't think these groups are very well organised but our officer in charge says they're a nuisance and we'll have to be on our guard.'

Heinrich thought back to a remark made by Hermann Goering at the Obersalzberg.

'The *Reichmarschall* told me we run a locomotive in front of our own. The big idea is that it spots trouble ahead or takes the first blow. I guess they're in radio contact.'

Fischer nodded, glumly.

'These saboteurs are getting hold of explosives. My Major told me some of them are miners from places like Poland. They work in the Bethune coalfield so I guess they can smuggle explosives out.'

He shrugged his shoulders to show little concern.

'I guess these attacks are rare so we should avoid them with any luck. Let's face it. This train's well-defended. It can withstand a heavy attack…so we should be fine!'

The two friends prepared to part for the night. Heinrich was not prevented from taking drinks and a bag of food back to the compartment. Others, too, had thought of the idea except they returned to their quarters plied with bottles of Austrian beers. As the *sonderzug* ploughed its way through the German industrial belt, many of its military passengers were celebrating with little thought for the future. Heinrich was startled when Fischer asked a curious question. It seemed he had undergone a change of mind.

'I've managed to get hold of a bottle of *schnaps!*' he laughed. 'The steward pretended to look the other way. Why don't we go back to your compartment and enjoy it on our own? I'm sharing with four others in a converted saloon. They're not my type. There's a couple of roughnecks from München and I think they're *Nazis.*' Heinrich sympathised but begged leave, expressing his desire for an early night.

'I've got loads of reading up to do, tomorrow,' he told Fischer. 'The *Reichmarschall* might send for me because I'm sure he'll want to know what progress I'm making.'

Suddenly, he realised he might have said too much. Fischer threw him a querulous look.

'I don't figure you, Müller…all this confidential work. But I promise I shan't enquire. Let's just knock off half a bottle together. We'll sleep all the better for tomorrow!'

Heinrich remained insistent causing his friend to grow suspicious.

'You puzzle me,' Fischer told him. 'All this secrecy. Are you sure you're not hiding someone in there? You haven't got a woman on board, have you? That girl of yours!'

Heinrich feigned amusement.

'You've caught me out!' he confessed. 'But don't tell the *Reichmarschall*. He'll be furious. I'll be in dead trouble if he finds out. So...'

He turned mock serious.

'...you mustn't betray me, Fischer!'

The two friends ordered a second coffee and chocolate biscuits. Fischer looked at his former school colleague quizzically.

'Should I believe you?' he asked. 'Something's going on but I haven't fathomed it out yet. But I'll get there. I'd feel easier if I'd seen those two children leaving the platform at Berchtesgaden with my own eyes.'

They downed their coffees and bade each other good night. Heinrich returned to his compartment in a troubled state. Fischer was no fool. He was smart and clearly dropping unsubtle hints. He turned the key to find the children drowsy and wanting no more than a drink before settling down for the night. He tucked them into their bunk beds and tried to make up a bedtime story. But he found it hard to concentrate.

To his relief, it was not long before both Sura and Johan were drifting off. He sat at his table illuminated by the small lamp. Fischer was one problem but getting the children off the train was a different matter. How could it be achieved and where could it take place? For one thing, it depended on the *sonderzug* stopping, but it had to be at night-time. A brief stop during the day would be of no value. He could hardly walk off the train, hand in hand with two children. For the first time, he found himself faced with the impossible. It was like being back on the Polish border all those weeks ago, although it seemed like a lifetime.

'I need a plan,' he thought, desperately. 'It's clear it must be in darkness. But where? And even if we got off safely… what then?'

It was not as if they were entering a neighbouring country in peacetime. The Germans had beaten the French some of whom were likely to turn hostile. He cursed himself for getting involved in a hare-brained scheme thought up by a teenager in Salzburg. He could not get Maria-Anna out of his mind; her brown eyes and fair skin, and a smile to charm birds from the trees. He wished she was with him, now. Maria-Anna had begged to come on the dangerous mission but Heinrich had refused her. With her at his side, he suspected things would be easier once the train adventure was behind them. Now, the responsibility was all his and he felt deflated and confused.

Heinrich threw his jacket on the cabin floor and turned out his lamp. He lay down, his head supported by his travel bag. It was infinitely worse than sleeping in Polish forests. The train wheels rumbled ceaselessly over tiny gaps between the rails. And when the *sonderzug* passed over multiple sets of points, the rattling and shaking were unbearable. That night, there was virtually no sleep for the former soldier. He tossed and wriggled on the uncomfortable floor glancing, every now and again, at the hands on his luminous watch. But the hours passed slowly. He managed to snatch only minutes of fitful sleep before grey daylight seeped into the compartment. There was no joy in watching the rise of the morning sun. Heinrich's only comfort was that Sura and Johan had somehow managed to sleep peacefully through the night, in the relative comfort of their bunk beds.

The next day proved even more difficult for the cooped up children but they bore their ordeal with stoicism. Regular reassurance was required from Heinrich, their effective jailer, for whom their regard grew by the minute. Once over the French border, the *sonderzug*, despite its elitist persona, was subjected to numerous delays. Down the grapevine, Heinrich learned that Hermann Goering was growing increasingly impatient and demanding the impossible from his unfortunate staff. The routine of his attending meals in the restaurant car continued as did the explicit bringing back of food and drinks. Carl Fischer made no more mention of his suspicions and the two were able to talk over old times. Events that, in effect, had taken place only a few years previously. They joked over the eccentricities of schoolmasters at their prestigious Viennese academy. It helped to pass the time. Fischer discussed with Heinrich what he intended to do after the war.

'Before conscription I was studying Civil Engineering,' he said. 'Hard going. My Maths isn't that brilliant. But I want to qualify and work for a major construction firm. The Todt Organisation, for instance.'

He turned to Heinrich.

'What about you?'

It was an innocent question and well meant. He had not really caught on that his friend found himself in a dire predicament about his future.

'I've no idea,' Heinrich replied. 'Maybe I'll be able to find someone to fix my shoulder better. But the longer I leave it, the less the chance of getting back to the violin.'

He looked rueful.

'Guess I'll have to teach,' he continued. 'Suppose that's not the worst thing. At least I get on with kids.'

He swallowed hard. It was a foolish if innocent remark. The comment was not lost on his companion but Fischer made no effort to follow it up. Heinrich swiftly turned the conversation to other matters.

'The *Reichmarschall*'s keen to see England for himself,' he said. 'He's convinced the British will sue for peace. I hope they do. It'll shorten the war.'

Fischer was not so sure.

'My father fought the British in the last conflict,' he said. 'On French soil. Mud-filled trenches on the River Marne. He hated it. Rats and exploding shells. He rates the *Englischers* as fighters and says they'll never give up. He was very worried when he heard I was travelling this way. Didn't want me getting involved with them in battle.'

Increasingly, Heinrich felt he could trust Fischer.

'Look…if we sign a Non-Aggression Pact with Great Britain, it would be the best thing for both of us. But what worries me is that our *Führer* might be thinking in another direction. Like…'

He paused, mid-sentence, and the two gazed thoughtfully out of the restaurant car window. Fischer narrowed his eyes, venturing to pursue Heinrich's line of thinking. They took care to check no other person was in earshot.

'Listen, I'm no military strategist,' Heinrich responded. 'But I've heard it rumoured the *Führer's* thinking of going further East.'

Fischer looked at him, somewhat startled.

'But that's all finished,' he said. 'Poland and Czechoslovakia have capitulated. And we've signed a deal with the Russians. They now have nearly half of Poland for themselves. Surely, we'll not renege on the Non-Aggression Pact. What are you trying to say, Heinrich?'

The de-mobbed soldier felt uneasy. Since the *Anschluss*, freedom of expression had become limited. Dangerous, even.

He looked Fischer straight in the eye.

'You're right, Fischer. I'm not suggesting the Reds will attack us. But what if we turned our guns on them? Once the war in the West is over, the *Führer* might take them by surprise. It's just a feeling I have.'

Fischer smiled but kept his voice down.

'Well Müller, my friend,' he whispered, 'you mix in higher circles than I do. You've even met the *Führer*, himself. And working direct to the *Reichmarschall* puts you in a privileged position. But I'll be straight with you. I think you're speaking nonsense!'

He paused to finish his dessert.

'Dangerous nonsense and I wouldn't put it round. I hope you're wrong,' he went on, 'because the last thing I want is to be packed off to Russia. Just imagine! All that ice and snow. And the blizzards. No! You've got that one wrong, Müller. Believe me.'

It was the second and final night of the journey. Tomorrow, the train would reach Calais. As Heinrich returned to his cabin, he realised time was creeping remorselessly up on him. Even now, he had no clear plan in mind with regard to initiate an escape. He had secreted a miniature bottle of French brandy in his pocket. The evening was drawing in. Once the children were relatively settled, after a last story, he poured out a glass and sat at his desk. Storming through the darkened French countryside, the great train thundered through the night on its final charge towards the Atlantic coast. Heinrich thought of Maria-Anna. What would she advise? In the swaying sleeping compartment, Heinrich felt very much on his own, lost and confused in a dilemma with no obvious solution.

XIX

The monotonous, over-worked farmland of northern France failed to inspire Heinrich. Although the brandy had helped him to sleep, he awoke feeling fuzzy and in a poor state to face the challenges of the new day.

To Hermann Goering's intense irritation, route priority appeared to be given to troop and supply trains moving up to, or returning from, the coastal ports. He fumed as his *sonderzug* found itself continually diverted into sidings with the military traffic granted preference. The *Feldmarschall* vented his wrath on the unfortunate inmates in the radio carriage. Shouting and waving his bejewelled *feldmarschallstab* baton, Goering presented a threatening figure in the cramped confines of the mobile radio unit.

It was a relief when the *Nazi* bully departed and returned to his luxury quarters. Meanwhile, Carl Fischer had managed to spend unofficial periods with the radio crew, joining them amongst the crowded collection of transmitters, aerials and receivers. Having been taught how to take down coded messages, he was flattered to be entrusted with short spells of routine, two-way Berlin communications. Fischer's companion excused himself to go to the toilet, leaving the young army recruit temporarily in charge.

'Make sure you write everything down, Carl. I'll look at it when I return. We're nearing Calais and I think it's dark, outside. I'll bring back a couple of coffees. And I'm desperate for a smoke.'

Having suffered unrelieved hours of claustrophobia the radio operator took his leave. Fischer sprang into action when the next message came in. He consulted the day's codebook and was shocked by what he read:

'*Investigate immediately. Possibility of Jewish stowaways on* sonderzug. *Thought to be children. Parents detained. Search train and report back.* Heil Hitler!'

Carl Fischer sat dumbstruck, radio communications apparatus swimming before his eyes. He steadied himself to log the communiqué, intending to alert his colleague the moment he returned. Of course! It made sense. He had been ninety nine per cent certain he had witnessed Müller inviting two young children onto the train. The very ones who had made a small presentation to Hermann Goering. He opened the log to note down the date, time and import of the Berlin message. Yet something held him back. In his grasp, he held the future, lives even, of two children and that of his friend from Vienna. Fischer appreciated he was dealing with dynamite.

He placed the torn off slip on the table in front of him. The log book beckoned. He took a deep breath and cursed himself. If only he had not shown an interest in communications and telegraphy he would not, now, find himself deep in a moral dilemma of his own making. His heart raced. If the train was searched, Müller would soon be exposed and brought to book; forced to explain his indefensible actions.

'So these children are Jewish,' Fischer thought to himself. 'What's Müller playing at? He could be shot. He's out of his mind!'

Carl Fischer's communications companion was taking longer than expected. His absence gave Fischer a brief opportunity to think. But his confused thoughts were starkly interrupted. The brakes slammed on in emergency and the *sonderzug* decelerated, clamped wheels skidding and screaming over the track. Fischer was hurled across the packed radio unit, striking his elbow on a bulky transmitter. As the train squealed to a final halt, the communications door was flung open and Fischer's radio mentor staggered in.

'My God! What's going on outside?'

The signals officer sat down at his desk and pulled on his headphones, his telegraph going into overdrive. He grabbed a pencil to feverishly take down notes.

'It's the locomotive ahead!' he shouted. 'They've radioed back. Looks as though there's trouble further up the line. God knows what's happening. It's pitch black outside.'

Carl Fischer hauled himself to his feet, slipping the Berlin communiqué into his pocket.

'I'll report back to my own unit!' he yelled. 'They'll order us out to search the line. They said this might happen!'

He threw his headphones on the desktop and fled down the corridor. His radio companion, intent on staying at his post, failed to spot Fischer had taken the wrong direction. The young Viennese hurried towards a nearby carriage where he knew he would find his friend. On reaching his goal, he rapped on the door. There was no response. Fischer looked round to ensure no-one had followed him.

'Müller! Are you there? Can you hear me?'

Fischer pounded the compartment door with his fist.

'Open up for God's sake! It's me…Fischer. *Open up!*'

It seemed an age before the narrowest crack appeared between door and frame. He could just make out Heinrich's anxious face.

'Let me in, Müller. I know about the kids. It's really urgent. You've got to listen to me!'

The door opened no further. Heinrich communicated through the gap, bracing his foot against the door to prevent it from being pushed in.

'What in Hell's going on?' he demanded. 'What's got into you, Fischer? You know I can't let you in!'

Fischer's temper blew.

'Don't be so stupid! I know your game. The authorities are onto you. I've just taken down a message from Berlin. They know about the children and the train's about to be searched.'

He pushed against the door.

'Trust me!'

Heinrich reluctantly opened up and Fischer pushed past him.

'You've got seconds!' he gasped. 'Get out now! The train's stopped for an emergency. It's your only chance!'

Carl Fischer glanced at two very frightened, white-faced children who were still in their bunks.

'There's no time to waste. I'll stand guard. I can't stay long!'

Heinrich Müller snapped into action.

'Quick!' he shouted at the petrified brother and sister. 'Shoes on…and coats. I'll do the packing.'

Carl Fischer contradicted him.

'No time to pack! Just get off this damned train! I'll open the door for you.'

He stepped back into the corridor. As he did so the compartment window shattered and glass splinters splayed over the compartment. A bullet hammered into the far wall, missing Sura's head by centimetres.

'Get down!' Heinrich yelled. 'Floor…crawl out!'

A second bullet followed, burying itself in a vacated bunk. Heinrich shoved Sura and Johan into the dimly lit corridor. Repeated crackling of small arms fire sounded from close by.

'Insurgents!' Müller yelled.

Carl Fischer helped the children out of the carriage. Sobbing, they tumbled onto the trackside.

'Quiet, you two!'

Heinrich jumped down to join them, aware that answering volleys were being returned by the *sonderzug* defenders. Short bursts of repetitive gunfire rang through the darkness. The guards on the *Luftwaffe* trucks joined in the action using automatic weapons.

'I've got to go!'

Fischer turned and raced down the corridor. He hurled himself into the radio unit to find the operator deeply engaged in communication with the advance locomotive.

He insisted Fischer stayed to help monitor the messages flying in. They heard shouting from outside the carriage as armed soldiers charged down the side of the train. With shaking hands, Carl Fischer retrieved the Berlin message from his pocket and opened the radio log to enter its brief details. He then slid the copied message into an appropriate file. The soldier recruit had performed his duty to the letter to which there could be no retributive come back. At the same time, he had risked life and limb to save his friend from Vienna, together with two children virtually unknown to him.

In the pitch blackness of the French night, Heinrich Müller urged Sura and Johan to run on ahead. Too terrified to cry out, they stumbled and tumbled over rough stone ballast spilling over onto the trackside.

'Keep going!' he urged. 'I'm right behind you. Don't look back!'

At that very moment, Heinrich lost his footing and pitched forward. Hastily scrambling to his feet, he ploughed on through the darkness but lost his orientation. He tripped over a signalling cable running parallel to the rails. A fierce stab of pain shot through his bad shoulder. Cursing loudly, he regained his footing only to crash headlong into the near invisible wall of a wayside hut. Heinrich lay prostrate and semi-conscious at the side of the main line to the northern French ports.

A hundred metres up the track, the *sonderzug* sounded its whistle. Its terrified engineer released his brake to urge the panting behemoth forward. As it ground away, the red light on the last carriage grew fainter. Silence prevailed as the renegades melted into the night. The incursion had lasted only minutes with German defenders suffering only minor injuries.

When Heinrich regained consciousness, he became aware of intense pain in his shoulder. Gradually coming to, he pulled himself up onto his knees to find a sticky trail of blood trickling from his bruised jaw. His brain suddenly engaged.

'My God…the children!'

Wincing in agony, Heinrich drew himself to his feet. Now, he made out the dim outline of the hut responsible for his misfortune. Limping round the other side, he hoped to find the children cowering in its cover. He called softly.

'Sura…Johan!'

No response. He tried again; louder this time. But to no avail. Heinrich looked round, hopelessly, making no sense of the darkened landscape in which he found himself. For the next few minutes, he continued calling into the night. Fighting desperately to get his mind together, Heinrich suspected the children had fled further down the track. Despite the agony of moving, he ploughed on, crying out every few seconds until he reached a minor road and barrier crossing.

A blinding light hit Heinrich between the eyes and a rough voice barked at him. The bright dazzle of a hand-held torch searched him up and down. He remained rooted to the spot. In the spread of the torchlight, it was just possible to make out two figures. Once again, a curt order in a harsh voice, possibly a foreign language. The torch-holder held his ground as a second man stepped forward. He carried a rifle pointed precisely at Heinrich's heart. In great pain, Heinrich signalled his passivity by feebly raising his hands.

'*Qui etes vous? Parlez!*'

Heinrich froze. He had learned only English in Vienna and possessed no more than a smattering of French. Trembling violently, he felt his stomach churn in the nightmarish situation in which he found himself. The man with the torch stepped up to him and shone its dazzling light directly into his face. Heinrich blinked.

'I speak English,' he stammered. 'A little English. Please…'

He stepped back a pace as the man with the torch menaced him with a cocked pistol held in his other hand. Stray light reflected onto the fellow's hard face and dark stubble beard.

'You…English?'

Heinrich shook his head. He trembled from head to foot.

'No!'

It was an unfortunate, if inevitable, admission. The two strangers exchanged words and the rifleman stabbed his weapon into Heinrich's ribs. His assailant searched for the correct expression.

'No English? No French?'

Heinrich shook his head, miserably. Again, the two assailants consulted each other.

'You…on train?'

There was little point in denying the truth. The men shot him looks of chilled hatred.

'German?'

Heinrich shook his head.

'*Östereichisches.*'

It hardly mattered. Being Austrian counted the same as being German, so they would surely kill him. He guessed these men must have been involved in the brief raid on the *sonderzug*. With his gun jammed up against Heinrich's chest, the torch man ran his hands over the young Austrian's body. He seized his wallet and examined its contents as best he could. He then consulted his companion who grunted some kind of accord. Heinrich suspected their first language was not French. The man grinned, showing his teeth, with no warmth in his expression.

'Me…him…'

He pointed to his friend.

'…*Polski!*'

He allowed the news to sink in and sniggered.

'*Komm, bitte!*'

Heinrich detected cynicism in his captor's mocking tone.

'*Welcommen, mein freund Kraut!*'

The gun man moved round behind him whilst the torch-holder illuminated the way ahead. Heinrich was only too aware of cold steel pressing into his spine. The two Poles escorted their prisoner down a lane winding away from the railway. Keen to reach their destination without delay, they maintained a sharp look-out for enemy patrols. As they chivvied their quarry along, Heinrich's thoughts turned desperately to the missing children. Sura and Johan were stranded out there; somewhere in the remoteness of the northern French countryside. And he, Heinrich, was powerless to help them.

'*Halt!*'

The two Poles knew just enough German to communicate with their prize capture. The torch bearer shone his light ahead. Its thin beam threw up the slender, steel girders of a small lift bridge crossing a canal. When they reached it, he was ordered to turn off the lane and pass down a narrow flight of concrete steps. When he reached the bottom of the run, the beam lit up a stretch of still water. He was then ordered along the grassy tow path running alongside the canal.

After five minutes, Heinrich's captors stopped and switched off their torch. One of the men put his fingers to his mouth and whistled. He waited a few seconds before calling a second time and was rewarded by a similar whistle, clearly a command to switch the torch on again. He issued a short pattern of flashes that were answered by a corresponding signal. Heinrich was rudely shoved forward.

Seconds later, the men used their light to fall on a thick cable roped round a stout metal bollard. It was just possible to make out the sombre prow of an industrial barge, lying low in the water. By the light of his own torch, a crew member climbed out, on deck, to put out a gang plank. Heinrich was prodded forward. He grabbed a hand rail as he stepped cautiously along the narrow deck running round the vessel. Someone at the stern waved a paraffin lamp whose soft light revealed the open door of the wheelhouse, overlooking the cargo hold. Heinrich was ignominiously shoved inside and ordered down a set of steep metal steps leading down to the bargee's smoke-filled compartment. Clinging to the descending hand rail, he saw that the cramped space was filled with a gathering of swarthy-looking individuals. The wary expressions on their faces varied between puzzlement and surprise.

The closeted inhabitants of the old barge sat round a small table staring suspiciously at the unexpected arrival in the dim, yellow light. One or two fired questions at Heinrich's captors who briefly explained the details of the capture before going back into the night to resume patrol duties. Heinrich Müller quailed before the cold glare of rising hostility.

XX

The atmosphere within the narrow confines of the skipper's cabin remained on a knife edge. Heinrich was tipped roughly onto a wooden bench at one end of the table. At first no-one spoke but, after a while, a thin-faced man with fair, short-cropped hair addressed the gathering. His French was beyond the limits of Heinrich's comprehension but the Austrian was in no doubt that his presence was under intense discussion.

The man glanced at his wristwatch and it appeared the meeting awaited a newcomer. Taken off guard, Heinrich was grabbed by the collar and hauled painfully to his feet. Two burly fellows stripped off his jacket and ran their hands over his body. In no time, they found his papers issued by the top echelons of the *Nazi* organisation. These included his identity and passport. He blanched as the documents were passed round the table for scrutiny. A young woman in a chequered head scarf showed particular interest. It appeared she carried authority within the group. Her appearance was typically northern French; thin face, high cheek bones and dark hair. After earnest discussion with her comrades she addressed Heinrich head on. The woman's German was Lycee grade and she ordered him to resume his place on the bench.

'Now we know who you are…Heinrich Müller born 1920. Place of birth Vienna. You fought in Poland against the brave defenders of that unfortunate nation. Now, if we are to *believe*,' she added cynically, 'you're discharged from the *Wehrmacht* and work as a "clerk" in the *Nazi* administration.'

She turned to her colleagues to give an explanation. A burly fellow with a wild moustache stood up, slamming his massive fist on the table as he did so. Heinrich, totally unable to make out a word he spoke, assumed he was not French. But he caught the key word '*Polen*'. Was he, then, a Pole? That would make sense, as Heinrich's captors on the railway were of the same nationality. If so, what were they doing in France on a commercial barge? Particularly, a vessel commandeered by French nationals and operating clandestinely against the German invaders.

Voices were raised with angry exchanges taking place between the antagonists. The fiery Pole appeared to be spokesman for a strong contingent of opinion. He jabbed a bony finger at the unfortunate Austrian then drew it across his own throat. Heinrich's heart missed a beat. The young woman leapt to her feet and demanded calm. Still fuming, the Polish worker returned to his place. The woman thanked him, curtly, before turning her concentration upon Heinrich.

'We're waiting for our leader who's been delayed. Tempers are rising. I can't guarantee your safety but we owe you nothing. You'll be interrogated and must answer all questions put to you. Failure to co-operate will lead to your immediate execution.'

Heinrich swallowed hard trying to keep down his inner terror and remained mute. The woman continued her diatribe.

'You'll be kept under armed guard…'

She was interrupted as an aggressive Frenchman leapt to his feet. He threw Heinrich's jacket he had been searching, onto the table. In his hand, he held a condemning piece of evidence that took his captive by surprise. An argument broke out, only pacified at the insistence of the woman. She glared furiously at the young Austrian.

'You claim to be a civilian,' she said, as Heinrich's war decoration was passed to her.

'So what's this?'

She flashed the *Ritterkreuze* in front of his eyes.

'A *Nazi* commendation? For war service? Look! There's a *swastika* at the centre of the cross!'

She made no attempt to hide her disgust.

'It soils my hands.'

There was no point in denying the obvious.

'Have you ever killed anyone?' she went on. 'A Pole perhaps? If you have, you're in appropriate company!'

She gestured towards the renegade Poles.

'These men escaped after their country was invaded and risked their necks getting here to fight with us. They're working at the pits around Bethune. People like you aren't fit to lick their boots. Now, they're caught up in your German advance.'

Her adversary remained mute.

'So what's a "war hero" doing on Goering's special train? Does that place you high up in the *Nazi* hierarchy? You don't look very old to me!'

It was now or never. Heinrich summoned up his courage and took a deep breath.

'I'm nobody,' he said. 'Merely a clerk seconded to assist the *Reichmarschall*. I didn't kill,' he went on. 'At least, not as far as I know. It's true I was awarded the *Ritterkreuze* in battle. Because I saved a friend's life.'

He trembled from head to toe. The young French woman took the opportunity to translate for the Poles in her midst. Heinrich's words seemed to have little influence judging from the growls and hatred aimed his way. She did not mince her words.

'These men want to take you outside and shoot you. We can easily get rid of your body. But my first duty is to hand you over to our leader, *Le Professeur*.'

By dint of personality, she managed to keep the furious Poles at bay. Her attention was taken by sounds above her head, hinting at urgent activity in the wheelhouse. Heinrich glanced up to see an elderly man in a long black coat gingerly descend the steps to the skipper's quarters. With one skinny hand, he gripped onto the hand rail. With the other, he steadied an ancient pair of *pince-nez* threatening to fall from his thin nose. His snow white hair had been carefully parted down the middle. The man looked frail and he was offered support at the bottom of the steps. One of the surly Poles vacated his seat and stood in the corner. *Le Professeur* glanced briefly at Heinrich and murmured something in

French. The company settled, accepting the old gentleman's authority. The woman briefly outlined the unexpected turn of events. *Le Professeur* addressed his companions before turning to Heinrich.

'I speak a little German,' he said. 'I learned your language in a prisoner of war camp in the last conflict. Twenty wasted months of my life. I was based near Mannheim.'

He paused.

'Audrey?'

Le Professeur spoke directly to the young woman.

'I'll question our prisoner and you can translate for our Polish friends, as we go.'

The young woman agreed and the occupants of the berth craned forward, eagerly. Heinrich's inquisitor began by asking him straightforward questions, even to the point of interrogating him about his time at the Salzburg Mozarteum. He then centred on the *Nazi*-issued documents and was curious about Heinrich's presence on a German armed train. Suddenly, the young Austrian's mind cleared. He seized the opportunity to explain the true purpose of his scary mission.

'Please, sir. I beg you to listen to me. My life is of no consequence. Out here in the countryside, and lost in the darkness, are two children. They're very young. Aged eight and eleven…a boy and a girl.'

His words were translated as his captors kept an uneasy silence. Heinrich went on to explain his role since rejection by the *Wehrmacht*. He was not interrupted although ordered to pause, at intervals, for the translation to be relayed to the spellbound listeners. As briefly as he thought necessary, he related his role in aiding Hermann Goering, although insisting he had no choice. He also hinted he had met other significant *Nazi* leaders through the strange connection of music. The precocious talents of the two Salzburgian performers were also mentioned.

The inhabitants of the below deck cabin kept a sceptical silence, suspicious of the distinct possibility they were being led up the garden path. Heinrich emphasised the point that the Salzburg children were of Jewish origin and there was every reason to believe their parents faced imminent arrest prior to deportation. The meeting continued for a few minutes longer before *Le Professeur* called it to a close. He advised taking a break for separate discussion with coffee. Heinrich was ordered back up to the wheelhouse and pushed onto the deck to sit cross-legged. No coffee came his way and two menacing Frenchmen stood over him with loaded pistols.

When the gathering re-convened, Heinrich was kept in the wheelhouse. *Le Professeur* had used his absence to address his fellow-resistors.

'We're only at the beginning of our work,' he said quietly. 'Our nation's in pieces but "*Résistance*" is being organised. We're handicapped as many of our young men have been taken off as war prisoners or forced workers. Those remaining are rounded up, by the hour, for labour in our own land.'

He passed a white handkerchief over his brow.

'I confess I'm something at a loss. I've no more idea than anyone else regarding the veracity of this so-called "Austrian's" account.'

An angry murmur of common agreement rang through the confined space. *Le Professeur* chose his words with even greater care.

'I'll order the prisoner down for one last round of questioning. Details of his story don't stand up. I ask you! The very idea of using Goering's special armoured train to smuggle two Jewish children out of their homeland! Seems like some kind of fantasy tale!'

Once more, the muffled sound of grim accord rumbled through the steely depths of the grain barge.

'Audrey,' he called. 'Bring him down…for the last time,' he added ominously.

The woman Résistance fighter ran up the steps to collect Heinrich, held under close escort. He was not invited to sit and immediately sensed the increased level of hostility towards him. *Le Professeur* removed his *pince-nez*, polishing their half lenses on his handkerchief.

'Young man, you've failed to convince us with your tale. We want to know why you were selected to work for the highest ranks of the hated *Nazis*.'

He stiffened in his seat.

'So…explain…your life depends on it!'

Heinrich Müller ran his hand anxiously through his hair and began a nervous and unconvincing account of his connection with Sura and Johan. He attempted to explain the association between his co-incidental work at Schloss Leopoldskron with the *Nazis'* mountain retreat, over the border.

'The *Reichmarschall* approached me and selected me to join his staff. I had no choice and that's why I carry these documents. He arranged for the train to travel to the Channel coast so he could inspect his beloved *Luftwaffe*. And he was keen to view Great Britain from one of your Atlantic capes. Somewhere near Wissant, I believe.'

His hushed audience did not move a muscle.

'I was ordered to accompany him but my main role was to work for him in Paris. Goering required a researcher to pinpoint the exact whereabouts of great French artworks. Many in *Le Louvre.*'

Heinrich sensed his listeners pricking up their ears.

'At first, I didn't really understand. But now, I've no doubt he intends removing your national treasures and taking them back to Germany. Some for his own purposes.'

Le Professeur shook his wizened head, angrily. He glanced round the company, little less perplexed than his aggressive comrades.

'My girlfriend back in Salzburg,' Heinrich continued, 'came up with the crazy notion of smuggling Sura and Johan onto Goering's *sonderzug*. I'd already told her about its proposed destination and she worked out it would place the children close to the French coast. The idea was to get them across the Channel to England. Although I didn't know how…'

His voice tailed off weakly and Audrey sought permission to speak.

'These so-called children…you know their names?'

Heinrich responded positively.

'Of course! How wouldn't I? Sura and Johan…they even slept in the bunks in my cabin.'

He broke down. Unable to hold back his sobbing, he reminded the group that the children in his care were still somewhere at large, lost in the dark vastness of the French countryside.

'They can't have gone far!' he insisted through his tears. 'Instead of wasting time on me, you should be out looking for *them*!'

Heinrich's head dropped into his shaking hands. Sensing his audience's restlessness, *Le Professeur* consulted his hostile colleagues.

'Our Movement,' he said, 'that aims to resist the enemy, is only just starting up. Yet we've already learned of *Fascist* collaborators willing to inform. What we have to decide, tonight, is fairly straightforward. It depends on what you wish to believe. Either this young man is telling the truth or, to put it plainly, he's spinning a pack of lies. If the latter, he's a *Nazi* spy planted by the *Nazis*, hoping to penetrate our Movement.'

A second menacing growl rolled through the close assembly. Heinrich's knowledge of French was insufficient to follow the entirety of the leader's argument. But he suspected the worst as *Le Professeur* drew breath to summarise.

'Before the Germans violated our sovereignty, we lived in a democracy able to welcome our exiled Polish friends. We found them jobs in the pits and offered accommodation. But, since the collapse, this has exploded in our faces. Now, loyal French men and women must be encouraged to fight for the very heart of our Révolution…*Liberté, Egalité et Fraternité*. What else is there? The only satisfactory means of solving this issue before us is to put it to the common vote. Even in the event of this young man being found innocent, some of you may worry that his continued presence may bring disaster upon us. We can't afford to make a mistake. *Caution must come before justice.* We owe that to our fellow comrades in the region.'

Heads nodded amongst the group members.

'Should it be necessary,' *Le Professeur* continued, 'I hold the casting vote as Leader. The result will be final.'

He turned to Audrey and asked her to make clear to Heinrich the full meaning of his decision. The young Austrian felt sick in the pit of his stomach. He had suffered adversity before, but now felt an even deeper sense of foreboding. His heart pounded. *Le Professeur* addressed his restless comrades.

'I'll ask you to raise your hands,' he said solemnly. 'If the majority verdict is "guilty" then we'll waste no more time. The prisoner will be taken down to the hold and eliminated. However, in the event he may be found 'not guilty', we'll need to consider what to do with him next. That's a separate issue.'

Le Professeur let out a deep sigh before initiating the vote.

'Comrades…those in favour of a guilty verdict…raise your right hands.'

Slowly, one after another, hands appeared above the heads of the resistors.

'Audrey, I count five. D'you agree?'

He coughed to clear his throat.

'Those who consider the prisoner innocent, raise your hands, too.'

Head swimming, Heinrich watched on helplessly as a mere two hands were lifted. They represented the opinions of the young woman and *Le Professeur*, himself. The leader looked grave and ill at ease but knew he must go through with his promise.

'Audrey…translate the verdict to the prisoner…the majority vote of this gathering. Don't delay. Simply inform him he is found guilty and will be shot.'

He fingered his *pince-nez,* nervously, as Audrey transmitted the verdict to the blameless Austrian. *Le Professeur* struggled to regain his composure.

'Bind his hands!'

He then turned his attention on two young men.

'Georges…Philippe…you know what to do. Make it quick.'

The two would-be executioners got up from their places and gravely ordered Heinrich to place his hands behind his back. They bound them tightly together before pulling out their weapons from holsters concealed within their jackets. Georges, a sullen-faced youth, pointed up the steps with his finger and Heinrich began the short climb to his execution. At this point the cabin door burst open and an excited young farmworker thrust his head through the open hatch.

'Guess what?' he cried.

He blinked in the light as he saw the solemn faces, below.

'Oh…sorry. I didn't mean to interrupt. I've been out on patrol. I found these two kids wandering along the lane. In the dark. Scared the life out of me they did. Don't even speak our language!'

He stopped short as his eyes fell on a young man on the first rung of the steps, bound and held at gun point.

'*Zut alors!* What's going on?'

Audrey seized control of a potentially incendiary situation.

'Two kids?' she asked. 'Where? Let's see them!'

The young farmer moved aside to reveal the pale, frightened faces of Sura and Johan staring down from the wheelhouse. The children shielded their eyes from the unaccustomed light. The prisoner roused himself.

'Sura…Johan…?'

The little Austrian girl could not hold herself back.

'Heinrich! Where've you been? We've been searching all over for you. *In the dark!*'

Georges, his would-be executioner, felt a heavy lump hit him in the chest. His pistol clattered to the floor as Heinrich Müller dropped faint, at his feet. Audrey sprang forward and knelt down to lay out Heinrich's prostrate form in the recovery position. She ordered a blanket from the skipper's bunk and slipped it over his unconscious body.

XXI

When Heinrich came round, he found himself lying on a bunk, head on a hard pillow. Struggling to raise himself, he found his arms no longer tied. Sura stood over him, clutching her toy dog. Was he dreaming?

'Bimperl?' he stammered, uncertainly. 'He's still with you?'

Sura smiled, the first time for many hours.

'*And* Ludwig as well!' she responded. 'Johan nearly dropped him in the canal. Typical…but he's fine!'

Audrey, the cool resistance worker respected by her rough colleagues, knelt by the side of the bunk and offered Heinrich a sip of water from a tin mug.

'Try to sit up,' she advised.

The captive did as he was told. Despite his confused state, Audrey sensed Heinrich was about to ask what would happen, next.

'Stay calm,' she said. 'Your life is no longer in immediate danger but my comrades are arguing about what to do with you. We've spoken to Sura and Johan. They confirm everything but it puts us in a very difficult situation.'

She was interrupted by the appearance of *Le Professeur*. The elderly leader approached the bunk and spoke quietly.

'How's the patient?'

When he saw Heinrich was on the road to recovery, he confirmed the Austrian's position remained precarious.

'I believe most of the comrades are prepared to let you live. But you'll remain under guard. One false move and I'll not be able to help you. They're brave men, three of them Poles from the Bethune mines. They can't return to their jobs without risking deportation. Now, they've no alternative but to live the life of renegades. God knows how long this will go on. For security reasons, I can't tell you more. Capture by the occupying forces means interrogation…and far worse from what I hear.'

Heinrich understood but felt a degree of confidence flow back into his veins.

'Monsieur, I'm truly grateful. Especially to your man who found Sura and Johan. I'll do everything necessary to co-operate with you. My concern is for the children. I'd hoped to get them all the way to the coast.'

With an effort, he raised himself up and shuffled into a sitting position on the edge of the bunk.

'I never really had it worked out,' he admitted. 'Is it still possible to find a small boat to get them to England?'

It was a naïve question and *Le Professeur* shook his old head. He knew there was not the faintest chance.

'I fear not,' he said. 'The enemy's organised coastal patrols on shore and at sea. Last week, a gang of brave fishermen from Gravelines was pursued and boarded. They were attempting to escape across *Le Manche*. They haven't been seen since and we fear the worst. The Germans have drawn a tight cordon along the Franco-Belgian coastline. I have contacts with mackerel boats allowed out to work but enemy patrol vessels keep them under constant surveillance.'

The news came as a nasty shock to Heinrich as this was not something he had anticipated. He glanced at the children who were able to understand the translated conversation in their native language. Audrey attempted to put on a positive front.

'I can't give you any details but it may be possible to find a temporary safe house for the three of you. There are good people around here. Others are too afraid. Defying the occupiers is a capital offence. We heard, only yesterday, of a couple outside Sangate arrested for taking in a fallen British fighter pilot. A neighbour in their street informed and all three were arrested by the *Gestapo*.'

Heinrich grimaced. He had heard rumours in Salzburg of the thuggish behaviour of the German Secret Police. The outlook appeared bleak. Audrey suggested that the conversation was not suitable for young ears but Heinrich contradicted her.

'With respect,' he said, 'I think it's best that Sura and Johan know just a little. At least they'll understand what they're up against.'

Glancing at the children he noted their strained, grey faces so unlike the buoyant children he had first met at Schloss Leopoldskron. *Le Professeur* turned to them and spoke quietly, using the German he had picked up as a former war prisoner.

'Little ones, there's much to talk about but it's best we spare you the details. You'll have to trust us just as you believe in your friend, here.'

He got up and invited Heinrich to join him in the skipper's cabin.

'Audrey, see that these two get at least a little sleep. They look all in.'

The cabin had been vacated, with no sign of the previous occupants. *Le Professeur* did not reveal to Heinrich the false compartment concealed behind the bulkhead in the forward section of the grain hold. He invited the young Austrian to sit at the table and went over to the wood burner stove. With care, he poured hot coffee warming in a tall, aluminium pot.

'We've had to think about the next move, young man, but you may be in luck. By good fortune, a resistance comrade from St Remee has made contact. He's offered his services to open up an escape route to the coast. But not in this area. I know the man and trust him, completely.'

He paused to give Heinrich time to settle and drink the welcome coffee.

'A feature of our work is that we don't give away details or information, other than what's absolutely necessary. For instance "Audrey" is not Audrey! I *cannot* reveal this fellow's identity to you. The reason's obvious...if the enemy attacks us tonight, and takes prisoners, the less information our people have to give away the better. *Comprenez?*'

Heinrich signalled his acknowledgement.

'What I can tell you,' *Le Professeur* continued, 'is that our friend is about to undertake a trial run for us. He's as brave as an ox. I'll attempt to persuade him to take you three along with him. If he's agreeable, you'll be placing your life in his hands. Whether or not he's prepared to risk his life for an ex-*Wehrmacht* soldier and two Jewish children is up to him. It's a big risk.'

The concept of some kind of priority list was something Heinrich had not considered. He thought hard. The germ of an idea began to take shape in his clearing mind. He finished his coffee and addressed *Le Professeur*.

'Sir, my motive, as you know, is to get Sura and Johan all the way to England. But there's something else.'

The leader looked at him sharply.

'Is that so?' he snapped. 'Then out with it, young man. Time's short.'

Audrey returned from the berth cabin where she had talked the children to sleep with a made up story, in halting German. She emptied the remains of the coffee pot and joined the two men at the table. Heinrich spoke quietly.

'I know this isn't the place to boast about my past, as you detest the *Nazis*, but I did get close to Hermann Goering. Like I told you, he insisted I became his research assistant.'

Audrey shot a knowing glance to *Le Professeur*.

'Goering's very boastful and can be very indiscreet,' Heinrich continued. 'Even in the presence of the *Führer*. He let slip one or two things that should have been confidential only to the high military command. He told me to my face that once Germany has conquered the West, and come to terms with the British, they will immediately look East.'

His small audience held their breath. It was *Le Professeur* who spoke first, barely hiding his scepticism. 'Go East?' he queried. 'But they've already *done* that! First the Czechs, followed by the Poles. Hitler's completed his aims.'

Heinrich begged to differ.

'With respect, sir, the *Reichmarschall* hinted…more than hinted…that the German war machine will next turn on the Soviets. The *Führer* has already issued orders for advanced planning.'

It was Audrey who challenged the preposterous possibility.

'Listen…I'm a Communist,' she said. 'So are many of my comrades. Everyone knows that Stalin and Molotov signed a peace deal with the Germans. Russia's too big a country to challenge. In any case, Hitler's gobbled up all the land he wishes to expand into.'

Le Professeur agreed. He foresaw no chance of an Eastern Front for the already stretched German resources.

'I'm sorry, Heinrich, if I may call you by your first name? But what you say is nonsense. The Germans have overrun France, the Low Countries, Denmark…Norway, even. What more do they want?'

He dug into his old jacket pocket for an empty pipe and put it to his mouth. Heinrich persisted.

'With respect, sir…Hermann Goering works very closely with Hitler and has his complete trust. The *Führer* doesn't always listen to his generals, despite their *blitzkrieg* triumphs. The *Reichmarschall* more than hinted to me that Hitler and von Ribbentrop have every intention of tearing up the Non-Aggression Pact between the Soviets and the *Reich*. Once the West is nailed down, the Ukrainian wheat plains will be too tempting. Goering called it the "bread basket" of the new empire. Hitler also has his eye on the might of Soviet industry. He intends turning the entire nation into slaves.'

Hunched over the table in the dim light of the single paraffin lamp, the three occupants sat in silence. Audrey was first to respond.

'Are you telling us that you heard this stuff directly from the mouth of Hermann Goering? Hitler's "Number Two."

Heinrich confirmed. *Le Professeur* gazed at the table top, intense thoughts racing through his agile mind. He stuffed the pipe back in his pocket.

'We've no reason to disbelieve you,' he said. 'It's possible you may be in possession of a priceless piece of information that the Allies would dearly wish to get their hands on. If this is the case, we must pass it on, directly, to London.'

He threw his hands in the air.

'*Mon Dieu!* We could be sitting on gold dust! This matter, alone, prioritises our mission to get you all across *Le Manche*.'

Heinrich's heart beat faster.

'We can always radio Heinrich's information to London,' Audrey suggested. 'We've established contact but carry little credibility. They're likely to ignore us. So it's essential to get you away from here and over to the British. If you're correct, this news might affect the whole course of the war.'

The small congregation lapsed into thoughtful silence. Audrey turned even more serious.

'There's a snag,' she continued. 'And a big one. There's no way we can *guarantee* your personal safe passage. Things can go wrong at any moment.'

Heinrich failed to comprehend.

'So,' Audrey continued, 'we must come up with a contingency plan. The Americans call it Plan B. For now, I can't think of anything better so what I have to offer will have to do. You have the knowledge in your head. If you're taken, it's lost with you.'

Her companions failed to follow her reasoning.

'If you were to commit this priceless information to paper it'll take on a second existence, chancy I admit.'

She delved into her pocket and pulled out a small notebook. Ripping out a single page, she got up to search for a pencil.

'Trust me,' she pleaded. 'It's the only way. Write down your name and your old *Wehrmacht* number and rank. Then, very briefly, your status with Goering. Simply state that Hitler plans to attack the Soviets, once the West is settled. And sign it.'

Heinrich hesitated.

'What d'you intend doing with it?' he asked. 'It's explosive. Totally incriminating. If I'm caught with this, the Gestapo will celebrate with the finest French champagne! I can't do it!'

Le Professeur sat dumbfounded with not a word to say. Audrey reinforced her point.

'This operation's no longer about you and the children. *The vital thing is this revelation.* If you're taken by the *Gestapo*, the opportunity is lost. But if the information survives, even on a piece of flimsy scrap paper, it has a second existence. An extra chance. With your signature and background it might carry weight.'

Heinrich sounded doubtful.

'Look…I said I'm a nobody,' he said. 'Even if the message ever gets to the British, with or without me, they'd think it was a "plant." It's worthless!'

Audrey fought the anger rising in her breast. Her temper snapped.

'For God's sake, do as I say! You're in no position to argue. Of course we can't tell London what to do or how to act. But, at least we can try. Surely, you can see that? They'll have other Intelligence to go on, anyway.'

Angry almost beyond control, she excused herself and ducked into the adjacent berth where the children slept soundly. She returned with Sura's most loved possession; a cuddly white dog with black spots.

'Bimperl!' she announced, crossly.

Searching in a nearby drawer, she took out a small pair of sharp scissors, a reel of cotton and a sewing needle. Audrey pushed the scrap of paper over to Heinrich.

'*Please*…I beg you. *Just do as I say!*'

Not bothering to disguise his reluctance, Heinrich picked up the pencil stub. As he did so, Audrey cut into the soft material within the belly of Sura's sleeping companion. She pulled out some of the stuffing whilst Heinrich completed his task. Examining his writing, assiduously, she folded the paper, twice. As her bewildered comrades looked on, she slid the tiny message into the body of the cuddly toy.

'And now…your battle award.'

She picked up the *Ritterkreuze* cross and ribbon and slipped it in, alongside the note.

'*Voila!*'

Whilst Heinrich admired the skill with which Audrey stitched up the incision, he could not stop himself questioning the unexplained inclusion of his *Ritterkreuze*.

'What's the point of including *that*?' he asked. 'The British won't know what to make of it. They may even think it's a joke!'

Audrey's impatience betrayed her growing fatigue.

'Maybe they will, maybe they won't,' she snapped, grumpily. 'But it adds to the authenticity. There's just a chance this message might alert our allies. There's nothing stopping them making their own enquiries. I don't want to be morbid,' she continued, 'but if you're captured, or somehow get separated from the children, this vital message might still get through.'

Le Professeur looked bewildered.

'It's crazy!' he muttered. 'I shan't say *"women"* because you'd kill me!'

Audrey shot him a dark look under her long eyelashes whilst Heinrich had the sense to hold his tongue. Audrey reminded him of another young woman, far away in Salzburg, who had postulated an equally preposterous scheme. He went along with *Le Professeur*, deciding discretion was the better part of valour.

Increasing fatigue overcame the three companions who were now desperate for sleep. The leader reached out to Audrey and placed his hand softly on top of hers.

'I'm getting too old for this work,' he said. 'You're well aware I was about to retire from my professional job and spend the rest of my life growing vegetables. Or walking my dog and fishing off Wimereux!'

He smiled laconically.

'Circumstances have determined I have a new career opening up. How long it'll last, I daren't speculate. However,' he continued, 'if something unexpected happens to me I have full confidence in the person who'll succeed!'

He squeezed Audrey's hand. In his heart, Heinrich knew the old man was correct. The Austrian's regard for the courage of the volunteer French fighters rose by the minute.

'The strange thing,' he thought to himself, 'is that I'll never learn the true identities of these formidable people.'

Le Professeur resumed control.

'I suggest, young man, you go back to the sleeping berth. There's still a couple of hours before the sun rises. *Attila*'s guarded day and night by our boys, outside. Some are out on patrol as I speak. Ready to alert us to danger. If an enemy patrol's sighted they'll give us time to disperse and hide all traces of your existence.'

He rose slowly from the table and stifled a yawn.

'*A demain, mes amis! Est-ce que c'est "bonne nuit" ou "bonjour?"*

xxii

Later that morning, Heinrich and the children were roused from their slumbers. Still half asleep, they breakfasted on brioches obtained from the *boulangerie*, at nearby Les Attaques. It seemed that activities upon the old grain barge were run like a professional enterprise.

'There's a grain store on the canal bank, at Les Attaques,' *Le Professeur* explained. 'Later this morning, the skipper plans to moor *Atilla* alongside. He'll take on a full load and go up to Calais to the dock silos. You must be away before then but you're in luck. Through a contact with the local *Gendarmerie*...I can say no more...we have a limited supply of Identity Documents ready to be filled out. One of our Poles has proved to be a gifted forger. He's working hard on your new identity papers as we speak. And we'll need a photograph although it takes time to develop the negative and print out to the right size. But we have our ways...*pas problem!*'

Le Professeur went on to explain that the children could easily be hidden but was less sanguine about Heinrich.

'*You* present us with a problem,' he said. 'You have little French…certainly not enough to pass a *gendarme* checkpoint. On the other hand, you speak German. We've thought of using that. If you leave French conversation to the person we'll entrust you with, you can use your own language on any German patrol that stops you.'

Heinrich looked up sharply.

'Sorry…I don't get it. Surely, German is the *last* language I should use?'

Audrey joined them looking gaunt and tired. She took her time lighting a cigarette, hoping its nicotine would revive her flagging spirits.

'You underestimate us, Heinrich,' she said. 'We've decided you hail from Alsace-Lorraine. You may not know this but, over the decades, the land between the Rhine and the French border has changed hands. Many of the people are fiercely French. The other half of the population clings onto its old roots to retain the German culture and language. It's an explosive set-up but since it's been overrun, the German Alsatians have been flaunting their ascendancy. They're making it very difficult for those who think themselves French.'

She inhaled deeply and relaxed.

'Which is where you come in! You will be "*Hubert Erhard*". Your disability prevents you from being called up for service. And you're a musician…of sorts.'

Heinrich admitted himself baffled.

'Of sorts?'

Le Professeur laughed, rebalancing his *pince-nez* .

'We've decided to apprentice you to an organ manufacturer! You learned your trade in Thann, in the

Haut-Rhin. That's where you were born and brought up. Now, you're about to take up your first appointment, here, in Northern France. It may seem like madness but we have our reasons. We can tell you no more, at present.'

The former violin student made no sense of the situation.

'I play the piano,' he said. 'Even tried the local organ, a few times, at our local church. But I wasn't any good because I couldn't figure out the pedals. And all those stops…too much to think about! That's why I stuck to the violin!'

The skipper called down from his wheelhouse.

'Received a signal,' he shouted. 'The lad out on the bridge has just given me a wave. I think your man's on his way!'

The two Résistance workers snapped into action. Audrey organised the children, handing over two parcels containing baguettes and a selection of *charcuteries*, *fromages* and *fruits*. She made doubly sure that Sura had Bimperl with her. *Le Professeur* took his time ascending the steep steps to the wheelhouse, followed swiftly by the others. Heinrich thanked the skipper and jumped onto the canal path. One of the Poles stood by the lift bridge and waved the party forward. He carried a metal winch in his hand. The children watched, fascinated, as he fitted it onto the winding mechanism. The windlass turned, bringing down the bridge's vertical road section. It lowered slowly into the horizontal plane, aided by the bridge counter balance.

Emerging from a cloud of dust, a dark green Citroen 23 *camion* chugged along the lane. Its driver leaned precariously out of his window, waving with one hand and sounding his horn with the other. The vehicle lurched as he fought to regain control, replacing his hands on the steering wheel. Unimpressed, the serious Polish guard waved the truck across the canal. Heinrich spotted the owner's name printed in bold red and yellow, on the side doors:

B.DEWYNTER ET FILS
ORGUES ATELIER
ST REME
GPFO

Sporting a lavishly-styled grey moustache, Bertrand Dewynter drew up and braked close to the reception party. He leant out of his window and called cheerily to his good friend, *Le Professeur.* Evil-smelling smoke from a half-finished *Gauloise* hanging over his fleshy bottom lip drifted out over the water.

'*Bonjour mes camarades…ça va?*'

It seemed the driver had not a care in the world but *Le Professeur* knew better. The two were old associates owing to the Résistance leader's former professional work in the area; schoolmaster, private piano teacher and church organist at the church in Guinnes.

M Dewynter had chosen to leave his son behind to keep the business going. Dewynter and Son was a well-established firm in the region, restoring and sometimes building whole instruments from scratch. Their reputation for excellence spread well beyond the immediate area.

At the crack of dawn, father and son had supervised the careful loading of pipes, large and small, for the Breton cathedral at faraway Rennes. The restoration was a prestigious commission of which they were duly proud. With necessary halts, Bertrand calculated the journey would take him over seven hours. He expected to be away for at least half the week supervising the installation of replacement pipes. These jobs were never easy and out of necessity involved liaising with noted organists, known to be fastidious in their demands. The sprightly organ builder recognised it was vital to establish good relations with the Brittany capital's eminent organists. But, in this tense time of occupation, Bertrand was equally keen to return to his premises that had so far been spared during the shelling and bombing.

The delivery of the Dewynter and Son pipes offered an ideal opportunity to co-operate with *La Résistance*. After Calais' hard fought final conquest by the Germans, Bertrand and Patrice had immediately offered their services to the growing clandestine movement. Prior to capitulation, they had helped smuggle two Allied airmen to the coast, south of Boulogne. It was a hazardous operation and father and son needed no reminding, if apprehended by the enemy, they would be interrogated and executed. Nevertheless, along with other volunteers, they were prepared to risk their necks for the Allied cause.

Aware of Bertrand's recent commission at Rennes, *Le Professeur* had approached him to test out the Brittany run as a potential escape route for hidden airmen. He hoped they might get close to the Breton coast, the Boulogne and Normandy areas being tightly sealed. Bertrand chose to keep his wife in the dark. Despite this, Diedre had every cause to feel apprehensive about her husband's activities. She planned to see him off with a flask of coffee and two stout loaves.

'My darling, you must take care. The Germans are everywhere. You make no effort to disguise your hatred of the Bosch. If they provoke you, *en route*, you must stay calm. I want you back in one piece…preferably still breathing!'

Embracing in true French fashion, his wife and son waved Bertrand off, ruefully watching the green canvas-topped truck roll out of the yard. Each organ pipe had been carefully wrapped and stowed. Sloping up from the truck rear to a high ledge, at the cabin end, the longer pipes had been tightly secured. It occurred to Bertran that the limited, dark space beneath them might act as a potential hideaway for RAF fugitives. Once loaded for transportation, it was not advisable to disturb the careful alignment of the delicate cargo. Using his extrovert personality, Bertrand hoped to convince any snooping guards to leave his precious pipes unmolested.

From the advantage of his driving seat, Bertrand Dewynter gazed down as his old chum, *Le Professeur*, hurried towards his truck. Audrey followed in his wake. Bertrand was puzzled when he spotted a young man approaching with two young children. The old comrades exchanged words and Heinrich grew nervous when the driver appeared agitated.

It was clear to Heinrich that *Le Professeur* was experiencing unexpected difficulty in persuading the noted organ maker to recast his mission from that of a trial run to the real article. Bertrand took a lot of talking down before reluctantly agreeing to carry unexpected passengers on board his *camion*. Flustered and muttering hot oaths under his breath, he jumped down from the cab and hurried round to the rear.

Meanwhile, Heinrich was handed his identity papers that had been rushed through. He had no idea if they were sufficiently convincing. Described as an 'apprentice organ maker', he knew he was in no position to argue. The Pole in charge of the bridge-winding singled Heinrich out and grasped him by the hand. He used the French he was beginning to pick up.

'*Bon chance, mon brave Östereiches!*'

The young Austrian smiled nervously and responded positively.

'*Merci, mon ami, Polski! Merci pour tous les choses.*'

Heinrich watched on anxiously as the red-faced M Dewynter grumpily unclipped clamps stretching the canvas cover over the rear. The driver did his best to control his seething anger but graciously helped the children to climb aboard. He pointed to a narrow gap between two of the larger pipes. Sura and Johan hesitated but Bertrand shook his head, indicating they must squeeze through. He then threw in spare sacking. Unaware that they were not French he suggested they sat on it. With the help of the *Résistance* miner, the organ maker shifted one of his precious pipes to all but close the gap between it and the next.

Le Professeur introduced Heinrich to his friend and the Austrian was curtly ordered into the cab. Fearing the imminence of a German morning patrol, Bertrand started up the engine and reversed the Citroen, aiming to re-cross the bridge. Hidden observers watched on as it disappeared down the dusty lane in a cloud of black fumes. Perched next to the driver, Heinrich regretted his limited grasp of French but knew he must attempt to placate his unwilling rescuer as soon as possible. Sadly, his attempts failed, lamentably, owing to M Dewynter's near total lack of German. As the kilometres rolled by, two enforced companions worked up a mutual but limited knowledge of English. It gave them time to develop a unique and idiosyncratic brand of *Franglais* helping them to progress towards basic understanding.

In the brief time available at the swing bridge, *Le Professeur* had gone to the trouble of explaining to Bertrand that Heinrich's assumed Alsatian identity might be of great value. It permitted him to converse in German, if required. His new surname, '*Erhard*', might likewise act as an advantage as it smacked of Germanic origin. This might prove beneficial should Heinrich hint to German patrols his family had always resented Alsace's historical seizure by the French. His only concern was that his Viennese accent bore little relation to that spoken in the Haut-Rhin *Département*. Nevertheless, Heinrich settled on playing a role well suited to his natural self, hoping to put himself across as a well-educated person from a good background.

As they approached Amiens, the young fugitive had a brainwave. He managed to explain to Bertrand that he wanted to study the organ promotion literature spread around in the cab. It struck him that the more he appeared conversant with the inner workings of the instrument, the better things might turn out. Bertrand, gradually reverting to his normal good humour, showed amusement as he watched his passenger eagerly devouring technical details of organ stops. Heinrich struggled with the dimensions involving Imperial units, the standard measurements of pipes. He was also staggered by the size of the enormous bass pipes demanded by great cathedrals. Having been brought up on the metric system, he attempted to work out the meaning of an 'Imperial foot'.

The musician in Heinrich responded to the nomenclature of the various stops. Bertrand was able to explain that he was only replacing relatively smaller pipes, none longer than eight feet. He pulled the details of his cathedral commission from his breast pocket

'Blockflöte?' Heinrich enquired, puzzled.

Bertrand laughed and began to whistle. For a brief moment he took his hands off the steering wheel and pretended to play a flute before regaining control. To Heinrich 'trompete' was obvious as was 'piccolo', a mere two feet. Likewise, 'voix humaine' and 'viole.' But he had trouble working out a number of the other stops.

'Posaune?' he asked Bertrand who obliged by blowing through his lips to achieve a passable rendition of a trombone. The two musicians giggled when the esteemed organ specialist failed miserably to imitate a high-pitched oboe.

'Hautbois!' Bertrand explained, apologetically. But his smile disappeared as traffic into Amiens slowed in front of the vehicle. They had no option but to join a queue. Fifty metres ahead, Heinrich spotted a road block. A large furniture van had been pulled over for intensive investigation. In fits and starts, the organ maker's *camion* crawled up to the lowered barrier. Bertrand coolly lit up a cigarette and waited for a patrol soldier to approach his side window. Heinrich, on the contrary, experienced fear of German troops for the first time. Theoretically, these young men were roughly his own kind. Only now did he appreciate how alienated he was from them and the potential threat they posed. His anxiety was not so much for himself but for the children, imprisoned in the back of the *camion*.

'*Vos documents de permit?*'

In a heavy accent, the young guard in gleaming helmet and mud-bespattered uniform demanded the required travel documents from Bertrand. He looked disdainfully at the description of the load and handed back the papers. Barely glancing at Heinrich, he raised his hand to the guard at the barrier. Bertrand smiled graciously.

'*Merci, monsieur! Cigarette?*'

The young soldier snorted.

'*Nein, danke!*'

The Citroen rolled on, using Bertrand's local knowledge to avoid the city centre. Heinrich noted further evidence of the German presence. Small military vehicles and motorcycles with side cars sped past whilst, on the far side of the road, a patrol of riflemen stepped in unison.

'God!' Heinrich thought, 'these people are my enemies. Now I know what it's like to be French!'

He glanced at Bertrand driving with one elbow rested, laconically, on his wound down window. He had already raised the hinged windscreen to permit an air flow to remove his foul-smelling cigarette smoke. Heinrich marvelled at the Frenchman's cool demeanour, vowing to steady his own nerves. They were on their way to the city of Rouen when Bertrand used the curious language they had invented between them to suggest a stop.

'*Les kinderenfants!*' he puffed.

Heinrich understood, much amused. But he was already concerned for the condition of Sura and Johan.

'*Kinderenfants? Mais oui!*'

Bertrand turned his truck off the main highway and into a rough side road, leading to a small forest. An unmade track appeared on the right, perfect for a temporary break and far from prying eyes. Heinrich leapt out of the Citroen to join his companion, at the rear. Bertrand worked at the clamps keeping down the canvas and opened the flap. He called lightly to the children and cautiously pushed the eight foot pipes apart. Two frightened faces appeared in the gap. Neither child looked well, hardly surprising given their bumpy ride. As Heinrich and Bertrand helped them out of their mobile cell, Sura and Johan's thin faces betrayed the agony of their ordeal.

'Hello, you two,' Heinrich called, sounding more cheerful than he felt. 'I'm sorry we couldn't stop, before now, but we've made good progress.'

After the four occupants had taken turns to relieve themselves amongst the cover of the trees, Bertrand and Heinrich set about preparing a picnic on the grass. Sura refused to join them, preferring the relative cover of the nearby forest fringe. Heinrich approached her, suspecting she might be close to breaking point. The small girl put her hands to her face and howled. Her chaperone attempted to put his arm round her thin shoulders but was thrust away.

'I want to go home!' she screamed. 'I want Mummy and Daddy!'

She stamped her foot and eyed Heinrich with anger.

'I hate you. Go away and leave us. We don't want to see you any more.'

Johan ran over to support his sister and stood combatively by her side.

'We know you're trying to take us away,' he shouted, angrily. 'We don't know where. And you won't tell us.'

Sura grasped his hand in hers.

'Come on!' she said. 'Let's get away from here, Johan. We'll find someone kind who'll help us. We're going home!'

Bertrand joined Heinrich at the edge of the wood. His friendly, round face could not disguise his concern. Placing his hand inside his jacket, he pulled out his wallet and opened it in front of the young rebels. He then carefully removed a photograph and showed it to them.

'*Mes grand kinderenfants!*' he told them. '*Je les adore… "liebe"? Un petit garçon et une fille!*'

He offered the somewhat crumpled photo to the Austrian children. Heinrich searched his mind desperately to find a way of making peace between them all.

'Please, Sura…Johan…you must trust us. We know it's horrible for you. You've been wonderful, so far, and we're half way through our journey. We've all left people we love. I've left my parents…and they don't even know! And…'

He wiped away a tear.

'…back in Salzburg there's the girl I love…with all my heart. I've had to leave her behind just as you've been separated from your parents. But there's something I want you to know…your Mummy and Daddy *trust* us. We'll never go back on our word to them. We promised to get you to safety. There was no safe place in Austria for you.'

He let his words sink in, appreciating the children were growing a fraction calmer.

'Can I let you into a secret?'

Tear-stained and miserable, the children agreed.

'This man…'

He indicated Bertrand.

'…is risking his life for you. *And* me. We met only this morning and he's as brave as a lion. If the Germans capture him, I can't even begin to tell you what they'd do. Bertrand has a wife and family. And as he told you, he loves his grandchildren.'

Heinrich smiled at Bertrand who worked out what was being said.

'The three of us are together. And it's Bertrand who'll get us to where it's safe. And when he's done that he'll do it for some other person he's never seen before!'

Wisely, Heinrich let his words sink home. Even at their young age, Sura and Johan were sensible enough to know he spoke the truth. With reluctance, Sura allowed herself to be escorted back to the truck. Johan felt for Heinrich's hand.

The picnic was a success and the children felt better for it. Bertrand managed to convey to Heinrich that Sura and Johan might take a short, accompanied break in the nearby forest. The organ maker stayed with his vehicle and watched the curious threesome disappear into the trees. They found a sunny glade where they could wander freely in the long grasses and enjoy the flowers. Close to the ground, a speckled wood butterfly fluttered onto a nearby leaf and opened its wings. Heinrich marvelled at its soft brown background, highlighting its cream-yellow markings.

'Sorry, you two,' he said gently. 'We must go on but we'll

stop again for another break. Tell me…how are Ludwig and Bimperl getting on? Are they enjoying the ride?'

Johan's little mouth puckered.

'Not really,' he said. 'Ludwig doesn't like being locked up. He's not a circus bear.'

Heinrich understood.

'And Bimperl?'

Sura brightened.

'Oh, Bimperl's fine. Perhaps next stop we can take him for a walk?'

They laughed. The spotted dog's exercise walk was agreed.

XXIII

Time ticked away, slowly, as the organ truck lumbered along open stretches of roads lined with tall poplars. Bertrand risked a second break before the important approach to Rouen. Sharing a Michelin Guide with Heinrich, he indicated that there was no way of avoiding German blockades. Having taken the advice of a friend, the night before over the telephone, he knew the occupiers were settling in and starting to exert themselves. But he was informed that searches were still at a minimum as the occupying forces were keen to keep roads open as they spread their tentacles across the land.

Bertrand's Rouen friend also explained that resistance was currently non-existent in the city and surrounds, and that the German forces were confident of keeping the population subjugated. So far, they had only experienced a negligible degree of rebellion and assumed, from the sullen expressions of the vanquished French, that the will to fight had gone out of the local people. On reaching the outskirts of the old city, Heinrich was disturbed to see the shattering effects of bombing and artillery action. Driving into the centre proved difficult as the roads were still strewn with rubble with numerous half-timbered buildings destroyed by fire.

Bertrand had planned to cross the Seine on the bridge, close to the ancient cathedral. The *Gendarmerie*, however, directed him to a crossing point further west where a traffic queue was building up. He was dismayed to find French policemen collaborating with their new masters. Armed enemy patrols looked on as the *gendarmes*, in peaked caps and black capes, blew their whistles and organised the traffic flow. To Bertrand's dismay, it appeared that a number of vehicles were being stopped and searched. When it came to the turn of the Citroen to pull up, a *gendarme* ordered both driver and passenger out onto the cobbles. His manner was brusque, presumably aiming to impress his German masters. Heinrich felt uneasy as the man called to a colleague to join him. Whilst they were satisfied with Bertrand's travel permit, Heinrich was ordered out onto the side of the road for questioning.

The newcomer, a tall man with a thin moustache, approached him with suspicion. He fired a volley of questions at the Austrian from which Heinrich could pick out only a few words. Fighting to keep panic at bay, Heinrich mumbled his name, recalling the phrase Bertrand had taught him on the way.

'*Je m'appelle Hubert Erhard. J'habite Thann, en Alsace. Il y a un problem?*'

Bertrand swaggered over and addressed the men with his *bonhomie natural*. He explained '*Hubert*' was a simple lad, his new apprentice and the best he could get in the circumstances. He was still teaching him the job. Bertrand explained poor '*Hubert*' had recently returned from an isolation hospital where he had been treated for Tuberculosis. That was the reason why he had not been called up for military service. However, it seemed the lad had a natural ear for music so, in the current emergency, Bertrand had taken him on. Regrettably, his established assistant had been drafted into the French Navy. The old organ specialist then invited the policemen to take a look at his truck. They followed him round to the rear where he got Heinrich to undo the canvas cover.

Neither *gendarme* had previous experience of organ pipes and music was of no particular interest. They found themselves mystified by the strange cargo, each metal tube lovingly wrapped and stowed. Bertrand went on to explain he was delivering them to Rennes and that these very pipes would be installed in the Cathedral St-Pierre. The *gendarmes* shrugged their shoulders with disinterest although one stepped forward to touch the nearest pipe. He felt through its cladding and made as though to shove it to one side. Bertrand pushed angrily in front of him.

'*Attention, monsieur! Ce sont delicates! Oeuvres d'art!*'

The *gendarme* brushed him aside and Bertrand lost his footing on the cobbles. Suspecting the sudden flair-up demanded investigation, a young German officer strolled forward. He spoke in his own language but it required no translation. The *gendarmes* pointed at the pipe cargo in the back of the truck and the officer laughed. Heinrich summoned up his courage and spoke to the man in his own language.

'These are hand-crafted organ pipes, sir.'

He pointed to the business details featured on the cabin doors.

'My master's been commissioned by the cathedral, at Rennes, so we're on our way to complete the delivery.'

The officer took a step back and adjusted his spectacles.

'You speak German?' he asked, astonished. 'Where did you learn to speak so well?'

'I'm from Alsace, sir,' Heinrich responded. 'My grandparents on my mother's side are German…the Klobes. We go back generations. You'll know our land was stolen from us by the French. Most of the kids at my school got by in both languages.'

He chuckled at what appeared to be a sudden recall.

'The French teachers beat us if we used our home German.'

The officer showed more interest. He hoped to come across as an equally-educated man.

'I think we both know our History,' he said. 'You'll be pleased now that Alsace and the Rhineland have been unified under German law?'

'It was always our dream,' Heinrich responded. 'I'd be happy to show you the pipes we've made. It's best I handle them.'

He bent to touch a four foot reed.

'This one's the blockflöte…the French use *our* language for some of the names. Next to it is a really important pipe…the diapason. It fills in the big background sound of the instrument.'

The German officer did his best to look interested whilst the *gendarmes* looked on in uncomprehending confusion.

'Would you like me to unwrap one for you?' Heinrich suggested, helpfully. 'The one over there is a clarion. The French would call it a "trompette." You may also be interested to know that the pedal board is German.'

The soldier glanced beyond the Citroen, concerned that the traffic was building up.

'I'm sorry,' he said. 'No time for a music lesson! Some other time, perhaps?'

He ordered the perplexed *gendarmes* away. They moved on to the next vehicle, a vegetable van supplying the local market. The officer relaxed and wished Heinrich and Bertrand well.

'Good luck, gentlemen! Your journey may go easier from now on. We haven't got Brittany fully occupied as yet. Although things will tighten up in the next few weeks.'

The officer allowed himself a quiet smile.

'We Germans are a musical race, you know. Your organ will help bring Bach to these ignorant French!'

Pleased with the joke he shared with Heinrich, he waved the truck on to approach the crossing of the River Seine. Driver and passenger held their breath. They knew they were fortunate, far more so than the citizens of Rouen whose inner city had been ravaged by bombing and artillery fire. Once across the bridge, Bertrand let rip a volley of French expletives, none of which required translation. To relieve the dreary business of being enslaved to the wheel, he reached into his pocket to pull out a flask of proof cognac. Unscrewing the cap, he toasted his new comrade in his best *Franglais*.

'*Très good, mon friend-ami Alsace! Salut!*'

He swigged down a considerable gulp of the French spirit and offered the flask to Heinrich who declined. For a second or two, Bertrand's driving became erratic. Heinrich assumed this was due to the cognac but was startled to find the Frenchman heaving with uncontrollable laughter.

The travellers settled down to the monotony of a few more hours driving, with two brief stops. At a small village, with no enemy in sight, Bertrand took the opportunity to use a public telephone in the local café. It enabled him to establish a contact supplied by the ever efficient *Professeur*.

Heinrich was surprised at the apparent normality of the sleepy scene around him. The occasional villager went about her business, with search patrols no longer posing a threat. This confirmed the German officer's point that the thinly spread invaders were concentrating on immediate military priorities. A nondescript truck transporting church organ pipes was hardly likely to attract attention.

The last of the sun was going down on the St Aubin road as they approached Rennes. Bertrand told Heinrich of the serious loss of life and infrastructure after the *Luftwaffe* had sent a bombing mission to knock out the city's railway sidings. Heinrich had difficulty in following the line of conversation but managed to glean that an ammunition train had been struck. Delayed troop trains had been lined up alongside and the casualty list was extensive.

The Citroen headed for the cathedral area. Bertrand was keen to reach his target before dark as a black-out curfew would surely be imposed by the occupiers. Fortunately, they had made good time. With daylight fading, Heinrich observed the main towers of the nineteenth century St Pierre, dominating the skyline. He was relieved when Bertrand finally pulled into a side street, granting near access to an obscure side entrance to the otherwise awesome building.

The organ maker left Heinrich sitting in the cab and hurried along the pavement to ring a doorbell. After what seemed to be an eternity, a young priest appeared and spoke earnestly with the driver. Bertrand signalled for Heinrich to hold on and remain with the vehicle whilst he was issued inside. After some agonising minutes the door re-opened. A young woman appeared at the threshold. She swiftly glanced both ways before running lightly over to the truck. Dark-haired and in a white blouse and navy skirt, she indicated to Heinrich to wind down his window. It came as a surprise to hear good German spoken in north western France.

'M Erhard? My name is "Michelle". Listen carefully. We have little time. I shall say this only once! Stay in the vehicle until after dark. The street lighting is poor. We'll come back and see to the children. You'll spend the night in the cathedral. That's all.'

Michelle had no time for pleasantries. She turned and hurried back to the cathedral, anxiously scrutinising the darkened street for danger. Heinrich sat tense as the side door opened, then closed behind her. He tried to settle but found himself fretting over the children. If only to offer reassurance, it was tempting to get out and call briefly to Sura and Johan. But he was aware the operation had reached a critical point when even the smallest error could ruin all previous achievements. Patience now played a major role and the agitated Heinrich sensed he must place his confidence in strangers not yet known to him. Above all, he must accept their instructions and follow them to the letter.

To his relief, Bertrand finally re-appeared at the obscure cathedral entry. He was accompanied by three rough-looking men who went round to the back of the vehicle. Heinrich joined them, noticing out of the corner of his eye two swarthy-looking individuals lurking on the opposite side of the street. He hoped they were look-outs. The organ maker gave orders and his assistants clambered aboard to handle the pipes. Before they started, however, Bertrand picked out the two central pipes and gave instructions for their wrappings to be partially removed. Each one was carefully manoeuvred out of the truck with their wrappings trailing over the cobbles. Sura and Johan were then encouraged to crawl out of their dark dungeon. Heinrich caught only the briefest glimpse of their terrified faces as they slipped into the narrow space between the pipes and their drapes. They kept their heads down to avoid being seen.

The small procession, concealing the fugitives, set out across the street towards the side entrance. In so doing, Sura and Johan were surreptitiously escorted into the building with Heinrich bringing up the rear. Michelle waited at the door and took charge. She directed her small torch into the increasing gloom of the echoing interior and told the children to follow. Bertrand then organised the transportation of the pipes to be placed near the organ loft.

Meanwhile, Michelle ordered Heinrich to move on. Hurrying forward in the fading light, he was barely aware of the golden interior of the great church. The small party crossed over to the nave where Michelle had arranged for a heavy slab of stone to be temporarily raised. She pointed her torch to reveal a secret staircase leading to the underground crypt. As they passed down into its chilly interior, Heinrich was aware that unseen hands replaced the slab, above their heads.

Michelle struck a match to light a paraffin lamp whose soft rays fell on the massive pillars supporting the building. She ushered her charges over to a side alcove where three mattresses and blankets had been laid out. At the same time, Michelle opened a wall cupboard in which she had stored drinks, apples and croissants. Unexpectedly, she permitted the otherwise stern expression on her face to drop. In the dim, yellow glow of the lamp Heinrich saw her enthusiastic smile for the first time.

'Please,' she said in adequate German, 'accept our hospitality. It's not much but times are difficult. I'll be your guide from now on and you must do everything I tell you.'

She looked kindly at the children.

'You understand, little ones?'

Still suffering from delayed shock, Sura and Johan gaped at Michelle with unseeing eyes. But they gradually came round and accepted the food. It was not long before they were devouring the croissants like tigers. Michelle took the opportunity to draw Heinrich aside.

'You'll not be here long,' she said quietly. 'Perhaps tomorrow. Maybe the next day. I'm waiting for instructions. The less I tell you the better. None of our names are real. We work under *nom de plumes.*'

Heinrich told her he understood and expressed his gratitude.

'*C'est rien!*' she responded, casually. 'We're determined to get these children away.'

She looked at them, kindly.

'I think you and Bertrand have been very brave!'

She turned to Heinrich and took him to one side in the shadow of a stone tomb.

'I must warn you. Getting through to the coast from here won't be easy. The occupiers are beginning to tighten things up but it shouldn't prove impossible. After that, we're in the lap of the gods… the sea gods!'

She shot him a searching glance.

'D'you believe in God?'

Heinrich looked down in embarrassment.

'Er…not really,' he said, apologetically. 'Not after what I've seen in this war.'

The young Frenchwoman did not challenge him.

'Perhaps you'd better start believing in Him, now?' she suggested. 'The House of God is a good place to start!'

Heinrich looked round and shivered in the creeping chill of shadowy pillars and ancient carved tombs.

'I don't expect God comes down here, much,' he said, gloomily. 'He's more likely to operate on the floor above!'

XXIV

Heinrich dozed fitfully on a thin duvet spread on the unforgiving stone floor of the cathedral. He was roused out of a brief period of slumber by the *Résistance* woman who appeared so calm in all her dealings.

'M Erhard, we have *brioches* for you and Sura and Johan,' she said in a very matter-of-fact voice. 'I can fill you in on the next move. Don't ask for details. It's best you know nothing. M Dewynter is a brave man. He's arranged to go on from here. It's some drive and we tried to persuade him to let us take over but he won't hear of it. In theory, he'll be visiting a small church to put in an estimate before returning to start his work in this building.'

The Austrian renegade felt at a loss. His identity had been altered and he was mixing with French strangers. He had fought bravely with *Wehrmacht* colleagues but now its soldiers were his enemies. It was almost as though his former self no longer existed. Keeping up the pretence of answering to a new name and existence was proving a great strain.

Bertrand Dewynter re-joined the stowaways having spent the night at an acquaintance's home, nearby. His welcome appearance lightened the atmosphere and he made a point of spoiling the children with *pain au chocs*. Sura and Johan were delighted with a sumptuous breakfast that raised their very dejected spirits. Coffee was served in the crypt as Bertrand outlined the situation. He was the one person who benefitted from operating under his own name.

'I don't suppose you know,' he intimated, speaking through Michelle, 'that my name is of Breton/Dutch origin? The Dewynters of Morbihan. We're an old fishing family but I broke away. No stomach for the sea! My old dad was disappointed when I left it to my brothers to carry on the family business. Crabs and lobsters…the Dewynters have been in it for generations. I was an embarrassment to them!'

Despite the language difficulties, Heinrich was beginning to piece together the clandestine role Bertrand had concocted. It emerged that Bertrand was acting as a conduit, today's journey being the first run. Heinrich accepted his role as 'guinea pig' over a potentially hazardous escape route. He was not aware, following the swift Fall of France, that the British wartime government under Prime Minister Churchill craved information on signs of German intentions. It feared an imminent threat of cross-Channel invasion so required up-to-date reports of signs of preparation. Clawing back valuable RAF crew was one thing but infiltrating agents into France was quite another. Since the Dunkerque evacuation, a two-way sea crossing had been established between river creeks in Cornwall and the distant Breton coastline. Charles de Gaulle's French Government in exile was already in contact with countrymen prepared to run the gauntlet. Determined to carry on the fight, foolhardy Breton seafarers defied the, as yet, minimal German sea patrols. Initially, even tiny boats such as cutter-rigged crabbers took part, some relying solely upon sails.

'*Eh bien, mon ami! Dormez well?*'

Bertrand did not wait for an answer.

'*Et les kinderenfants?*'

Heinrich finished his coffee, relieved to see his trusted older friend and his idiosyncratic form of Germanic *Franglais*. He requested Michelle to translate for him.

'So what now, Bertrand?' he asked. 'Where are we heading and how long will it take? I'm concerned for Sura and Johan.'

The cheerful organ maker shrugged his shoulders.

'Still a good distance to go. I'm under orders not to reveal much to you. Let's just say I have a false letter inviting me to take a look at an instrument somewhere on the Breton coast.'

He paused to let Michelle catch up.

'It's a good excuse and takes us all the way. We're loading some dismantled pipes of this botched Rennes instrument so we can keep the children concealed. I'm afraid they'll have to share the journey with a couple of large petrol cans. Fuel's becoming scarce. The Germans are clamping down on supply.'

His guffaw echoed through the crypt.

'But we have our contacts. Well, at least for now!'

Heinrich wondered how far away the ultimate destination was from Rennes. Brittany appeared to be a big place. The matter-of-fact Bertrand confirmed they were still in for a long haul.

'I intend driving cross-country,' he said. 'No point taking the Lorient route. The port will be crawling with the Bosches.'

He pulled up short.

'Begging your pardon!'

Heinrich took no offence at the translation.

Michelle shook her head.

'He's so tactful!'

She continued her translation as Bertrand continued in his outspoken manner. The young Austrian interrupted.

'Michelle, what happens to us when we get to wherever we're going?'

Bertrand smiled as Michelle shared the question. He shook his untidy, grey locks and raised a cautionary finger to his fulsome lips.

'Ah…secret!' she interpreted. 'If something bad happens, you know nothing. You won't be able to give anything away. We still need others to help us get through. Their identities are not for your ears!'

Heinrich sensed the precarious mission balanced on a knife edge.

'*Eh bien!* We leave in half an hour,' Bertrand explained. 'You see to the kids and I'll supervise the final loading. Don't worry. *Le vieux Bertrand* will get you there!'

Something niggled at the back of Heinrich's mind. His knowledge of the geography of western France was virtually non-existent. But this did not prevent him from wondering how an overt organ *camion* would not raise suspicion. There was no justifiable reason for it to stray off course. It made no sense but Heinrich kept faith in his bluff driving companion.

After smuggling Sura and Johan back onto the truck, the party set out on the final stretch. The day turned out bright and sunny with the green Breton countryside in full summer glory. Twice, Bertrand pulled up in quiet spots to release the children and take comfort breaks before relaxing on the wayside grass with a picnic. He insisted on an extended afternoon stoppage on the high moors and it was easy to be seduced into the feeling that no harm could befall them. The bare, windswept terrain came as a shock. Further on, Sura and Johan enjoyed a final brief break in a forest. The real world of destruction and violence seemed to have by-passed this peaceful paradise. However, with less than half an hour before reaching their destination, time-conscious Bertrand insisted on bundling his passengers back into the vehicle.

With the aid of Michelin maps, Bertrand managed to convey to Heinrich that the Breton coast would soon be in sight. Also, that the quicker route through Brest had to be avoided as the occupiers were moving to take over the main French Naval base. The good news was that the rest of the sprawling Finisterre hinterland was too expansive for the Germans to patrol.

Heinrich's heart leapt as the promising sight of a spectacular, rocky bay hove into view. Craggy outcrops and arching sediments, historically metamorphosed by sub-terranean igneous activity, stood isolated from the cliffs. Beyond, the blue sea sparkled in the late afternoon sunshine. Its wrinkled surface was broken by protruding rocks, treacherous to inexperienced sailors. Bertrand's face was all smiles.

'*La mer!*' he announced. '*Mon frère Jean-Pierre…*'

He searched for a German word.

'*Mein brüder!*' he announced triumphantly 'H*aus joli. He live!*'

His companion struggled to make sense of the chaotic language as the organ truck rumbled down to the sea. Heinrich gazed at the peaceful scene. It all seemed too simple. Merely stepping on a boat and setting sail for England? He poured over the map and came to a stark realisation. Whereas the original, short *Pas de Calais* crossing had once seemed feasible, it now appeared there was a far greater expanse of sea between Brittany's outpost and England's nearest point.

Heinrich's heart took a hopeful leap when the *camion* passed an outlying road sign reading 'Camaret-sur-Mer.' At last, all was revealed. As they wound their way through narrow streets tightly packed with white-washed cottages, he knew the hoped for destination had been reached. Bertrand judiciously manoeuvred his way through horse-drawn fish wagons and headed along a thin spit of land. It formed one side of the old harbour. Beyond that rose the towering bulk of an ancient brick and stone-built fortress. Heinrich spotted its defensive slit windows. On the far side, a fortified wall protected the port's austere guardian from attack by sea.

'*La Tour Vauban!*' Bertrand announced, helpfully.

He burbled on in fast French, oblivious of his friend's failure to comprehend. They pulled up on the crowded quayside by a buttressed, stone church and its dominating grey-tiled roof. The organ maker pulled out a new packet of *Gauloises*. On his side of the open cab, Heinrich caught the first scent of sea air, a mixture of salt, dried seaweed and fish. The harbour was packed with boats at their moorings, each small and rugged-looking after years of battling the sea. Rickety wooden fishing sheds, nets strung outside, dominated the busy scene. Old salts in berets, sea boots and canvas jackets sat on stools repairing fishing gear. It was Heinrich's first ever glance of the ocean and its mercurial ways. The Austrian landlubber could not help mentally contrasting the scene with the land-locked solidity of suburban Vienna.

Half-dead cigarette drooping over his bottom lip, Bertrand opened the cab door and jumped down. He shouted at Heinrich to do likewise and join him at the rear. Wrestling with the canvass ties, they threw back the cover to release the incarcerated prisoners. Blinking in the unaccustomed bright light, the wan faces of the two young Salzburgers lit up in wonder at the lively scene before them. Previously, Sura and Johan had only seen seaside pictures in school textbooks.

Heinrich felt concern. Was it wise to display themselves so openly? However, when he looked about him there was no sign of enemy presence. It was as though the small port had remained untouched by war. Bertrand took the children by the hand and strode cheerfully over to a nearby building, dominating the quay.

'La Chapelle Notre Dame-de-Romacour!' he shouted back. 'I wonder if it needs a good organ mender?'

Of course! It suddenly made sense to the Austrian visitor. Heinrich trailed his three companions as they stepped into the gothic-arched entrance opposite the tall bell tower, overlooking the harbour.

'Clever old Bertrand!' Heinrich thought to himself as he entered the cool interior.

Having taken brief, mental notes of the resident instrument, the organ specialist led his party back out into the sunlight. Johan ducked as a bold herring gull circled low over his head. He raised his hands to shield his eyes as the fearsome bird screamed at him before heading out to sea. Bertrand gathered his charges together and herded them along the quayside. He could have been taken for their grandfather, out for the day, inspecting the motley collection of brightly-painted vessels. Heinrich was fascinated by the knotted moorings slipped expertly over stolid bollards. But, above all, he was overjoyed to find Sura and Johan revelling in the new fishy sights and smells. It was a joy to see them sparking back into life and responding to a vibrant new world. The memory of the agonising road trek from Calais was already beginning to be pushed to the recesses of their young minds.

XXV

Bertrand treated his new-found Austrian friends to an ice cream of their choice. The children pretended to offer licks to Ludwig and Bimperl, still intact after the exacting journey. Leaving the truck on the quayside, he led the way back to the port and its cramped streets. A little way up the hill and leading out of the town, he sought a larger house beyond the fishermen's cottages. Dull grey-rendered walls with long, shuttered windows. The dreary, matching shutters were hooked back in their permanent places. Imposing railings fenced off a small front garden comprising mostly of gravel and a few nondescript plants. Bertrand pushed open the ornamental wrought iron gate, stepped up to the entrance, and invited Johan to pull the doorbell chain. The children were intrigued to hear a faint metallic response from the interior. An approaching figure was visible through the lead panes of the narrow windows.

A babble of exuberant French ensued as an elderly woman came to the door and confronted Bertrand. She appeared in a full black dress nearly down to her footwear and, on her grey-white hair tied into a bob, she wore a hand-embroidered lace cap. She beamed at the children and ushered her guests into the reception. They stood there, overwhelmed, hardly knowing how to respond.

'*Ma soeuer…sister?*' Bertrand attempted. '*Madame Dewynter! Married to my cousin.*'

Sura and Johan solemnly shook hands whilst Heinrich bowed, graciously. *Madame* swiftly closed the door and ushered her visitors into a spacious room of old upholstered chairs, plain oak floor and sash windows. On the table, a generous spread of hospitality had been prepared for the, by now, ravenous guests. Heinrich made out only a little of the rapid-fire French conversation between Bertrand and his rosy-cheeked sibling. Meanwhile, the children settled down to a welcoming feast set before them.

In fact, Heinrich's comprehension of French was improving faster than he thought. Despite *Madame*'s marked Breton accent, he was able to glean that the party would spend only a little time in her home. Indeed, they were expected to move out that night. After the feast, Sura and Johan were taken out to relax in the small rear garden not overlooked by neighbours. They were greeted by the family dog who took special interest in Bimperl. The small, untidy buff-coloured terrier, answering to the name of Merlot, happily scampered after a ball thrown for him. Wrestling it from the firm grasp of his terrier jaws was another matter. In no time, he and his new playmates were the best of friends. Heinrich parked himself on a peeling white wrought iron garden seat and looked on, at last able to relax.

"We'll leave the children out there,' Mme Dewynter smiled, addressing her brother by the window. 'Let them relax. I can't imagine how awful their ride must have been. Especially with your notorious driving! But they've done well. And now look at them! *Jouifs?*

Bertrand confirmed and did his best to explain the presence of Heinrich.

'I know you've been filled in on his background but we can trust him. He's definitely not an enemy. If the Gestapo get hold of him they'll make mincemeat of his carcass.'

His sister's demeanour changed. She possessed more knowledge than might appear.

'You go, tonight,' she said, solemnly. 'High tide's a few minutes before mid-night. The boat from England with Breton sailors will stand off. There's a light wind forecast so it can stand offshore and send in a dinghy. We understand there's an agent from *Londres* who'll be brought here before he's moved on. They tell me he's *Parisienne* but I can forgive him that. His mission is to get to the capital and establish contacts. He's a radio man so he'll be sending back reports.'

Bertrand turned serious, barely recognisable from the formerly cheerful *camion* driver.

'Brittany's got a crucial role to play in this war,' he told his sister. 'I understand the tunny fishermen are already making contact with British fishing fleets. It's our hope that tonight's crabber will slip away, unnoticed. But it won't be too long before the Germans set a curfew on night sailing. Not that it'll work out. They'll soon discover it's the tides that dictate comings and goings. They'll be forced to permit night fishing. At least, that's what we're banking on for the future.'

His sister listened quietly and got up to look out of the window. She was happy to see the frolics of the dog and the children.

'Two friends,' she said, '…let's call them Bastien and Hugues. They'll act as escorts to the beach. They've investigated a little cove round the headland, well out of sight of the port. Hugues will take your Austrians down to the beach with Bastien acting as look-out. There's plenty of cover. Hugues will signal to the crabber with a lamp and guide their dinghy in. *Nous sommes rest ici, mon frère*, and pray to the Good Lord for a successful operation.'

She crossed herself.

'If the boat doesn't turn up we try again, tomorrow night. On the later tide. If nothing happens, the operation's aborted and we'll await further instructions. Bastien is our radio man. He joined our group, recently, and we're lucky to have him. If all goes well, you'll soon be on your way back to Reme.'

The jangling bell in the kitchen responded to a tug outside the front door. *Madame* scuttled into her formally furnished front room. From behind long drapes she surveyed the new callers. She went to the door to let in two young men. They took turns to kiss the respected old lady on her soft cheeks.

'Hugues…Bastien. *Bien venu!* Our guests have arrived and you must meet my brother, Bertrand. He's driven from Calais. He'll stay the night with me and hopes to leave in the morning. His part of the mission's over, thank God. He'll be relieved to hand over the last part to you.'

Hugues, a swarthy fellow with wiry black stubble untouched for days, accepted Bertrand's offered hand. He shook it warmly.

'We're honoured, *Monsieur*. You've driven all the way from Calais? How is it up there?'

Bastien, a pale serious young man, stood awkwardly lumping what seemed to be a heavy load in a large canvas bag. He did not waste time asking for a private base. *Madame* escorted him up the stairs. At the top, she showed him into the nearest bedroom and closed the door quietly behind him. Heinrich wandered in from the garden to be introduced to Hugues who had no German. The fisherman showed him little warmth and did not offer him his hand. He turned to Bertrand.

'It's on, *monsieur*,' he said, quietly. 'We leave after dark. We'll do our best to get your people away but the main objective is to link with the agent coming in from England. Bastien's gone upstairs to establish radio contact with local helpers. He's setting up, now. He hopes to be able to receive and transmit from here. So he's running a test.'

The two Frenchmen settled into a discussion of the current political and military situation. Neither held any respect for the Pétain Government about to appease its conquerors. Hugues launched into a diatribe of invective, cursing the failed French military leadership.

'We fishermen are so lucky!' he said. 'Our work ensures we stay here, on the coast. But many of our school friends are now missing after joining up. No-one has any idea where they are. Dead or alive. Now it's our turn. We must get behind this unknown French General, in England, and do our bit for the war.'

He spoke with vehemence.

'It's far from over. *Certainment!*'

Madame left the men to finalise the planning of the night's mission. Making extravagant use of hand gestures, she communicated to the children that they should take the opportunity to sleep. She had already spotted the strain and tiredness in their eyes and feared for the hazardous events ahead of them. Sura and Johan willingly followed *Madame* up the uncarpeted stairs to a pretty bedroom. Slipping off their shoes and socks, the children crawled onto the luxury of a soft bed, losing consciousness in seconds.

Madame Dewynter stepped quietly down the stairs to suggest coffee, all round. She then bustled off to her kitchen before returning with a tray of wide-brimmed cups, milk, sugar and biscuits.

'The radio fellow, Bastien,' she said. 'I don't know him. How does he like his coffee?'

Hugues suggested his colleague would opt for *noir café sans sucre*. The men fell back to their discussion whilst *Madame* handed a filled cup and saucer to Heinrich. She smiled sweetly and indicated the stairs. Heinrich was happy to oblige and mounted them with care. He knocked quietly on the temporary radio shack door before opening it with his spare hand. He then entered to find the quiet Breton wearing a head set, hunched over a bulky two-way radio telephone. Bastien had already plugged in his microphone in the attempt to establish contact with fellow resistors. He looked round, sharply, when Heinrich approached the table on which the twenty kilo 'portable' radio set had been placed. With its solid aerial extended full length, the operator tuned a small dial, searching for the appropriate frequency. He made no pretence of his annoyance at being interrupted and gestured to Heinrich to vacate the room. The Austrian placed the coffee cup on the table, leaving Bastien struggling to make contact.

Opposite the radio base was the double bedroom in which the children were now sound asleep. Heinrich opened the door, a fraction, and peeped in. Ludwig, Johan's one-eared bear, lay in the child's arms whilst Sura snored, lightly. Heinrich closed the door and made his way back down the stairs. He was not aware that Hugues and Bertrand had slipped out to carry out a final reconnaissance at the selected cove. He took advantage of their absence to relax in the relative peace of the rear garden, taking with him a local newspaper abandoned in *Madame*'s sitting room. In the fading light of the afternoon sun, Heinrich struggled through the French news stories surprised, although delighted, to find he was picking up the new language. Flicking through the pages, he found advertisements easiest to puzzle out. Heinrich's attention was alerted to a promotion for domestic radio sets. His attention was taken by a rounded Bakelite model with a prominent dial boasting national and foreign stations.

Something triggered in his mind…the set, upstairs, manned by a *Resistance* fighter! Where had he seen something like it, previously? With a jolt, he sat up on the hard garden seat. The *sonderzug!* Carl Fischer, with his fascination for radio communication, had dared to show Heinrich the latest portable *Wehrmacht* two-way set. Using the VHF signal it had only a limited range as receiver/transmitter. Applying the American vernacular, Fischer had jokingly referred to it as '*walkie-talkie*'.

Heinrich's heart beat fast. The sturdily constructed radio in the bedroom over his head bore a striking similarity. But he swiftly discounted the possibility. He was, after all, no expert on receiver/transmitters. In all likelihood, most models shared similar features, allowing for developments and advances. *And yet?*

His attention focussed on the esoteric world of radio engineering, Heinrich failed to spot Merlot trot across the small lawn to sneak into his outside kennel. Merlot had good reason, delighted with his new acquisition. Stretching out on an ancient rug, he contentedly chewed at Bimperl, his toy canine counterpart. Merlot had no intention of destroying Sura's treasured sleeping companion although he worried at it with his terrier teeth.

Puzzled and deep in thought, Heinrich folded the newspaper and returned indoors. *Madame* bustled away in her kitchen *domaine.* He gave her a hand, the endless peeling of potatoes and carrots being a skill he had acquired in *Wehrmacht* training. *Madame* Dewynter graciously accepted his offer and handed him a small, sharp knife. He heard footsteps on the stairs and Bastien's mournful face appeared round the kitchen door.

'*Madame*, forgive me, I'm not getting much joy detecting a signal from our comrades out on the cliffs. So I'm taking a break. I've run out of cigarettes so I'll slip out for a few minutes. Will I have to go all the way down to the harbour?'

The kindly Breton woman knew of a nearer *tabac kiosk* and gave instructions to find it.

'Don't hang around,' she told him. 'Supper's on the way!'

Just for once, Bastien's grim countenance betrayed the faintest trace of a smile before he slipped out of the house. Allowing about a minute for the radio operator to turn the corner, Heinrich put down his half-peeled potato and asked to be excused. He ran lightly up the stairs, turning immediately into the radio room. The bulky metal box stood on the table where he had first spotted it. A vertical steel aerial stuck out from its top terminating, at the apex, in horizontal cross arms. He hurried over to search for clues regarding the transmitter's origin. It took only seconds to find what he was after.

'*Lorenz*' – the manufacturer's name was easy to spot. '*Torn.Fu.b. 1 Watt.*'

Two or three short-phrased notices guiding the operator were stamped on the front. They were printed in German. Heinrich felt sick. Whose side was Bastien on? Could he be trusted? Surely, the French comrades were too smart to be taken in? He closed the door, quietly, and slipped back down the stairs.

Before supper, Heinrich asked Bertrand to join him in the garden. Despite their limited conversation ability, lacking both in vocabulary and grammar, the Austrian managed to convey to his friend the gist of his concern. However, he was not prepared for Bertrand's instant repost. The old organ specialist laughed off the possibility of penetration of the underground organisation. He insisted all men were vetted and secure, suggesting the two-way radio was in all likelihood lifted by a French sympathiser drafted in to work for the occupying forces.

Heinrich felt he had no alternative but to trust Bastien and the fine people who, thus far, had proved bold and brave.

Somewhat shamefully, he dismissed the notion that a comrade might be working for the other side. The irony of his position did not escape him. By now, Heinrich accepted he was a non-national. A non-person. Neither Austrian nor French. He had no option other than to retain faith in strangers generously prepared to risk their lives for him.

Left alone, Sura and Johan would have slept through until morning. But after the adults had finished *Madame*'s excellent supper, and drunk a toast to the mission's success, the children were gently awakened. Despite their sleepiness, both children sensed mounting excitement as they tucked into the meal put aside for them. Heinrich had assured them that the final stretch of the journey would be relatively straight forward. He elected not to over-play the difficulties.

'We leave for the coast, within the hour,' he said. 'I think you'll love it. Big adventure. Are you up for it? I'm just as excited as you two. There'll be a boat lying offshore to take us over to England.'

Sura grew thoughtful.

'Why can't we stay with *Madame*?' she said. 'She's kind and we already know a bit of French. We feel safe here.'

Heinrich understood but once again made light of things.

'You *are* safe here,' he responded. 'But that might not last too long. The German army's already taken over the nearest big town. So we think it's best we hop over to England whilst we can. You'll be perfectly safe, there.'

He pretended to drag up a memory.

'Your aunt, outside London, has a piano. A good one. *Madame* Dewynter doesn't have such a thing. Just think… you'll soon be playing again!'

Hugues broke up the conversation and called Heinrich into the entrance hall. He attempted to explain that Bastien planned to go on ahead. It seemed that radio reception from the house was variable and he wanted to get nearer the headland to secure final contacts. Bastien shook hands gravely with his colleagues and wished them luck.

'You know your way from the dropping-off point, Hugues,' he said. 'I'll set up on the cliff top. Our friends will be out there in the darkness keeping a look-out for you. If there's any trouble they can find me. Just one thing.'

He held up two woollen scarves.

'I'll drape one of these on a rock on the side of the path dropping down the gulley to the beach. If you find this white one you can proceed. If it's the red one, you must abort the mission, immediately. The safe house is the farm close to the dropping-off point. If you're forced to use it, the farmer knows where to conceal you. You remember the code word?'

Hugues nodded.

'You may have to lie up for twenty four hours,' Bastien continued. 'Then we'll move you on. Is that clear?'

The radio man's sudden eloquence caught Heinrich by surprise. He caught the gist of Bastien's last-minute instructions. Suddenly, he appreciated that solemn Bastien held a high place in the local *Résistance* hierarchy. Perhaps equivalent to *Le Professeur* back at Les Attaques? It was reassuring having him on board. What Heinrich did not know was that it was not Bastien but *Madame* Dewynter, herself, who was the local leader.

'We foresee no problems,' Bastien said tersely. 'No reports of German patrols in the area. I double-checked that by land phone.'

Aided by Bertrand, he strapped his cumbersome apparatus on his back and staggered out. Although he did not possess a strong, muscular frame, he made light of the twenty five or so kilograms combined weight of radio and battery. Bastien had arranged to meet his transport around the corner from the house.

An hour later, a small black car drew up outside. Bertrand spotted it from the window. He checked his watch. The car signalled twice with its headlamps.

'This is it,' he said.

Sura and Johan tried to contain their excitement and Heinrich warned them not to say a word. They embraced all round as *Madame* struggled to hold back tears, clucking over her small charges. Heinrich drew Bertrand to him and hugged him warmly. He had rehearsed his lines but his French pronunciation still betrayed his Germanic origin.

'Bertrand, my great friend. We're forever in your debt. God bless you. We'll meet again!'

It was the organ maker's turn to grow tearful. He planted a fatherly kiss on Heinrich's cheek and bent down to cuddle the departing children.

'Go on! Shoo!' *Madame* demanded. 'You're wasting time. We shall pray for you.'

She made the sign of the cross over her ample bosom. Bertrand and Heinrich bowed their heads and likewise crossed themselves. From the driving seat of a two door

Renault 8, the chauffeur grew impatient and indicated to his passengers to move. Heinrich and the children squeezed into the rear with Hugues sitting in the front. The car moved off slowly, the driver creating as little acceleration noise as possible. Within minutes, it had left the town behind to cross the open headland, towards the sea. Hugues turned round and whispered back to Heinrich. The Austrian leaned forward to find Hugues attempting to hand him something in the dark. A solid object of cold steel was pressed into his hand. He needed no telling. It was a pistol.

'*Attention, mon ami! Achtung!*'

Startled, but determined to keep the presence of the weapon hidden from Sura and Johan, Heinrich slipped it into his jacket pocket. Ensuring the safety catch was on, he made the correct assumption the pistol was loaded. It seemed an unnecessary precaution as the uninterrupted transfer had worked like clockwork. The car pulled up at the dropping-off point and the driver extinguished its headlights. Hugues got out first, holding the door back for Heinrich and the children to emerge. He whispered an urgent word with the driver and organised his turn around before the lights were once more switched on. Isolated on a remote Breton headland, there was sufficient moonlight for the party to detect the worn gulley path leading to the sea cove.

Sura and Johan played their full part in the adventure, stimulated by the sound of gentle waves lapping on the nearby beach. The sharp tang of salt filled their nostrils.

'*Voila!*'

Hugues, leading the party down the winding, stony path, spotted a white scarf draped over a large fallen rock. The mission was on. Out there, somewhere in the pale reflection of moonlight on the waters, a small craft stood by ready and willing to carry the party to England.

XXVI

The remorseless tide crept in. Craggy headlands stuck out from the crumbling cliffs. A curved expanse of sand and pebbles swept left and right from the gully entry to the beach. Hugues lit a match as light clouds drifted across the moon. He shielded its light, as best he could, under his open jacket. The brief flare was enough for him to check his watch.

'Just over an hour from now,' he whispered, taking precautions despite the apparent absence of any threat. 'Bastien will co-ordinate the watchers above us. They'll signal to the boat from the cliffs.'

He pointed at the dark skeleton of a small boat rusting away on the rocks.

'Head for that,' he said. 'Then stay on the seaward side and don't show yourselves. I'll contact Bastien to tell him all's well. If you see a light from sea, don't hang around waiting for me to get back. Go out to meet the dinghy as the drop-on/drop-off must be done with speed.'

He handed Heinrich a small torch.

'In my absence, take this. Don't use it unless you have to. The dinghy will only flash, periodically. Two short flashes and one long. You answer with two long flashes and one short. I'll be back soon!'

Hugues turned and ploughed through the loose shingle as quietly as the shifting pebbles permitted. Left on their own, the three Austrian renegades settled uncomfortably with little protection from the wrecked hull.

Back at Camaret, *Madame* Dewynter gazed at the mound of plates heaped at the side of her enamel sink. But her thoughts were elsewhere. She urged Bertrand to give her a hand. His attention was taken by a scratching sound at the back door. *Madame* asked him to open it and let in a determined Merlot. The terrier sprang through the gap, proudly bearing his new trophy in his jaws. His mistress filled a bowl of left-overs from the butchers. Her back was turned to her brother so she did not see his staggered look of dismay. Bertrand's jaw dropped.

'*Mon Dieu!* It's the girl's sleeping toy. Bimperl…!'

Madame shook her head.

'What a shame! Sura loved that little dog. Well,' she burbled on, 'there's nothing we can do about it. I'm sure Merlot's very grateful.'

She watched from her sink as Bertrand snatched Bimperl from the terrier's grip. Powerless to stop him, *Madame* Dewynter stood transfixed as her brother headed for the front door.

'Don't wait up for me!'

Madame sprang to life and scuttled after Bertrand but there was no point in shouting and attracting attention down the street. All she could do was watch his disappearing figure under the dim lights of the occasional public lamps.

'The fool! What's he think he's doing? He could jeopardise the whole operation for the sake of getting that wretched thing to a little girl!'

She threw her washing-up cloth into the sink. Meanwhile, her brother headed for the port and his parked *camion*. Few people were out on the street and the last person he wanted to run into was a *gendarme*. Breathing heavily, Bertrand staggered into his cab and glanced anxiously round the harbour for signs of activity. The last of the boats were casting off, taking advantage of the tide. It was now or never. He started up the engine and drove slowly along the quayside with full headlights.

Each second was precious but Bertrand resisted the temptation to increase speed. He waved to the port *gendarme* who was content to let him pass. The Citroen picked up as it mounted the gradient beyond the village. Despite the unwelcome dark with no familiar signs to help his navigation. Yet Bertrand was confident he would locate the drop-down spot that led to the beach where he and his siblings had once bathed as children. In any case, Hugues had entrusted him with the whereabouts of the safe house, at the top of the cliff.

Parking his truck, Bertrand thrust Bimperl into his pocket and started down the old smugglers' path. He tumbled awkwardly when clouds obscured the moon but struggled back on his feet, determined to make contact with the escape group.

'They're out there, somewhere,' he thought desperately. 'All I can do is keep my eyes sharp and hope for a signal exchange.'

It was at that moment that the moonlight fell on an object crumbled on the tideline of washed ashore seaweeds. He froze on the spot. A body? Crouching low, he crept up to the still shape. Bertrand's heart raced. He knelt down, maintaining a sharp look-out for danger. Other than the rhythmic wash of the incoming tide, an ominous silence pervaded the gruesome scene. Bertrand turned the head of the corpse to one side. A thin line of blood congealed over the lower lip. The soft rays of the moon illuminated a young man's face, eyes wide open and frozen with shock. Bertrand gulped, fighting hard to prevent himself from vomiting. It was Hugues!

He looked away but the stoic fighter in him rose to the fore. There was no purpose spending even precious seconds on the body. It was his own life that was now in peril and he sensed evil lurking in the dark surrounds. The murderer might be watching him from behind the nearest gorse bushes. With no means to defend himself, Bertrand got to his feet. He feared an assault, at any moment, but sensed safety lay in reaching the protection of the scattered rocks. Step by step, he clambered clumsily over the first line of low rocks and spotted a massive boulder fallen from the cliff face.

Bertrand flattened himself on the wet sand and crawled, crabwise, to the inviting shelter. His hands scraped against razor-sharp barnacles. Letting go, he lost his balance and his left knee and thigh slipped into a rock pool. Soaked through, he cursed and crawled round to the other side of the intrusion, hoping he was not being followed. There was no telling if the murderer had departed the scene. Caution ruled Bertrand's every move. Little by little, he grappled his way towards the incoming tide, his dark form merging with treacherous stretches of dark wracks.

Was that a light? Brief white flashes from out in the bay. It was answered by a beach signal away to his left, little more than fifty metres away. Just for a moment, Bertrand caught the huddled outline of the torch bearer and two smaller forms at his side. Could it be Heinrich and the children? Or was it a trap? A false messenger luring the innocent dinghy to unexpected arrest?

He decided to wait for the next communication. The interval passed like an eternity before a second sea signal flashed across the water. Nearer this time. It received an instant response from the shore, granting Bertrand a brief opportunity to work out the shapes of the senders. His heart was in his mouth. He had no choice but to risk crawling across to the beach signaller. If the enemy had taken control of the beach reception, Bertrand could at least shout out a warning to the boat. If the torch flasher was genuine, then the take-off would go ahead as planned. His mind flashed back to the murdered Hugues. He desperately wanted to contact Bastien up on the headland but had no method of contact.

Further stabs of light from the approaching dinghy. The answering response from the beach momentarily lit up the skeleton of an abandoned fishing smack. There was no choice. Bertrand raised his cumbersome, middle-aged form and crawled over to the spot where the light had last flashed. He took the plunge and called out.

'Who are you? Identify yourselves. It's me…Bertrand!'

He held his breath and waited for a response. It came immediately in a broken French/Viennese accent.

'*Bertrand? Ist vous? Je m'appelle Heinrich! Ist moi!*'

The organ maker crawled his way over the final stretch of rock to join his friends. There was no time for greetings. He pushed his hand deep into his pocket and pulled out Bimperl before handing him over to a shocked Sura. She hugged her inseparable companion to her breast. Bertrand indicated that she should undo two of her blouse buttons and keep Bimperl safe. She did as she was told. Heinrich caught on, immediately, and told the little girl to make sure she did not neglect Bimperl a second time.

The tide lapped only thirty metres or so from the fishing wreck. A light flashed close in. Heinrich made out a tiny rowing boat, crewed by two burly fellows stroking muffled oars.

'*Venez!*'

He urged the children to follow him. They clambered over the jagged rocks, slipping and grazing their knees. Plunging up to their waists, Sura and Johan were grabbed by strong hands and hauled into the tiny rescue dinghy. The craft threatened to capsize as a dark figure jumped off the other side and headed for the shore. Staggering under the weight of heavy equipment, the French agent ran for the cover of the rocks, disappearing into the night.

Heinrich hesitated. He had ignored his friend. Turning away from the sea, he called back to Bertrand. A shot rang out followed by an agonised cry echoing around the enclosed cove. The young Austrian recognised the voice. Defying the pleadings of the oarsmen, eager to get off the beach, he pushed the small dinghy back into the waves.

'*Allez!*' he commanded. '*Allez vite!*'

His mind raced.

'Sura…get Bimperl to the British. There's a message inside his tummy!'

He turned away plunged back through the swirling waters.

'*Tell them…the British. D'you understand? Promise!*'

The boat backed off, skilfully turned by rowers who headed back to the waiting crabber. A child's anguished cry carried on the wind. Heinrich splashed back to the shoreline. The clouds let enough light through to identify the spot where Bertrand lay groaning. A torch flashed on, dazzling Heinrich's eyes. Blinking in its glare, he saw the bearer held a gun in his other hand.

'I'm sorry, Heinrich, but your little French adventure is at an end!'

The words made no sense to Heinrich although he recognised the voice.

'Yes,' the gunman confirmed. '*C'est moi! Bastien!* Stay where you are and don't move.'

Heinrich required no translation. He watched in despair as the *collaborateur* lowered his weapon and pointed his weapon directly at Bertrand Dewynter's temple.

'The old fool's a menace. He deserves to die.'

Bastien prepared to pull the trigger. In a flash, Heinrich remembered Hugues' pistol in his jacket pocket. He slipped the safety catch and levelled his aim at Bastien's ribs. The sharp report of the shot echoed off the rocks. Bastien coughed and collapsed, slumping into the nearest rock pool. Heinrich had killed his first opponent in the war. He hurried over to Bertrand who was still breathing but deeply shocked. The old man managed to point to his left arm. Heinrich whipped off his own jacket and tore at his shirt. He then wound the strip tightly round Bertrand's wounded limb. Pulling him up on his good side, Heinrich lost no time in dragging his French comrade away from the fatal spot.

'Keep going, Bertrand!' he shouted in his own language. 'You can do it. I'll get you back. Don't give up!'

Nearer to the land, three torch lights flashed on. Over the sounds of the waves, Heinrich detected men's harsh voices. The lights were moving away from him and it crossed his mind that he and Bertrand might not necessarily be the immediate targets. He manoeuvred his friend into the shelter of a giant boulder and observed dark silhouettes of crouched, helmeted figures heading over the rocks. The hunters were seeking bigger prey intent on ensnaring the secret agent, whose arrival had been anticipated, even before the smuggling expedition set out from Cornwall.

Heinrich craned his neck round the corner of the protective rock. A hundred metres further on, a platoon of determined soldiers crowded round a focussed pool of artificial light. They hemmed in a lone figure standing with hands raised over his head. Minutes later the German captors, satisfied with their successful night's work, marched off the beach with their prize. The operation had been planned with consummate skill and the fact that minor players had been permitted to escape was of no consequence. What they did not know was that the chief architect of the deadly operation lay dead, face down in a shallow rock pool. Within the hour, his bleeding torso would float up on the tide to be carried further down the rocky coast.

XXVII

The two sea-faring Bretons headed their tiny craft into the heaving waves. Their worst fears were justified. Looking back onto the darkened foreshore they saw, to their dismay, a concentration of lights on one spot. The game was up and the agent they had successively landed never stood a chance. Clearly the Germans had responded to a tip-off. Did this mean a patrol boat would be speeding out to intercept them? There was no option other than row with all their strength towards the brave, little two-masted lugger, running in for the rendezvous.

Sura and Johan huddled in the bottom of the boat, spray spuming over the bows and soaking them. They were stunned by the inexplicable desertion of Heinrich. Why had he abandoned them? A light flashed from less than twenty metres away where the crabbing boat hove to, sheets let out and bows into the wind. Willing hands reached over the gunwale, encouraging the rowers with their hazardous transfer. The children were hauled aboard, unceremoniously, and the dinghy secured at the stern. Urgent Breton voices shouted over the bluffing of the wind.

'Pull in the sheets!'

Both of the crabber's small red-rust sails filled and tightened. The vessel carved into a mounting wave. Standing at his short main mast, skipper Henri urged his tiny crew to increase the distance between themselves and the shoreline.

'I knew it. Wind's getting stronger. Forecasters got it wrong!'

He felt confident that a German patrol boat would be lucky to spot *Emigrant*. In the fleeting moonlight, he recognised the contours and hazards of the bay he knew like the back of his hand. The immediate problem was to navigate Point-de-Pen-Hir, a prominent headland fraught with danger and semi-submerged rocks. Right now, the hazards acted as protectors. A fast pursuit boat with no knowledge of the obstacles stood every chance of foundering.

Henri instructed Jean-Pierre, one of the rowers, to fit up Sura and Johan with heavy jumpers and oilskins. No matter that they were several sizes too large. Huddled on a cross bench the children shivered, too weak to protest as the crabber tacked into the wind. The skipper had already put the earlier disaster out of his mind. He concentrated on the immediate concern of smuggling out the two children. But had he not been told there would be a third passenger for England?

The swell increased as the five metre crabber bucketed up and down in the heavy seas exposed beyond the headland lee. *Emigrant* performed as she had a thousand times before, perfectly designed to handle anything the sea might throw at her. With his Breton sea nose, Henri sensed a severe storm on the way. No matter. The load was light and he had confidence in his two companions and their ability to handle threatening conditions.

The clouds thickened, blanketing both moon and stars.

'Jean-Pierre,' Henri yelled into the howling wind. 'Take in a reef!'

Emigrant heeled over, the angry sea threatening to wash over her port gunwale. The air filled with salt as the tough little lugger bucketed up and down, scaling and descending water mountains but defying the storm. Jean-Pierre lashed the terrified Sura and Johan to the base of the mast before turning to bale out the fast-filling waters. Meanwhile, the skipper fought the tiller, straining with every ounce of strength, to turn the boat into the teeth of the gale. He feared he would be swept back to the shore and dashed on the rocks.

The lugger pitched and rolled. Chilling sea spray struck the roughened cheeks of the sailors who were determined to save both boat and passengers. The contest continued for what seemed to be an eternity. At any moment, the tiny boat might disappear beneath the churning foam stirred by a furious sea god.

'*Mon Dieu!* The mast's going!'

Henri's plaintive shout went unheard but Jean-Pierre and Marcel needed no telling. As the crabber headed up a monstrous wave, the clouds lifted fleetingly to reveal the mainmast cracking in two with the main halyards flying free. Marcel threw himself over the stricken children as the wooden spar above them splintered to be whisked away on the angry waves.

Up on the tiny flimsy fore-mast, the remaining sail hung on, offering the faint hope of steerage to the skipper still wrestling with the tiller. The tussle between sailors and elements continued for a further two hours. Marcel stayed close to the terrified children but continued baling. Henri stuck to his task. Mainmast or no mainmast, he felt confident *Emigrant,* his pride and joy and his father's before him, would ride out the storm. The tumult relented as the winds decreased, causing the waves to moderate with only the occasional monster threatening to catch the skipper out.

As the clouds dispersed, a pale glow appeared above the eastern horizon. The battered crabber's position was well out to sea, all but stranded in the middle of the English Channel. Battered *Emigrant* was a sad sight as Henri coaxed his hardy little craft in a northerly direction. De-masted and losing her crabbing pots, she struggled towards her destination on a westerly wind.

'Ship to starboard!'

Henri stiffened to attention, still hugging the tiller. *Emigrant,* low in the water, did not permit him to get a glance of the vessel Jean-Pierre had spotted with his sharp sea eyes. Henri weighed up the odds. Had they been pursued? Surely not. Not in that storm. But he knew the feared E-boats patrolled the straits between Finisterre and England. Jean-Pierre struggled to keep his footing with no mainmast to cling onto.

'Trawler!' he yelled, indicating the direction with his free arm. 'She's seen us! Heading our way!'

Jean-Pierre was right. Henri caught a brief glance of the vessel. Had they managed to get further across the Channel than he imagined? There was no time to work out his position. The bulky silhouette of an armed trawler appeared out of the darker western horizon. Its strong steel bows plunged towards them, black smoke pouring from its single funnel. As it drew nearer, the crew of *Emigrant* made out the stark image of a single gun on the prow. Faces were visible on the small bridge. The Bretons' hearts leapt. This was no enemy boat but an armed trawler requisitioned by the British Royal Navy.

Henri hove to. Tough seaman that he was, he fought to hold back tears. The other craft cut its speed, slowed to a stop and lay off. Jean-Pierre waved and cheered as he spotted the Royal Ensign fluttering proudly at its mast. The trawler lowered a boat with two men into the last feeble throes of the storm and rowed across to the beleaguered crabber. They tossed over a rope and drew alongside. The hardened trawler men were struck with the sorry sight of two soaked and terror-stricken children. Sura and Johan who were lowered carefully down to them. Jean-Pierre joined them to help them up into the rocking rescue ship. The rowers then returned for Marcel and his stoic captain. The British trawler skipper knew no French whilst Jean-Pierre's smattering of English did not allow for the strong Hartlepool accent. *Emigrant* and its dinghy were taken in tow, bobbing up and down in the wake of the trawler.

Hot tea and chocolate were handed round on the bridge before the traumatised children were taken below to be given dry clothing. The Breton sailors willingly accepted the offered comforts as *HMT Basset* shuddered to the throb of her increased engine revolutions. She turned for her base at protected Portsmouth, more than four hours away. Henri, Jean-Pierre and Marcel found themselves invited back up on the bridge where they shared their fellow sailors' respect. The 460 ton Dog Class trawler ran up to maximum ten knots whilst its radio operator contacted Portsmouth to expect its arrival with passengers.

In the increasing red glow of the rising sun, *HMT Basset* made good headway towards land when suddenly a shout went up.

'Single aircraft...port bow!'

The trawler master issued urgent instructions as the ship geared up for imminent attack. Sailors scurried onto the deck to mount the main gun. Others ran to the two .303 calibre Lewis guns. From his vantage point on the bridge Henri watched in transfixed fascination. His eyes widened as an indeterminate dark speck in the sky swiftly morphed into a menacing aggressor.

'Messerschmidt 110!'

A fighter-bomber! The crew had confronted their deadly opponent before. The twin-engined attacker swooped out of the sky on its run-in. *Basset*'s Lewis guns opened up, blazing a trail of bullets at the assailant.

'Hard to port!'

Basset's master barked out his order in the nick of time. The helmsman swung his wheel hard over and the trawler turned away, thick smoke belching from its stack. Cannon shells fired from the Messerschmidt threw up angry plumes of spray. Henri ducked as a second burst of fire struck the hull of the converted trawler. He gripped onto a hand rail and pulled himself up. The Breton skipper's heart missed a beat as the enemy's bomb bay opened to permit two menacing bombs to head towards them. How could they miss? Henri stood, mesmerised, as they struck the surface merely metres from the stern and disappeared beneath the waves. As the *Luftwaffe* aggressor re-gained height, *Basset*'s Lewis guns trained their fire on its retreat into the clouds. The 110 appeared to suffer minor damage as bits of metal flew off its damaged tail fins to drop into the sea.

'Engine room. Full speed ahead!'

HMT Basset shook, turned back on course and ploughed through the waves. Her gunners remained at their posts but the Messerschmidt's pilot and gunner had already made the decision not to try for a second run. The attack was over in a matter of seconds but the naval vessel's master maintained a sharp watch.

Four hours later, an outline of the sandstone cliffs of Monk's Bay, on the Isle of Wight, appeared over the horizon. The trawler pressed on to approach close to a circular island tower, standing out above the sea surface. Pointed out to sea, its mounted guns had *Basset* in their sights but permitted her to pass, unchallenged. A radio message between ship and defence tower cleared her way to enter closely guarded waters.

As *Basset* continued her final run into Portsmouth, the Breton sailors were intrigued by the sight of a second tower in the midst of the shipping lanes. Standing thirty metres out of the water, its Bofors gun and ready crew were visible from the deck. Sura and Johan, now recovered from their trauma, were taken up on the bridge as honoured guests. They took turns viewing the approaching mainland through ship's binoculars, their first sight of the land of refuge. For the first time in days they were within spitting distance of safety. Pursuit was no longer a possibility. Henri stood between the brother and sister, his weather-roughened hands placed gently on their slight shoulders. He turned and grinned at the English helmsman. The trawler man's concentration lapsed momentarily as he raised a thumb in cheerful greeting.

Sura's imaginative mind inevitably turned back to the night's adventure but most of all to the inexplicable desertion of Heinrich. She could not think why he had opted not to continue with the rescue mission. It had been their most intense moment of vulnerability. She felt for her brother's hand. From now on, it seemed that eight year-old Johan would be the only person in the world she could safely depend on.

XXVIII

The huddled outlines of close-clustered buildings became more defined as the Dog Class trawler made its final approach up Spithead towards the docks to offload its precious passengers. On the starboard side two Royal Navy frigates bustled out on anti-submarine operations. As they steamed past, Johan gazed at them in awe. He had no idea that warships, bristling with gunnery, could be of such dimensions. *Basset* rocked to and fro on the disturbed surface of the frigates' disturbed wake where river met sea.

The trawler ran past The Hard, a tight conglomeration of inns, workshops and businesses fronting the narrow sea entrance to the closely guarded naval base. Coal smoke drifted lazily from blackened chimneys. His young eyes boggled at the towering superstructures and flag displays of tied-up naval vessels. The great yard and city stated its bold intent to take battle to the enemy.

Basset homed in on a pre-arranged landing stage to unload and take on new supplies. Other than a few scrambled hours sleep, there would be no rest for her crew, soon to resume attacks on prowling U-boats. Helped down the gang plank in sailors' clothes several sizes too big, Sura and Johan gripped onto their treasured possessions, Bimperl and Ludwig. These were now their only material contact with the world they had left behind. Skipper Henri, Jean-Pierre and Marcel bid their young passengers emotional goodbyes. They then strode away to assess the damage to the battered hull of their crabbing lugger, detached from *Basset* and tied up to bollards further along the quayside. *Emigrant*'s dinghy was nowhere to be seen.

Two middle-aged women in round-brimmed hats and green-grey buttoned uniforms approached the children. The trawler master saluted them, respectfully.

'Good morning, ladies!' he said. 'Glad they got the radio message through. Two young stowaways on board. Not a word of English between them. Thank God you're here. No idea what to do with them!'

He winked at Sura and Johan.

'We couldn't leave them stranded at sea!' he added cheerfully.

He turned to shake the children's hands in turn.

'Best of luck, youngsters!' he continued, aware they did not understand his words. 'Next time you go sea-bathing make sure you take a change of clothes with you!'

Sura and Johan smiled uncomprehendingly as the gnarled seaman returned to his trawler. Suddenly, they felt very alone. All the people who had rescued them – and their numbers had mounted – could no longer protect them. Now, they stood alone in a foreign country isolated by a language they did not speak. One of the uniformed women bent down kindly and addressed them in a soft voice.

'I'm Austrian born,' she said in their own tongue. 'That's why they selected me. My husband's English. I've lived in this country for nearly twenty years. So welcome to England. This is Mrs Harbutt. We've been asked to look after your welfare. You can call me Mrs Leaming. I've learned it's best not to use the term "*Frau*" over here. Not right now, anyway!'

Sura and Johan gazed at her in astonishment. It seemed, every few days, they were passed from one set of adults to another.

'*Guten morgen, Mis…*' Sura replied.

She stumbled over the pronunciation of the woman's English married title.

Mrs Harbutt proffered her gloved hand.

'How d'you do?' she asked, rather stiffly.

Johan noticed the silver badge on the peak of her hat. It showed the outline of a scarlet crown and the letters 'WVS' in the same colour. Her friend took up the conversation, once more, indicating a black saloon car with another uniformed woman driver sitting at the wheel.

'We've arranged transport for you,' Mrs Leaming explained. 'We'll take you up to our headquarters in the town and find suitable clothes. I expect you'll both be starving. Organising food and clothing is what we're best at!'

The children, struggling to cope with their new circumstances, allowed themselves to be escorted to the car. The woman chauffeur stepped out and opened its doors, inviting them to sit in the back on cracked leather seating.

She was younger than her colleagues with pretty brown curls poking out from under her severe hat.

'*Wielkommen, mein kinder!*'

They were the only German words she knew. She had rehearsed them to herself on the drive to the docks, embarrassed she might fluff her lines when the key moment arrived. Mrs Harbutt slipped alongside the driver whilst Mrs Leaming sat in the back with her new charges. Her native German was slightly rusty but she had little difficulty in communicating with her young charges.

'We'll be taking you up to the church hall to get you kitted out,' she explained, kindly. 'After that, you'll stay with me for a little while. My husband's serving overseas so I'll be glad of the company. I was told you might have relatives here in England but no-one seems to know who they might be, or where they live.'

The saloon jolted over the cobbles of the dockyard road and drove through the strong gates guarded by armed marines. It continued through the busy, narrow streets of the naval area humming with activity. Five minutes later, they pulled up at a side building to a church. The driver got out to help the children and the two ladies went on ahead to announce the presence of the new arrivals. Sura and Johan were ushered into a busy room where several WVS women stood sorting out donated clothes on trestle tables. They chatted noisily as they sifted through the offered garments.

'Follow me!'

Mrs Leaming escorted her new charges to a table at the end of the room on which plates of biscuits and home-made cakes had been laid. A couple of the volunteers stirred large aluminium pots of tea before firmly applying their lids. From their kind expressions, it was clear the children were objects of interest and welcome.

'No doubt our small friends would prefer "pop",' Mrs Leaming suggested, lightly.

She pointed to two large, screw-topped glass bottles each containing brightly coloured, artificial fizzy drinks. The children's eyes shone.

'I don't think they'll like Dandelion and Burdock,' their new friend advised the serving lady. 'Pour them each a glass of orange pop. They can choose whatever they want to eat.'

Sura and Johan soon lost their shyness and tucked into the offered fare. Johan was amused at the sudden appearance of a bright orange stain on his sister's upper lip. He had no idea that he, himself, had developed a similarly-coloured moustache. The children were led into a side room where Mrs Harbutt had assembled a collection of children's clothes that had been washed and ironed. Sura and Johan were invited behind a screen to try things on and encouraged to come out for the ladies' expert approval. It did not take long before both were kitted out with smart-looking outfits that suited them well enough. Mrs Harbutt even offered to run a comb through the children's hair but discovered it caked with salt, a sharp memento of their recent intrepid cross-Channel journey.

When they returned to the car the chauffeur headed towards Copnor, turning off the Stubbington Road, and pulled up in a quiet side street of modest semi-detached Victorian villas.

'Here we are!' Mrs Leaming told the children. 'That's

my house. The one with the white front door and stained glass windows.'

She was pleased to be granted the unexpected opportunity to use the language of her earlier years. Stepping out, the brother and sister clutched onto Bimperl and Ludwig as they were shepherded through the wrought iron front gate and up the small path to the entrance. The car drove away leaving the two ladies and the children on the front door step. Mrs Leaming inserted a key into the lock and ushered her new residents inside.

Once settled, it was clear that the exhausted Sura and Johan were dearly in need of sleep. Their Anglo-Austrian landlady showed them the way, upstairs, to a back room containing a pair of matching single beds.

'Oh dear!' she said. 'In the rush, we forgot to look out night clothes. Not to worry, we can pop back to the church, tomorrow, and find pyjamas for you both!'

Neither Sura nor Johan were in the least concerned about the lack of nightwear. It was a little bit like being home, again. They sensed a safe presence that had been absent on their precipitous adventure, half way across Europe.

As evening drew in, Mrs Leaming ventured quietly up the stairs suspecting her young guests would still be sound asleep. Knocking quietly and entering on tip-toe she took in the sight of two refugee children making up for the hours of rest they had previously been denied. She thought of her own children, likewise a son and daughter. The boy had won a University award whilst the girl was half way through nurse-training at Southampton. Her eye was caught by the sight of Bimperl, Sura's beloved dog, fallen on the rug by the bedside. She bent down to pick him up but, as she did so, her sharp eyes were drawn to crude stitching across the belly of the cuddly toy. Sura stirred.

'Where am I?'

She sat up and rubbed sleep out of her eyes. Mrs Leaming perched on the side of the bed and handed Bimperl to her.

'You're in England, my dear. Your brother's with you. All's safe and well.'

'Where's Heinrich?'

Mrs Leaming looked up, sharply.

'Heinrich? Is he a friend?'

Sura came to, slowly.

'Yes,' she said in a whisper. 'He's our best friend. But he didn't come with us. We don't know what happened to him.'

Their new carer felt at a loss and handed the little girl her toy dog.

'Here!' she said. 'He slipped onto the floor so I picked him up. Looking at the stitches in his tummy he seems to have been in hospital, recently!'

Sura grasped Bimperl to her breast. Suddenly, she remembered Heinrich's urgent instruction in the dark, churning waves on the Breton beach.

'Bimperl's very brave!' she said. 'Heinrich said we had to show him to someone in England. There's a message inside his tummy!'

Johan was now awake.

'A French lady sewed something inside Bimperl,' he joined in. 'We heard her say the British would be interested. We didn't understand.'

Mrs Leaming looked a little crestfallen.

'Why Bimperl?'

She excused herself and went into the bathroom to fetch a pair of sharp nail scissors. When she returned, the two children were sitting up in their beds looking better for their much needed sleep. She approached the subject with some delicacy.

'Sura, with your permission...are you saying we should take a look inside Bimperl's tummy?'

The young girl pulled a face, but agreed and handed over her precious dog.

'I'll be as gentle as I can possibly be,' Mrs Leaming assured her.

With the greatest care, she snipped skilfully at the stitching. Sura and Johan looked on. As the incision grew, it became obvious to Mrs Leaming that something had been deliberately sewn into the small toy. She snipped neatly through the remaining stitches and held back the sides of the material.

'Good heavens!' she exclaimed. 'What have we here?'

She eased out a rather bedraggled-looking scrap of folded paper. Turning on the bedside light, she unravelled the note to find words written in pencil. Clearly, the paper had suffered the trials of the sea crossing and details were hard to make out.

'Heinrich Joseph Müller,' she read. '...Grenadier. I think that's what it says. And regiment details, possibly. Then there's a number...a long number. I don't think it's to do with the telephone.'

She gasped and held her hand to her mouth.

'Oh my goodness! It's written in German although the wording's rather faded.'

Sura interrupted as she struggled to read the contents.

'Heinrich was our friend,' she said. 'I told you about him. He wrote the message on the French barge.'

Mrs Leaming shook her head. She felt inadequate, quite unable to deal with this new situation.

'French barge?' she enquired incredulously. 'They told me you started out on a small fishing boat.'

Johan tried to help her.

'That was later,' he said. 'When we escaped from the train in France, Sura and I got lost in the dark.'

The Portsmouth WVS woman felt increasingly out of her depth. She re-read the words again in the attempt to comprehend the faint, pencilled wording.

'*Urgent. Pass on to British authorities. Repeat urgent. Hitler plans to attack Soviet Russia. Word of Reichmarschall Hermann Goering. Berghof. June 1940.*'

The normally phlegmatic citizen volunteer struggled to make sense of what was happening around her.

'Hermann Goering?' she said, disbelievingly. '*The* Hermann Goering? Even *I've* heard of him!'

'Yes!' Sura responded, brightly. 'We met him. He's quite nice, really. He liked our music and we gave him flowers at the station!'

Lost in a greater state of confusion, Mrs Leaming attempted to calm herself. She placed the small piece of crumpled paper on the bedcover. Her eye caught a faint splash of colour further inside Bimperl's unstitched midriff.

'I suspect there's something else hidden inside your little friend.'

With nimble but shaking fingers, she gently teased out a rectangular, coloured ribbon from the stuffing. To her astonishment it was attached to a small iron cross. She found herself gaping at the hated swastika emblem at its centre. Mrs Leaming shrank back and dropped the object on the floor. Against her will, she retrieved the cross and battle ribbon and laid them out on the bed then coughed to clear her throat.

'Have either of you seen this, before?' she asked.

The children laughed.

'Of course we have!!' Johan replied, spiritedly. 'It's Heinrich's *Ritterkreuze*. He won it in Poland being brave. But he's not a soldier, any more. He said he wasn't any good at it. And then he got wounded…'

'In the shoulder,' Sura interpolated. 'That's why he couldn't play his violin.'

Mrs Leaming sat speechless but there was more to come. Johan took up the confusing narrative.

'The *Führer* gave it to him,' he said. 'Pinned it on his chest. We were there. At the concert. The *Führer*, himself!'

Sura confirmed the story. Her expression darkened.

'So we want to know what happened to Heinrich. He did his best to help us on the train. We think he's the bravest person in the world.'

Sura stifled a sniff. Helga Leaming, born in southern Austria and married to a serving British soldier, craved for the support of her absent husband. She stood up slowly. Somewhat against her natural inclination, she picked up the military decoration and its puzzling, accompanying message.

'I'm happy for you two to get up when you like,' she said quietly. 'Don't hurry, my dears. Come downstairs when you're ready. I haven't introduced you to my cat, Lily. You'll like her. She's a tortoiseshell.'

In her confusion, it was all she could think of saying. Suddenly, an idea struck her and she excused herself.

'I think I should make a phone call, if you don't mind. The only problem is that I don't really know who to!'

XXIX

Eleanor Harbutt was a sensible woman. Married to a senior officer in the Hampshire Police Constabulary, she was the first person friends turned to in times of need. However, when the phone rang shortly after her return home, she was surprised to find her friend Helga on the line. Further, that her WVS colleague appeared agitated. Struggling to half-grasp the import of Helga's whispered words, she warned her friend to say no more.

'People might be listening, my dear. We can't be too careful. Goodness knows what you have in your possession. It may be utter nonsense. And probably is,' she added. 'Nevertheless, I'll contact George, at Headquarters, and seek his advice.'

Eleanor Harbutt was as good as her word. At first, her stolid husband was inclined to discount any possibility of a message being sent from the heart of the German *Reich*. Nevertheless, his policeman's instinct told him he would be advised to raise the matter with his superiors. Two hours later, he contacted Mrs Leaming, direct.

'Helga…it's George…Eleanor's husband. Please listen carefully. I can't say much…orders! Expect the arrival of someone from London, in the morning. He'll be on the first train down to Portsmouth. Whatever you do, don't discuss this matter with another soul. Not even these children staying with you. It may all be a cock and bull story but the security people are sending someone to investigate. That's all I can tell you.'

He did his best to reassure his wife's old friend.

'I'm authorising an overnight armed guard on your house. Front and rear. A sergeant will arrive and identify himself within the hour. Just stay calm. That's all. Good night!'

Helga was astounded. Stay calm? A security official from London? The thought of having an armed guard outside her small house filled her with new anxiety. Did it mean the children were under some kind of threat? Her anxious mind swirled with wild thoughts. Johan intervened.

'I like your cat,' he said, chirpily. 'What's his name?'

It seemed to Helga she was living in parallel universes.

'My cat? Oh…er…Lily, actually. She's a "she"! Lily loves being stroked under the chin.'

Sura joined her brother and was immediately won over by the contented purring of the tortoiseshell pet commanding her regular spot on Helga's sitting room sofa. Her chosen position was within close range of the heat generated by the brightly burning coal fire in the hearth.

'You must forgive me,' Helga told the children. 'All this has come as a bit of a shock. I'm afraid I don't have any toys. I don't suppose books will be much use to you. But if you look in my front room you might find something in the far corner between the piano and the window. Some of Beth and Donald's old stuff might be there.'

Lily decided she had received sufficient attention and jumped off the sofa to cosy up to the fire guard. She curled up into a snug ball and closed her eyes. Sura followed Johan out of the sitting room. Almost immediately, Helga was surprised by an excited, loud whooping sound. Johan came hurtling back into the sitting room.

'You've got a piano!' he cried. 'A real piano. Can we play it? Have you got any music?'

Helga hurried into her formal front room to find Sura lifting the lid, about to try out a few notes.

'It's a Brimsmead upright,' Helga told them, although unsure of her reason. 'I have it tuned twice a year. My tuner gets cross with me because he says I should try to keep it at an even temperature. My husband and I only use this room in the warmer months.'

She turned a little stern.

'I don't mind you playing with it but please don't lift the keys up, or hammer them too hard. It's not a toy!'

The Brimsmead was her husband's pride and joy. Helga's daughter had taken her grades on it.

'Just handle it gently,' she urged. 'I don't want it damaged.'

Johan had already lifted the lid of the accompanying stool to sift through assorted music stacked neatly inside.

'Ah! *Rosamünde*,' he pronounced, opening the cover and passing it to his sister. 'Austrian edition!'

Sura adjusted the height of the stool. Then, delicate hands arched over the keys, she began to play the opening page. Her new carer knew enough about music to recognise the child's confident, musical touch. Johan stood to one side and slightly behind his sister to turn the pages. Helga Leaming listened in astonishment, enchanted by Sura's fluency. There was not one note out of place. It was as though a teacher had set Sura the piece, the week before, and asked her to perfect it before the next lesson.

The impromptu performance was interrupted by a loud knock on the outer door. Helga begged to be excused. As she hurried into her small entrance hall, she noted through the stained glass the bulky, helmeted figure of a policeman. She opened the door and invited him inside.

'Good evening, ma'am! Sergeant Petley from your local station. Sorry to disturb you but I think you'll know what this is about?'

The sergeant adjusted the cape round his shoulders and indicated to a younger, thin-faced policeman, hovering at the gate. Large torches hung from their belts.

'That's my colleague, P C Hobbs. Sensible lad. He'll be wanting to take a look round outside. Is the side gate open?'

Over the next few minutes, Helga found herself brewing tea for the policemen whilst listening to the strains of extraordinary music streaming from the front room. Sergeant Petley commented favourably but lost no time in getting down to business.

'Suggest you close the curtains in that room, ma'am, if the children are going to have a go on your piano. The constable and I will patrol, front and back. We'll be very discreet. Funny old world. Can't imagine why anyone would wish to harm a couple of kids. I gather they're not related to you?'

Helga attempted to explain the position.

'Sura and Johan,' she said. 'I've no idea how long they'll be here. We only met, yesterday, down at the docks. I'm really not sure I'm up to all this.'

The sergeant smiled. He removed his helmet to sip the sweet tea offered.

'You're doing fine,' he said. 'I must ask you to make sure you keep those noisy little blighters inside and away from windows. Well…no time like the present. Best start our watch. You've got a telephone, I understand? I don't think my whistle will be much use up here.'

Helga closed the front door quietly behind the policeman and returned to her front room. The piano playing continued. But she was surprised to find young Johan had taken over from his sister. His small hands flew over the keys, ending together with the three rallentando chords of the finale. He turned round and grinned at his admiring audience.

'Mozart!' he announced. 'We used to live near his house in Salzburg!'

All of a sudden, the child broke down in tears. Sura threw a sisterly arm round her distraught brother. Helga felt an instantaneous pang of motherly love. She dashed forward to comfort the children, aware that Sura was holding back her emotions. But it all flooded out. For the next hour or so, the three individuals clasped onto each other as the tearful story of the extraordinary journey unfolded in bits and pieces.

Helga suggested they moved to the back room to the cheering warmth of the fire. She made a hot chocolate drink for Sura and Johan who sat with Lily purring between them.

'When are we going to see Mummy and Daddy again?' Johan wailed. 'When are they coming?'

The WVS woman from Portsmouth could offer no answer. She found Sura's doubts even more disturbing.

'Mummy and Daddy told us we couldn't stay as Salzburg was getting horrible for people like us. At school, some of the children called us "*Juden*". They teased us. Daddy said it would be better to go to England to our aunt.'

Helga cottoned onto Sura's remark.

'You have an aunt in England? D'you know where she lives?'

Sura shook her head.

'London, I think. Or somewhere near London. Heinrich has the details. He was supposed to take us to her. But…'

She broke down in a further fit of tears.

'What's going to happen to us?'

Helga Leaming's brain raced. She was beginning to piece together the separate pieces of a metaphorical jig-saw. The truth dawned. These very talented children hailed from an Austrian-Jewish family. Their parents had taken the decision to arrange for their escape. Did they hope to follow?

Helga had followed the developing political situation in her native land as best she could. There was surely no chance, whatsoever, that the parents could get out of the tight *Nazi* grip. In effect, the children were orphans. They had no parents to care for them and no near contact. Only Britain offered sanctuary. Over the wireless, before the start of the war, she had heard about *kindertransport* from Germany and Austria. Sura and Johan were now refugees with no home. What was to be done? There might be a

Jewish organisation she could contact. But would they be able to find the whereabouts of the children's relative, living 'somewhere near London'?

Tucking Sura and Johan into their beds with Ludwig and the re-stitched Bimperl, a deep thought entered Helga's moral mind. She hesitated. Before committing herself it might be advisable to discuss the matter with Eleanor, in the morning. If only her husband could be at her side and not stationed in India. She shepherded the children to her daughter's old bedroom. Beth used it only rarely on fleeting visits home. But if the truth were to be told, Helga Leaming had already come to a firm decision, not of the mind but her heart. She knew she had no need of well-meaning advice from family or friends.

Quietly re-ascending the stairs, she opened the children's door to no more than a crack. Helga remained outside, eyes filling with happy tears. Gently blowing the children kisses she closed the door and went downstairs again. Lily had jumped back to her sofa command spot.

'Well, my old friend,' she said, dabbing her moist eyes with a handkerchief, 'I think you're going to have to share your home with two new friends.'

A contented smile spread over her kindly face.

'Sura and her brother may be here for some time!'

XXX

Latchmere House, built in the early nineteenth century by an English entrepreneur, lay close to Ham Common, on the outreaches of South West London. Behind a high, forbidding brick wall, the mansion dominated large grounds. Plain and unprepossessing in its design, the sloping, grey slate roofs and chimneys were easily visible from the road. At his grand, mahogany desk, Lt Colonel Robin Stephens sat fuming. Known for his quick temper and intolerance, he adjusted the monocle in his right eye and swept his hands over immaculately combed and plastered hair. He got up and shouted at the private soldier dealing with matters in his outer office.

'Stones…get Captain Short in here at once…if he's still here!'

The Private jumped to attention and picked up the phone. Stephens stormed over to the window and gazed out on the lawns.

'No bloody organisation,' he fumed. 'Only established in this God-forsaken place five minutes and they expect us to run it like an established grocery store in the High Street!'

He went back to his desk and looked again at the paper that most recently graced the in-tray. Colonel Stephens addressed the passive walls of his new headquarters.

'What kind of nonsense is this? Some account of a failed attempt to run one of our trained agents into France? Then the moronic French compound their folly and fail to pick up an agent on his way to us!'

His assistant tapped on the open door and timidly entered.

'Captain Short's on his way, sir. He was just about to leave.'

Private Stones heard light footsteps hurrying over the hard, wooden floor of the outer office and stiffened to a salute.

'Cap'n Short, sir!'

Leaving his two superiors to themselves, the young man closed the door behind him and sank down on his hard seat.

'God almighty!' he whispered. 'Old *Tin-Eye*'s been in a right mood, all day. What gets into him? God help the Captain.'

Colonel Stephens' explosive mood cooled as swiftly as it had boiled.

'Short, my dear fellow! Sorry to delay. I need to chew something over with you. Appreciate your angle…that sort of thing.'

Captain Short, squat, round and owlish in appearance greeted his mercurial superior with uncertain *bonhomie*. The two men were complete opposites. Short's naturally pleasant nature had a calming effect upon the Colonel. The two represented both sides of the same coin, with each contributing equally to a productive relationship. Short was invited to take a seat.

'Whisky?'

He assented and asked that it could be watered.

'Problem, sir?'

Stephens strode across to the large, plain window.

'Take a look at that paper in my tray, Short. Just received the thing from SOE. "*Special Operations Overseas,*" as they call themselves.'

He snorted.

"*Botched Operations Overseas*" more like it. I'll be brief. They've got themselves into the business of running agents into France. The Calais crossing's out so they've picked some unheard of spot in Brittany. The PM's backing them. You know what Churchill's like. He wants every bit of information they can pick up on the Invasion.'

He gulped his whisky.

'We all know it's coming.'

Captain Short scrutinised the paper in the light of a shaded desk lamp. The Report marked '*Top Secret*' attempted to provide a garbled version of the recent drop-off failure close to Camaret-sur-Mer. He shivered at the thought of a newly-trained agent suffering capture the moment he set foot upon the Breton shore. Looking up, Short ventured to break the Colonel's animated flow.

'Bad news, sir! The Jerries must have been waiting for the poor sod. Mission blown…which means only one thing. SOE's local ring is penetrated. God help the agent fellow. Shot already I expect.'

Colonel Stephens turned back from the window.

'He won't be the only one. They'll be making arrests left, right and centre. But just as bad...the Froggies failed to pick up a contact the French *Résistance* was sending our way. We'd been tipped off about it. Extraordinary business. Some gobbledegook about a German deserter willing to talk. Carried information but not about the Invasion. Claimed access to Hitler's innermost secrets. Load of poppycock if you ask me!'

Colonel Stephens resumed his seat, his glass now half empty. His deputy tried to take stock of the situation.

'D'you think it might have been a fix, sir? A smart way of finding out the time and route of the SOE drop?'

His thinking moved on.

'Sounds suspicious to me! I'd be more convinced if this so-called deserter had made it to our shores. At least we could have had a crack at him...we've got all our facilities, here. Softly, softly catchee monkey.'

His boss agreed.

'Softly, softly's the best way. It should be our Camp 020 motto,' he said. 'I've spent half the day fighting off the Home Office. They want us to declare our existence to the International Red Cross. I bloody well refused. We've got three Kraut spies in our cells, right now. Next thing, we'll be expected to hand out food parcels to the buggers. And letters back home, I suppose...

> "*Dear Mother. Don't worry about me. I'm in good hands and the British are very kind. It's a shame you can't visit me here, in Ham. Please send Bratwürst. Your loving son, Hans!*"

Captain Short choked on his drink. His boss operated on a fuse only millimetres in length but fought hard to preserve the anonymity of Camp 020 whose spare rooms were filling with captured *Reich* spies. Between them, the two Intelligence officers had worked out a method of interrogation. Despite his bluster, Stephens had successfully initiated a subtle approach to gain prisoners' confidences. After confession, they could be sent for hanging.

'There's something I don't get in this SOE message,' the Colonel continued. 'It mentions two young children were picked up instead of the so-called agent. Austrians, apparently. Jewish origin. Don't see the connection. They were brought across the Channel in a crabbing boat that got rescued in a storm. Now, they're holed up in God-forsaken Portsmouth.'

The Colonel came to the point.

'The Hants Police tell us these children possess some kind of "crucial message" for us. Can you believe that? This Kraut deserter chap ducks out or gets killed but still manages to set up a couple of kids to bring over priceless information!'

Captain Short could not help but smile. It was the sort of stuff he had once read in Boys' Own Magazine.

'A likely one, sir!' he joked. 'May I go home now? My good lady's cooking something special. Shepherd's pie, she said. I'll get it in the neck if I spoil her good efforts!'

The boss of Camp 020 looked him straight in the face.

'Of course! But get to bed early because I want you on the new electric train service to Portsmouth, first thing in the morning. Trains every half an hour from Guildford. Permission to travel First Class!'

His subordinate colleague pulled a face, knowing the Colonel would not take offence.

'You're not serious, sir? Chase off to Portsmouth to interrogate children I've never met? Hardly my line of work. How old are they? I'm not especially good with kids. Not other people's, anyway.'

Captain Short summoned up his courage.

'With respect, I've more important things to do. Right here in 020. I'm just getting through to an agent we picked up near Dungeness. Feel I'm getting somewhere with him. We share things in common. He likes French wines.'

Colonel Stephens raised his hand and asked his subordinate to listen.

'*We* can deal with your new prisoner. There's something odd about this story, Short. There's a funny smell about it. In my nose. Call me ridiculous…it won't be the first time. No…I want you down there if only to eliminate the possibility of it being even slightly relevant. We can't ignore it. That's an order, my dear fellow. "*Old Tin-Eye*" commands!'

The deputy spy inquisitor shook his head, wearily.

'Well, if you say so, sir. But just one thing. My German's improving fast but I need a trained translator with me. I could easily get hold of the wrong end of the stick. There's that Miss Rutter in the typing pool. Naturalised British and fully vetted. She's fluent and might go down better with children than me. To be honest, I'd hardly know where to start.'

The Colonel beamed.

'I haven't told you all,' he said, airily. 'The Hants Police tell us a paper message has been discovered sewn into the tummy…if that's the word…of one of these children's teddy bears, or some such thing. With some kind of Nazi military award.'

He paused to let the information take effect. Captain Short wondered if his leader was beginning to lose his marbles. The Colonel interrupted his deputy's thought process.

'To be more accurate,' the Colonel continued, 'the child's comfort toy isn't a teddy bear but some kind of cuddly dog. Made its way across the English Channel…at night! So don't complain. Take a day out. And enjoy the break. Car to Guildford's booked. I'll speak to the Rutter girl. She's on late duty so I'll send her home, early. She'll travel with you, tomorrow morning. Local Police will meet your train at Portsmouth Station. That's all!'

The two men downed their whiskies. Captain Short bade his superior officer goodnight and walked out to his car, turning over in his head the prospect the next day would bring.

'Ah well,' he pondered. 'At least I'm not going to be late for Janet's shepherd's pie. Tomorrow's another day.'

XXXI

The road journey to Guildford was uneventful. Olga Rutter sat demurely in the rear of the army-requisitioned saloon, her gas mask parked over her knees in case of an air raid. Captain Short felt he owed her an explanation as to why she had suddenly been uprooted from her normal routine.

'Thank you for coming, Miss Rutter. It's an odd business but we're going to need your language skills. One thing I must impress upon you. You're already sworn to secrecy regarding your work at 020. Whatever unfolds today must *never* be divulged. You know the rest so I say no more.'

He briefly outlined the mission, playing down its potential significance.

'I suspect it's all a waste of time. But the Boss has decreed so we minions must obey. The important thing is to treat these children with sensitivity. That's where you come in!'

Olga Rutter felt out of her depth.

'I can't possibly see what use I'll be,' she apologised, modestly. 'This is rather above my grade but I'll try to do whatever you require, sir.'

The brand new 4COR Southern Railway electric express made light work of the taxing inclines beyond Guildford. Secretly, Captain Short regretted the lack of a decent steam locomotive at the helm but he conceded the recently introduced electrics made light work of the gradients. Likewise, he was impressed with the comfort of the seats of the First Class compartment.

'The buffet's just along the corridor. We're too early for lunch but they'll offer a light snack, no doubt. Don't forget your mask. Tea or coffee?'

Travelling First Class was a novel experience for the young typist. She was more than happy to indulge in the luxury and put it down to experience. The train made good time to Haslemere before continuing its final run down to the South Coast. As the first signs of conurbation swept by, Olga assumed the journey was nearly complete.

'So smooth!' Captain Short commented. 'No puffing and panting. I might get used to it, in time, but I miss the smell of good coal smoke! By the way,' he added, placing his bowler hat carefully over his brow, 'from now on you refer to me as "Mr Davidson." I'm something at the Home Office, largely to do with child welfare. You'll be my assistant…a Miss Parker. I'm sure you'll be able to cope with that?'

Olga Rutter/Parker giggled and assured the Captain she would do her best to play her part. At the grand station of Portsmouth and Southsea, an unmarked police car awaited the passengers from London. Its driver checked their identities before showing them to their seats, unaware of the significance of the owlish gentleman in buttoned raincoat and bowler. Only the black umbrella was missing.

'It'll take about ten minutes, Mr Davidson,' he said. 'Not far. Be there in a jiffy!'

The car purred away from the splendid frontage of Portsmouth's sand-bagged main station. Traffic was sparse and the visitors were soon alighting at the correct address. To their surprise, a Police Sergeant answered the bell. He, too, demanded to see their papers. 'Mr Davidson' declined.

'I don't think so, Sergeant. I think you already know we've been sent down by the Home Office. The welfare of the children is at stake.'

Sergeant Petley gave the man from the Ministry a knowing look.

'I understand, sir. Whatever you say, Mr Davidson. This way.'

He introduced the new arrivals to Mrs Leaming who stood nervously in her hallway, unsure of her role. Very sensibly she suggested tea.

'You'll be wanting to meet Sura and Johan,' she said. 'Do come in and I'll introduce you. Does one of you speak German?'

Mr Davidson reassured her that his female assistant spoke the language like a native and all would be well. Sura and Johan sat apprehensively on the sofa. Lily perched on Johan's lap. He fingered her furry neck during the introductions. Both children relaxed upon discovering the unassuming lady visitor spoke their own tongue. Miss Rutter assured them they had nothing to fear.

Meanwhile, refreshments were introduced by Mrs Leaming who subtly closed the door behind her and went back to her kitchen. Mr Davidson spoke first.

'We're very pleased to meet you both!'

The children relaxed as the skilled inquisitor gently took them through their journey of several days and nights, strange locations and hair-raising events. He established the initial meeting between themselves and Heinrich Müller. Using Miss Rutter's subtle abilities, he soon confirmed Sura and Johan had, indeed, found themselves at the epicentre of the *Nazi* political machine. After about three quarters of an hour, he suggested a break. It granted the opportunity for the children to relax a little whilst he felt the need to consider what he had learned thus far.

'You'll excuse me,' he said. 'Miss Parker, would you be kind enough to ask Mrs Leaming to pop in? I suggest we reconvene in three quarters of an hour.'

Helga Leaming was ahead of the game. On her kitchen table lay a spread of sandwiches with thin slices of cold beef, Spam meat as an alternative and salads. Miss Parker and the children sat down at the table whilst Mr Davidson donned mackintosh and bowler and took his leave. He had a quiet word with the Sergeant who was about to be replaced on duty and strolled off down the quiet suburban street.

It was all very puzzling. The authenticity of the children's story was unassailable and he was not prepared to challenge it. He even accepted their account of the concert and medal award ceremony at Hitler's Berghof. Mr Davidson had taken particular trouble to enquire about the alleged clandestine journey on Goering's *sonderzug*. Once more, the story held up. Before they broke for lunch, he had taken the children through the escape, in some detail. It seemed they had saved the young Austrian soldier's life seconds before he was about to be executed by the French resistors. None of this could have been rehearsed or orchestrated. The young man had somehow made contact with the *Résistance,* in Normandy. Was this a ruse? Did he have it mind, all along? In one way, it seemed he did but the plan had not worked out. It raised a doubt in his convoluted mind.

Mr Davidson found himself at the gates of a small suburban park. He wandered along the winding path to find a bench to sit on. Bit by bit, he planned his questioning for the post-lunch session, aware that he must not over-stress the children. On his way back to the house, it occurred to him that the final leg across the Channel to England, allegedly planned by Heinrich Müller, had also not worked out. The actual crossing had been made, days later, in far away Brittany. Was this significant? Only the children could provide the answers. As he turned into the street, a thought struck him forcibly. Colonel Stephens was wrong! *This story was not poppycock.* The children were not capable of such invention. Thus, there was a stark choice. Either the role of Müller was honestly-motivated or the children had been cleverly hooked into a brilliant *Nazi* plot.

Was Hitler planning a peace deal with Britain to take her out of the war on reasonable terms? The Intelligence Officer was only too aware of individuals highly placed in the Government and high society who were prepared placate the *Führer,* at the drop of a hat. Lord Rothermere of *The Daily Mail,* for instance, and Foreign Secretary Lord Halifax. It was rumoured that *Nazi* sympathisers ran higher up the social scale, even to members of the Royal Family.

It was a cunning scheme! If Hitler could make peace and cease hostilities with British and Empire forces he would be freed up to turn his ambitions East and attack the Russians. What a get-out for the British! They could treaty with the German Regime whilst continuing to rule a world Empire, unmolested. It placed the *Nazi* regime in an ideal political position to counter the inevitable Marxist threat to world capitalism. Imperial Britain would retain its global interests on the understanding that they would not oppose *Nazi* aims to conquer the prize of the fertile plains of Eastern Europe. Potentially, there were other gains. For instance, the rich Romanian oil fields and total take-over of the Soviets' manufacturing industries. All to Hitler's advantage and his crazed droolings of a *Reich* to last a thousand years.

'My God!'

Captain Short, alias Mr Davidson, found himself in the biggest quandary of his life. He turned into the short garden path of Mrs Leaming's residence aware that the second part of the children's account was yet to be revealed. A young policeman stood at the door. He had been properly briefed and knew to let Mr Davidson into the house.

Over the course of the next hour, the inquisitor gently guided Sura and Johan through the final episodes of the adventure. The story appeared to get increasingly bizarre. Escape from a French canal barge in an organ maker's Citroen truck. Children hiding beneath the pipes and spending a night in the dark crypt of a cathedral. The very strange matter of Heinrich Müller sharing the driver's cab with an organ specialist and their arrival in Brittany to be secreted in a safe *Résistance* house. Finally, he listened intently to what the children could tell him of the dramatic last seconds on the wild Breton beach. Clearly, they had expected Müller to get on the boat yet he had spurned the chance. For some reason the fellow had turned away and splashed his way back to the shore.

'Sura, tell me,' Mr Davidson said gently. 'Tell me about your little friend…Bimperl?'

The little girl was happy to co-operate.

'Oh, he's fine, now,' she told him. 'Since Mrs Leaming mended him. He's got new stitches.'

Mr Davidson asked Miss Parker to pop out to Mrs Leaming and ask her to join them. He also required to examine the stuffed toy. Above all, his attention was centred upon its former contents…the German military gallantry award and the hastily scribbled note. He studied the message, word by word.

'Thank you. You've all been very kind. And wonderfully co-operative. I think we should stop here. Sura and Johan…I can't thank you enough. I really don't know how you came through all this. You're very brave both of you! If I had my way I'd find British military medals for you both!'

He rested his chin on his cupped hand.

'I think you know that not a word must ever be spoken on this matter. It may turn out to be of some considerable importance.'

Mr Davidson took Sura and Johan's hands in his.

'I really mean it, you know. You will promise?'

Despite their limited understanding of the complex situation, the two young Austrians agreed.

'We promise,' they said, in unison.

Mr Davidson stood up and Miss Parker joined him. He expressed his gratitude to Mrs Leaming and all she had done for the children.

'I don't expect we'll meet again,' he said. 'But permit me to say it's been our privilege. We wish you all well.'

Sura stepped in front of him and barred his way to the door.

'You haven't asked about Mummy and Daddy,' she said. 'No-one will say where they are. They told Maria-Anna they'd follow us to England. But we don't know how!'

The sharp Intelligence Officer looked down at her.

'Maria-Anna?' he asked. 'Who's she?'

Sura glanced quickly at Johan.

'She's Heinrich's girlfriend. Well, we think they're in love…'

Johan agreed.

'We saw them kiss! She lives in our city. That's how she met Heinrich.'

Mr Davidson ushered the small party back into the warm room.

'Tell me…this Maria-Anna. She wasn't on the train with you, as well?'

Sura laughed.

'Of course not! She had to stay because Heinrich wouldn't let her come. But he misses her terribly. He said so on the train. It was Maria-Anna who worked out the plan to get us away from Salzburg. Not his. She got very cross with Heinrich when he said her idea of getting us on Herr Goering's train was stupid. They had a row! She told me!'

No-one spoke. In the induced silence, Mr Davidson realised the story had plunged to a deeper level.

'Maria-Anna went to talk to our parents,' Sura said quietly. 'They trusted her and agreed to let us escape.'

The three adults found themselves at a loss for words. Finally, Mr Davidson coughed nervously and took great trouble over his next question. He spoke slowly, carefully selecting his words.

'You say it was *her* idea? Are you *sure* of that? *This is very important.*'

Sura and Johan glanced at each other and mumbled their agreement. Mr Davidson bit his lip.

'This story gets ever more complicated. You're giving me so much to think about I worried that my brain's about to burst!'

His good humour lightened the situation and they all said their farewells. In the drive back to the railway station, the occupants of the car sat in silent thought. Even in the train hardly a word passed between them. Captain Short, his own persona once more, permitted his mind to sift through all the evidence he had to consider. Finally, with the rocking motion of the train, he drifted off to sleep. The subtle interrogator was aroused by Miss Rutter as the London-Portsmouth express braked to pull into its Guildford platform.

'The car's waiting for us beyond the taxi rank,' she informed her mentor. 'It's a lot easier being myself again!'

The good-natured Intelligence Officer was relieved to be back in his normal surroundings.

'That was quite a day, Miss Rutter. But you're to wipe it from your memory. I'll have a word with your section leader.

Your help to me was exemplary and you kept the children very much at ease.'

He placed his hand on her arm.

'Well done!' he said. 'Remember now…not a word. You had to take the day off because you were feeling under the weather.'

They parted company when Miss Rutter got out at the service-supplied digs she shared with two colleagues. Captain Short had further to go to reach home. He speculated on how he should present the evidence to Colonel Stephens, on the morrow.

'I'm sure he'll insist this is a cunningly worked out *Nazi* plot. Brilliant in its execution. Maybe it is but, right now, I simply don't know where I'd put my money. If only it was possible to interview this Müller fellow. So annoying that he never made it across the Channel. If he had, we'd have dragged the truth out of him, one way or another.'

It had been a full day. He turned his key in the front door latch and entered his home. The sound of merry audience laughter boomed from a large wireless speaker in the lounge.

'*ITMA!*' he thought. '*It's That Man Again!* Janet loves Tommy Handley.'

The Captain hung his coat on its hook by the front door and placed his bowler, precisely, on the round hall table. His mind switched back to the course of the day's events.

'Heinrich Müller. Nondescript grenadier yet personally decorated by Adolf Hitler. Is he genuine or just naïve? It doesn't add up. Of course, from what the children told us he's very young. Can he really be in with Goering and Co?

Playing their very dangerous game of international chess? Somehow, goodness knows how, we have to find out.'

He smiled quietly.

'Whoever this Heinrich Müller is we could certainly do with him on *our* side!'

XXXII

Next day dawned clear and bright. Olga Rutter's office friends were pleased to see her back at work. She brushed aside their discreet enquiries, citing a bad headache. Meanwhile, Captain Short got in early, even by his standards, and sat behind his desk pondering the imponderable. It was not long before he received a summons from 'Old Tin-Eye's' lair.

'Ah, there you are, Short! Good trip? Perfect weather for the seaside!'

His deputy smiled, thinly.

'Very good, sir. Lots to talk about. Can't make head or tail of it. Certainly not a waste of time.'

His boss walked over to the French window, pushed it open, and invited the Captain onto the adjoining patio.

'Go for a stroll?' he suggested. 'Start at the beginning and end at the end. Quite simple!'

Captain Short hesitated. Then the two men set out along a gravel path in the direction of the tennis court. Colonel Stephens pre-empted his colleague.

'Surprise me!' he challenged. 'This story's all tommy-rot...or is it? I'd have never packed you off to Portsmouth if I hadn't felt something in my guts. Odd business. My angle is that the Germans have been bloody smart. Thinking about it all night. What's your angle?'

The captain was hardly surprised by his boss's penetrative insight. Despite personality differences, their minds worked alike.

'You may be right,' he said. 'Either that or totally wrong. It's one thing or the other. The children are genuine. Well, they couldn't be otherwise, I suppose.'

The two men walked on in silence. A blackbird sang from a nearby tree.

'I've been doing a bit of my own ferreting,' Tin-Eye informed his colleague. 'You shoot first. Then I'll tell you my slant on this.'

For the next few minutes, the skilled inquisitors toured the grounds. Captain Short took his superior through the whole of the previous day's events and produced the *Ritterkreuze* along with the scrappy note. He pointed out the apparent contradictions and non-sequiturs in the story.

'It twists and turns,' he said. 'Full of contradictions and impossibilities. Like you, I lay awake last night thinking. In the absence of the main protagonist we can't prove a fig. But the children told me something that I hadn't anticipated. *Nazi* plot, or no, they claimed a young girl in Salzburg schemed up the whole wheeze. It's laughable. But those two kids are OK. They wouldn't make it up. It really does seem that their Jewish parents were under threat, like all Jews under occupation. This was the only way out for their children. Crazy! Yet this Heinrich Müller fellow went along with it. He had all the facilities, so it appears. God knows how he managed to bamboozle the Jerries.'

Colonel Stephens looked serious and polished his monocle with a silk handkerchief.

'Right! You've actually told me nothing. We can't prove this thing either way on such scanty evidence. So let me tell you what I've been into, lately.'

His deputy relaxed. At least his boss had not chewed him up, something he had half expected.

'For your ears, only, dear boy!'

Stephens replaced the monocle.

'Been doing a bit of my own research. Fellows at Headquarters jolly helpful. Have you heard of *Otto*? *Operation Otto?*'

Captain Short shook his head.

'You recall the Soviet-German Non-Aggression Pact, signed last year? Gave Hitler the go-ahead to invade Poland. Well, it's not quite that simple. My pal tells me they've had enquiries from Moscow. NKVD boss Pavel Fitin. Nasty bit of work but a worried man. Word is that Hitler's set his generals a task. Massive attack on Moscow before winter sets in, this year. He's looked at the Ruskies' Divisional strength and concluded his lot would wipe the floor with the Red Army.'

Captain Short intervened.

'I thought *we* were the opposition! Certainly feels like it. Invasion in the next few weeks? Don't tell me the madman's thinking of going East at the same time? It's not on!'

His Colonel snorted.

'Word is they think they can win in ten weeks. God knows what the creep's up to, but the Soviet military are taking it seriously. *Operation Otto*...Bob's your uncle!'

He paused.

'Except there's a fly in the ointment. Big fly. Stalin, himself. Refuses to listen and banking on the Treaty. Claims it's all a big Western plot taking in the Yanks. Conspiracy Theory. So he's not taking a blind bit of notice of his Intelligence reports. What d'you think of that?'

It was gargantuan stuff but hard to assimilate. Captain Short struggled to get his head around the swirling, political ramifications. His boss offered more.

'All fits in! Hitler sweeps through Western Europe. Virtually no opposition. Does a deal with the Brits. Turns round the other way and strikes like an adder at the Soviet Union. No point in giving them another year to prepare because they're in a right bloody shambles. The Dictator's sacked half his General Staff and shot most of the best generals. Army's under-equipped and split two ways. One facing Europe; rest facing the Japanese. It's the Japs Stalin most fears, which is why he's got his best troops stationed along the Mongolian border. That's where he feels they'll strike. Hitler's worked that out, cunning sod. So he's planning to attack whilst the going's good. That's the unofficial *spiel*.'

The two men rose from their seat and walked slowly back to the main building. They maintained a silence until they reached the garden entrance to the Colonel's office. He ordered tea.

'By the way, I haven't mentioned a thing around here about *Operation Otto*. Keep it under your hat. But it's for real. It could be our life-saver. I'm going to get this stuff through to the Big Wigs so they can take a look at it.'

Captain Short felt fazed.

'So it looks as though I wasted my time down in Portsmouth, sir? Very small beer compared to what you've just told me. In fact…inconsequential!'

His superior surprised him.

'D'you really think so? Doesn't prove a thing, admittedly, but *corroborates* what the NKVD boys say in Moscow. The really weird thing is that the message your children smuggled over appears to stem very nearly from the horse's mouth. Goering's good enough for me. He's been Hitler's pin-up boy since the *Luftwaffe* demolished the French Air Force. Sun shines out of every orifice!'

Tea was brought into the meeting. Captain Short asked the million dollar question.

'So what do we do now, sir? We can't *sit* on this stuff.'

Colonel Stephens stared hard through the steel-rimmed monocle.

'We're in this together, Short. If we fail to convince our overlords then I'm going to get this material to Churchill, himself. By hook or by crook.'

He broke off.

'By the way, you don't seem to have spotted the fallacy in the story you went off to investigate!'

His deputy wriggled in his chair.

'There are many things I haven't spotted,' he said modestly. 'Tell me!'

Stephens laughed uproariously.

'Go back over the whole tale,' he advised. 'A German

High Command plot? I very much doubt it. They don't have that kind of imagination. My money's on the children's tale!'

Captain Short was intrigued. A week later the two subtle interrogators of Camp 020, top secret outpost of the British Secret Services, were sitting in the recently appointed wartime Prime Minister's Downing Street office. Their superiors had deliberated over the pros and cons of the case and reached a similar conclusion. Winston Churchill sat hunched over his desk, jacket tossed carelessly over a nearby chair. Over the top of his half-glasses he glared at the two visitors before blowing cigar smoke in their direction.

'Make yourselves comfortable, gentlemen. I know the sun's hardly over the yard arm but you'll be taking something stronger than morning coffee, I thoroughly hope?'

Orders were issued and a flunky duly appeared with the required beverages and a double brandy for the PM.

'I've worked through the Report you sent. Fascinating reading but I'll need to put you both through the mill on this one. Never did take prisoners…metaphorically speaking,' he hastily added. 'Now, first I want to see this bit of paper you've brought along with you. Ah! And something else, that gallantry award issued by the Nasties? They'll never give me one!'

He chortled at his own double joke.

'How did you get hold of it, young man? Fire away!'

xxxiii

The Aftermath – October 1945.
Dame Myra Hess sat in her North London garden reflecting on her life over the previous five years. Since her insistence to return to war-ravaged London from the USA, she had worked hard to provide lunchtime concerts to London workers at very low cost. Having been turned down by the BBC, Dame Myra had approached Kenneth Clark, Director of the National Gallery, in Trafalgar Square. Kenneth Clark was only too delighted to re-open the gallery, all its major treasures having been evacuated to safe-keeping in far-flung parts of the country. Its grand rooms stood stripped and bare.

By the cessation of hostilities over eight hundred thousand Londoners, on Mondays to Fridays, had queued at the Gallery. The tickets cost one shilling and granted them access to the world's great music in a time of hardship and despair. Never demanding a professional fee, Dame Myra, one of the world's most renowned interpreters of Mozart, Bach, Schuman and Beethoven, had personally performed in one hundred and fifty Gallery concerts.

The Music of Freedom

In the golden September sunlight, Dame Myra opened a letter stamped with a Portsmouth post mark. An admirer, no doubt. In all likelihood one of her admirers who had enjoyed wartime performances at the National. Its contents took her by surprise,

Dear Dame Myra,
I hesitate to write appreciating how very busy you must be especially now that international concerts are possible once more. I write as a humble piano teacher in Portsmouth and wish to bring to your notice two remarkable young pianists. I have had the privilege of teaching them over the past few weeks following their recent return to Portsmouth. Sura Steaffel (16) and her brother Johan (13) were evacuated along with the resident who has offered them shelter after their flight from Nazi persecution. In order to avoid subsequent blitzing of Portsmouth their carer, a Mrs Leaming, moved up North to Doncaster. She took her Brimsmead piano and was fortunate to find a gifted teacher for the children, a Miss Elsie Werren. (Elsie and I studied at the Royal Academy together.) Even after all these years, no word has come regarding the fate of the children's Austrian parents. It is assumed they lost their lives as a result of the atrocities of the Hitler regime. Johan also plays the violin so brother and sister are able to perform chamber pieces by leading composers. I do hope you will not mind my contacting you but feel certain I have very rare talents in my care. Would it be possible for the children to travel up to London in the half term holiday (they are at school here) and perform for you? I would very much welcome your opinion as I feel that their

gifts should be granted a grander stage than I can provide here in Portsmouth. Please do not imagine I am wasting your time. I would be terribly grateful to hear from you and accordingly enclose a stamped/addressed envelope.

Most sincerely,
Dorothy Martins (Miss) LRAM

The international concert pianist gazed out on the autumn blooms adorning her garden. She smiled. This was not the first time such a request had been made but previous instances had generally involved London-based children. This was different and it interested her.

'Elsie Werren?' she thought to herself. 'I seem to have heard the name. I've heard Doncaster is a musical place. I wonder what drove her away from London?' she speculated. 'The Blitz, possibly?'

Dame Myra acted at once and just over a week later two nervous teenagers, accompanied by their kind adult guardian, Helga Leaming, found themselves on the great lady's doorstep. Each held a leather music case with their most practised pieces. They were made welcome and helped to feel at ease. Dame Myra put them gently through their paces on the fine instrument in her drawing room. The children were enchanted by its fine tone and light touch.

'Fine playing, my dears! Sensitive and musical. I need to hear your Bach. I assume you play him?'

Sura delved into her bag and pulled out a book of *Two-Part Inventions*.

'I don't play Bach that much,' she said, confident in her near fluent English. 'I find him very difficult!'

Dame Myra agreed.

'He's quite awful! Ties my fingers up in knots but I wouldn't be without him. We always start the day together. He sets me up. Then I tackle other things.'

The impromptu concert continued. Both were asked to sight read and drew applause from the increasingly impressed Dame. She held up her hand.

'That's quite enough for one session. Now, I have this letter from your new teacher in Portsmouth, a Miss Martins. She thinks very highly of you both. Are you likely to stay down there now that the war's over?'

She had hit a nerve. Johan's face clouded.

'We've no idea,' he said, looking round anxiously at Helga Leaming sitting unobtrusively in the corner of the elegant music room. 'We love it in England but really we're Austrian. People are trying to find our parents but we never hear anything.'

The Dame noted his deep-felt dismay.

'My past relatives are German and I was brought up in a Jewish Orthodox family here in London. So I do understand. I hope you may hear good news soon.'

She changed the subject, quickly.

'Now, as to the immediate future. Let's assume you'll remain over here for some time yet. I'll communicate with your good teacher in Portsmouth. She's done the right thing bringing your talents to my notice. I'd like to demonstrate them to a wider audience. I don't know if you've been told, but I've spent the last few years organising concerts, here in

London. We defied Hitler's bomb threats and they proved very popular. I'd like you two to take part. We could call it your London debut!'

The two teenagers sat stock still. The offer sounded daunting.

'One thing I can assure you,' the great pianist continued, 'I'll be on hand to supervise you so there's no need to feel nervous. Our concert-goers are very understanding.'

It was time to go. Sura and Johan waved back to the great pianist from the gate of her neatly tended front garden. Helga Leaming, lost in a state of semi-disbelief, led the way to the nearest bus stop.

'Well!' she said. 'Aren't you lucky? You've met the great Myra Hess! Come on, now. We'll find a Joe Lyons Tea Room and I'll buy you each an ice cream.'

She corrected herself.

'Well, what passes for ice cream, these days. Curse the rationing!'

The electric train ride back to Portsmouth excited Johan. He wandered down long, inter-connecting corridors, looking in at comfortably-off passengers in the First Class compartments. It reminded him of a train journey of what seemed a lifetime ago. A journey spent in a cramped compartment with two narrow bunks. His mind flashed back to Heinrich. Only occasionally did Johan now think of him. The young teenager continued on his way back to join the others in their Third Class carriage.

'We'll never see Heinrich again,' he thought, miserably. 'He disappeared from our lives. Just like our parents.'

Thirteen year-old Johan pulled himself together, with fortitude beyond his years.

'Sura and I are on our own, really. But maybe we can do something together in music?'

It was a hopeful thought but the young refugees' future was not foreseeable.

London was picking itself up after scores of thousands of homes, businesses and factories had been destroyed or damaged. Yet especially in Dockland, in the East End, the chirpy spirit of the citizens was undiminished. Prime Minister Churchill, whose unflinching defiance of the *Nazi* menace would make history, had failed to win the July General Election. Instead, Labour Party leader Clement Atlee had been voted into power. A new Leader. A new era. The current keyword was 'austerity' with Britons continually urged to tighten their belts. The long and difficult haul to recovery would continue for years.

The queue of lunchtime concert-goers straggled down the long flight of steps to the National Gallery and along the pavement. There would not be many more concerts at the Gallery as it was about to be refitted to re-house its treasured exhibits. The exciting news was that Dame Myra Hess was making a personal appearance. Having enthusiastically handed over their entry shillings, the early queuers rushed for the front seats. Those failing to find a seat in Room 36, the glorious centre gallery, sat on the floor. Many attenders took advantage of the austerity sandwiches available and sipped hot drinks. They looked forward to the great Dame who gave them Schubert and Brahms before announcing a change in the scheduled programme.

'Ladies and gentlemen…thank you for coming and supporting us over so many years. Today, I have a little surprise for you. Only recently, I had the pleasure of meeting two young pianists brought to my notice by their teacher. I shall say no more. It would be wrong of me to make a pre-judgement so I'm happy to leave that to you. But I'm sure we're all in for a treat!'

Her light-hearted speech typified the warm relationship she had built with her loyal audience.

'I should explain,' she continued, 'that Sura and Johan are sister and brother. They came to us, in the most extraordinary circumstances, all the way from Austria. Not as you might expect before the war, but actually during it!'

She paused to let the information sink in with the intrigued concert-goers.

'Please will you welcome our young guests? The Steaffel children…Sura who's sixteen and Johan, thirteen. First, they'll play two of the late Mozart piano duets. And after that they'll perform, separately. If you're very lucky, I *might* be able to persuade Johan to get out his violin. Sura, I'm certain, will wish to accompany him.'

She gestured graciously to her rapt audience.

'She'll do it rather better than me!'

Dame Myra put her hands together inviting the sister-brother combination to step through an open door and approached the piano. They cast nervous glances at Helga Leaming and Miss Martins who sat together on the front row. Beneath the gallery's stunning glass dome, the teenagers adjusted their individual piano stools and swung into their Mozart. Too shy to do their own announcing, Sura and

Johan relied on Dame Myra to intervene between works, providing brief details of their next offering.

Enthusiastic applause echoed through the bare gallery, rebounding off the dome and rounded alcoves. An encore was insisted upon and Johan delighted the listeners with a tactful violin tribute to the country that had granted him refuge. He and his sister had practised to perfection Edward Elgar's popular *Chanson de Matin*. At the backs of their minds, the teenagers also wished to secretly acknowledge the part played by French people in their escape from tyranny.

After a final word from Myra Hess, the audience began to disperse, many returning to local shops in The Strand or Whitehall government offices. Sura and Johan came back on the stage to collect their music. Approaching them down the emptying central gangway, a young woman held out two small bunches of flowers. Sura looked up. Her eyes met those of the young woman whom she recognised, at once. Her jaw dropped and she found herself unable to speak. Johan, too, stood transfixed. Clutching his music, he recognised the diminutive figure bearing flowers as Maria-Anna, the girl who had helped them escape from Salzburg.

The performers dropped their music and raced towards her. Audience members making their way out smiled, indulgently. Maria-Anna's flowers were crushed to her bosom as the three Salzburgers hugged each other. No words passed. Only tears of joy. Extracting herself from their clutches, Maria-Anna presented her bouquets. She then asked the stunned performers to accompany her to the rear of the room. With a broad smile she indicated the presence of a young man, sitting by himself, on a seat close to the wall. His hair was neatly brushed and he wore a well-fitted dark suit, white collar and tie. He struggled to get up, using a walking stick to aid his movement. Heinrich Müller held out his free hand as Sura and Johan stumbled along the row of chairs towards him. His radiant smile told Sura and Johan all was well. Throwing inhibitions to the winds, they embraced, and were immediately joined by Maria-Anna. Johan, excited beyond belief, imagined he was dreaming.

'Heinrich?' he gasped. 'Is it really you?'

The young man looked him in the eye.

'Of course, Johan! Didn't you expect me?'

Neither brother nor sister knew how to respond. Heinrich turned mock serious.

'You look very grown up.'

He turned to Sura.

'And what about you, young lady? It is you? I don't suppose you still have Bimperl?'

The spell was broken. Everyone laughed, the considerably sophisticated Sura seeing the funny side.

'Oh yes!' she said. 'Bimperl's still with me. *He's a war hero!*'

Heinrich screwed up his face.

'A war hero? How's that possible?'

'Don't you remember?' Sura responded. 'The little boat on the shore. That terrible night. You thrust Bimperl into my arms and told me to get him to the British!'

Mrs Leaming and Miss Martins joined the party. Sura continued.

'In England, Helga unstitched him and found the note and your medal. Isn't that right, Johan? You said to get the message all the way to the British. Bimperl,' she added proudly, 'eventually met our Prime Minister!'

Heinrich was bowled over by Sura's claim. He could not help his incredulity.

'Bimperl met Mr Churchill?'

Before he could ask further questions, Johan confronted the Austrian with the puzzle that had dogged the siblings during their five years' refuge in England.

'Why didn't you come with us, Heinrich? On the boat, I mean. You turned back to the shore.'

Heinrich swallowed and pitched for an explanation.

'I had to go back,' he said. 'There was no choice. I went back for my friend. D'you remember? M Dewynter…the organ builder. You spent a lot of time in the back of his truck!'

The teenagers recalled the brave French patriot who had risked life and limb to get them to the coast.

'M Dewynter was shot on the beach. Even now I don't know how I got him off. But we struggled back to the truck and drove away. Just in the nick of time. The Germans came after us. Running up from the shore with torches and dogs. They took shots at us!'

It was Sura who asked the key question.

'Then what did you do?'

The tiny group waited with bated breath.

'It was simple,' he said. 'I joined the *Résistance* and fought the Germans. Especially after the Allies landed in Normandy. That was only last year. There's so much to tell.'

Helga Leaming, fully comprehending the German conversation, asked Heinrich how he planned his future.

'My future's already begun,' he replied. 'Once the fighting was over I contacted Maria-Anna, back in Salzburg. I invited her to France. More than that…yesterday, I asked her to marry me. I'm still waiting for an answer!'

Sura slid her arm into that of the shy Salzburg receptionist and drew her close.

'Yes, Maria-Anna?' she said.

The gentle Salzburg maiden blushed.

'Of course I will,' she answered. 'Why d'you think I came here? I shall never let Heinrich go again!'

The few remaining concert-goers gawped at the spontaneous display of joyful celebration. Heinrich threw his good arm around his new *fiancée,* kissing her on her soft lips. Johan and Sura danced a jig round the happy couple. Finally, Heinrich recovered sufficiently to explain the future he hoped to spend with her.

'I shall ask Maria-Anna to work with me in Remy,' he said. 'You may remember…there's a famous organ builder there with his son. Business is already looking up and he's asked me to join the firm. *Monsieur* wants me to be his advertising manager and look into expanding the export business. Work's coming in because of all the war damage. So I hope to be coming over to England, too. Even our cathedral in Salzburg was heavily bombed.'

'*Bonjour mes amis!*'

An older man, dumpy in body and with an uncontrolled grey moustache. He beamed from ear to ear as he spotted Sura and Johan.

'*Mes petits favoris!*'

He held out his strong, stubby arms and engulfed the young astonished pianists.

'*Maintenant, mein kinder,*' he said cheerfully in his best German-styled Franglais, 'we all *allez pour une* nice *Anglaise tasse de the!*'

He rolled his eyes feigning disdain for the cross-Channel beverage much decried by his countrymen.

'*Je crois que ç'est le thé Anglais est* disgusting. *Ugh!*'

The small party of friends, old and new, danced down the steps of the National Gallery and crossed the road to Trafalgar Square. In the bright sunlight, its newly-restored fountains exploded in heady plumes of sparkling water. The Frenchman threw a critical glance in the direction of a mighty, soot-encrusted column. He eyed the top, a diminutive, blackened figure of an English Admiral who had defeated the might of Napoleon's battle fleet. Bertrand Dewynter shrugged his Gallic shoulders and heaved with laughter.

'*Eh bien! C'est la guerre. Vive La France et vive L'Angleterre!*'

He raised a clenched fist to the sky.

'*Et vive L'Europe libre! Unité!* Always!'

Heinrich Müller, musician, soldier, rescuer and *Résistance* fighter slipped his arm around the young woman he loved with all his heart. He turned to Sura and Johan.

'*An die Musick!*' he said softly.

They smiled and understood. At their feet, a motley flock of pigeons rose from the paving stones and circled the historic square. A street violinist struck up a lively tune. London was at peace.